Voyage of Strangers

Praise for *Voyage of Strangers*

"At times heartwarming, at times horrifying—two words that rarely appear together. A deft juggling act indeed."
—Kenneth Wishnia, author of the award-winning Jewish-themed historical novel *The Fifth Servant*

"Beautifully written prose and meticulous research make each scene come alive. Zelvin ratchets up the conflict and suspense so I found myself reading late into the night. Anyone who loves a historical adventure rendered by an expert needs to read this novel."
—Libby Fischer Hellmann, author of *Set The Night on Fire*, *A Bitter Veil*, and *Havana Lost*

"Zelvin combines two historical injustices into a compelling and meticulously researched narrative that brings the stories from the impersonal historical to the immediate personal."
—Rabbi Ilene Schneider, award-winning author of the Rabbi Aviva Cohen mysteries

*To Maralyn
all the best*

Voyage of Strangers

ELIZABETH ZELVIN

Elizabeth Zelvin

LAKE UNION
PUBLISHING

Text copyright © 2014 Elizabeth Zelvin
All rights reserved.

Published by Lake Union, Seattle

www.apub.com

Amazon, the Amazon logo, and Lake Union
are trademarks of Amazon.com, Inc., or its affiliates.

ISBN-13: 9781477825167
ISBN-10: 1477825169

Cover design by Cyanotype Book Architects

Library of Congress Control Number: 2014937374

Printed in the United States of America

Table of Contents

Cast of Characters

Known to history

Christopher Columbus, Admiral of the Ocean Sea

King Ferdinand of Aragon

Queen Isabella of Castile

Diego Columbus, a Taino interpreter

Don Juan de Fonseca, Archdeacon of Seville

Melchior Maldonado, former envoy to the Holy See

Don Diego Columbus, the Admiral's younger brother

Michele de Cuneo of Savona, a childhood friend of Admiral Columbus

Antonio de Torres, ship's captain

Dr. Diego Alvarez Chanca, physician

Fray Bernardo Buil, a cleric

Fray Ramon Pane, a cleric

Guacanagarí, a cacique

Alonso de Hojeda, ship's captain

Gines de Gorbalan, ship's captain

Mosen Pedro Margarit, a soldier

Don Bartholomew Columbus, the Admiral's older brother

Guatiguana, a cacique

From the author's imagination

Diego Mendoza, a marrano sailor

Juan Cabrera, a sailor, his enemy

Hutia, a Taino, his friend

Fernando, a sailor, his friend

Rachel Mendoza, his sister, also called Raquel or Rafael Mendes

Doña Marina Mendes y Torres, his aunt, a converso

Don Rodrigo Maldonado, her suitor

Javier, her footman

Hernan and Esteban, her men at arms

Cristobal, a Taino captive, Hutia's father

Rosa, a mule

Drina, a Rom girl

Shandor, her uncle

Marko and Tshilaba, her parents

Baxtalo, her dog

Queen of the Roma, her great-grandmother

Don Francisco Espinosa, a merchant noble of Seville

Doña Beatriz, his wife

Paquito, Horacio, Faustino, and Leon: their sons

Adelina, Eulalia, Graciela, and Aldonza: their daughters

Amir, a Moorish slave

Fray Alonso, an inquisitor

Captain Olivero, a Genoese shipmaster

Tiboni, a *nitaino*

Tanama, a young Taino widow

Iguana and Aguta, players of *batey*

Yayama, Fernando's Taino mistress

Pilar, a Spanish widow

Benito and Ana, her children

Part One

NAVIDAD

Prologue

Hispaniola, December 24, 1492–January 4, 1493

I crouched in the crow's nest of the *Santa Maria*, praying to Ha'shem that I would succeed in coaxing my tinderbox to strike a spark. That spark must then ignite two short lengths of cable, dipped in lamp oil and wedged upright in an open leather pouch filled with sand, before anybody on deck noticed that I was not among them. It was the twenty-fifth day of Kislev in the year 5253 according to the Hebrew calendar: the second night of Chanukah, the Festival of Lights. It was also December 24 in what the others, including Admiral Columbus, called the Year of Our Lord 1492: Christmas Eve.

My breath caught as the candles in my improvised menorah flared up, then settled down to glow with a steady flame. To my relief, they did not smoke or flicker. The consequences of getting caught were too dreadful to contemplate: hanging, here or back in Spain, for practicing my forbidden Jewish faith, and a flogging I might not survive for that most terrible of transgressions at sea, kindling unauthorized fire on a wooden ship.

I muttered the *b'rucha* rather than praying aloud, as I sometimes did when the ship was scudding along under full sail and the wind's howl drowned out my song of praise to Adonai. I would not have risked even that, but the watch had just changed, and all who could do so had dropped where they stood onto the deck and fallen at once into a heavy slumber.

They had good reason. My fellow sailors had been carousing without cease for the past two days. We had been besieged by visitors from the villages beyond the shore of the beautiful bay the Admiral had named Santo Tomas. More than a thousand of the folk we call Indians had swarmed onto the *Santa Maria* from canoes, along with half as many more who came swimming out to us, although we had anchored a full league offshore. All were unclothed, even the women, and all bore gifts, evidently valuing a calabash of water or a strange, sweet fruit as highly as a nugget or ornament of gold. Though I would not confess it even to Fernando, my only friend on board, I had never seen a naked woman before. I accepted the fruit and water with thanks—none offered me gold—and shied away from the questing hands they laid upon my person, which made them laugh. The older seamen had no such inhibitions. I kept my eyes on Admiral Columbus, who was dignified and gracious as always.

"Mark how freely they give, Diego," he said softly at a moment when only I stood near him. "It is easy to recognize when something is given from the heart."

My heart swelled with pride as always on the rare occasions when he spoke my name, tacitly acknowledging his old bond with my father, which must never be mentioned. Yet it also felt ready to burst with grief, in spite of the Admiral's kindness. These naked and untutored folk welcomed strangers to their table, just as we had at Passover back in Seville, before we were driven out. Now we were all strangers in a strange land ourselves, my parents and my sisters far off in Firenze no less than my comrades and I on this unpredictable voyage.

My lip curled when it occurred to me that the villagers' offerings of gold resembled the coin we gave to children at Chanukah. It was at that moment that I conceived the plan of lighting my own menorah. I could not try it on the first night, when the decks were still crowded with visitors and not a man aboard had gotten a night's sleep since we first greeted our Indian guests. Just as the excitement had seemed to be dying down, it was roused again by the arrival of gifts for the Admiral from a cacique named Guacanagarí, the king or prince of this region. Chief among the gifts was a magnificent mask with nose, tongue, and ears of hammered gold, along with baskets heaped with food, skeins of spun cotton, gold, and parrots that screeched, flashed brightly colored feathers, and dropped dung all over the vessel. Guacanagarí also invited the whole ship's company, and the *Niña*'s as well—for the *Pinta* had gone off on her own some time before, and we were fearful of her fate—to come ashore and feast with him.

"He's inviting us for Christmas dinner," one of the seamen said, and all around him laughed.

"*To* dinner or *for* dinner?" another asked, and they laughed again. In fact, it was the warlike Caribe who were said to eat human flesh, not these amiable Taino.

But then all realized that if this cacique had so much gold to give away, it followed that he must know the location of the mine for which we had long searched. Even Admiral Columbus's eyes blazed with gold fever, for he longed to be able to lay a vast treasure at the feet of the King and Queen as repayment for the cost of the voyage. Our Indian interpreters from the other islands, at his urging, questioned many of the local folk, but their dialect was different. Indeed, I thought these fellows had told us nothing but what they believed we desired to hear from the day we carried them aboard our ships. For many had escaped, and I believed that none of them stayed with us willingly, but only out of fear of our muskets and steel swords.

At any rate, the Admiral determined that we would keep Christmas with Guacanagarí.

"Our Lord in his goodness guide me that I may find this gold," I heard him pray.

So we weighed anchor and bade farewell to the bay of Santo Tomas and its friendly people. By nightfall on Christmas Eve, we had reached the great headland that I could still see from the crow's nest if I looked astern, though in the dim light of the waning moon, it seemed no more than a looming black shadow. There was little wind, and the ship barely rocked as it moved onward, following the *Niña* ahead. Being a caravel, she was always a little faster than our sturdy tub.

I was just thinking what a blessing it was to have calm seas for my devotions—I knew from experience that the whole mast, with the crow's nest atop it, swung wildly in any kind of swell—when a tremendous jolt and shudder knocked me off my feet and into the menorah. Luckily, the leather flap closed as I fell heavily against it, driving the candles into the sand and extinguishing them. Stuffing the pouch into my shirt along with my tinderbox, I shinnied down the ropes and leaped softly to the deck, giving thanks to Ha'shem that my feet were bare and the night so dark that no one noticed.

The crisis was severe, for as we learned later, we had run aground upon hidden shoals while all on watch slept, even the helmsman and the gromet, or ship's boy, he had ordered to take the tiller. The next two hours were a time of chaos and confusion, shouting and a frenzy of activity in our desperation to save our ship. Whenever I paused in my labors, my heartbeat pounded in my ears. We were only a league offshore. If the *Santa Maria* broke up, I could swim ashore, as my father and the Admiral had in their youth when wrecked together off the coast of Portugal. That was the origin of their lifelong friendship, and my father, grateful for every day of his continued life since then, had made sure I knew how to swim at an early age. But the whole Ocean Sea separated us from the lands and people we knew. What if we were stranded on these shores with no means of return? We must not lose the ship!

Indeed, we might have saved her if the *Santa Maria*'s master, Juan de la Cosa, had acted as he ought. The Admiral, seeing what must be done, gave immediate orders. But de la Cosa failed to obey them. Instead, he ordered his closest cronies to launch the ship's boat and flee with him to the *Niña*, determined to save their own skins at the cost of ours if need be. This so shocked all who remained, even the Admiral, that the master and his small band were gone before any thought to prevent them.

Meanwhile, increasing swells drove the *Santa Maria* further and further onto the coral reef. By the time Vicente Yañez, who commanded the *Niña*, had ordered the fugitives back and sent a boatload of his own men to help, it was too late. With horror and despair, we watched the timbers of the hull come apart at the seams and the sea come rushing in. Before dawn, the Admiral was forced to command all to abandon ship and leave the dying vessel to her fate.

The disaster changed all our plans. We labored mightily to salvage the contents of the *Santa Maria*, while the Admiral wept. Thanks to Ha'shem for the goodwill of Guacanagarí. The cacique offered the help of his tribesmen, food for all, housing in his village to relieve the overcrowded *Niña*, and many pieces of gold. He shrewdly surmised that these would dry the Admiral's tears and go some way toward consoling him for the loss of his flagship. By the day after Christmas, he had come to believe that the shipwreck was the will of the Almighty, meant to guide him to make a more permanent landing in this hospitable place, to which a better-equipped expedition could return to seek the fabled gold mine of Cibao. Our whole company applauded this new plan, being equally eager for gold. Only I failed to join in this feverish enthusiasm, having seen well enough how the possession of riches could lead to the envy and malice of others, as it had for the Jews of Spain.

It was decided to build a fort upon the shore within sight of the wreck of the *Santa Maria*. Many clamored for the privilege of being left behind to man it when we returned to Spain, having not only gold but the availability of the friendly native women as inducements. All awaited eagerly the Admiral's choice as to which of us would go and who would remain. I was happy enough working hard at building the fort, which the Admiral declared would be called La Navidad.

For good measure, I made a new friend. The Admiral had enlisted Taino from the nearest village to labor alongside us. The youngest of these seemed drawn to me as the closest to him in age. At first, he fingered my garments and asked questions beyond the smattering of Taino that I had learned earlier in the voyage. When he saw I was eager to understand, he began to teach me the language. Curious as he was about me, I was equally curious about him. What did he make of these strange white-skinned men with our birdlike yet vulnerable ships and our metal tools and weapons? What did his bright black eyes read in our faces? Could he discern the dark soul of Cabrera, the sailor who had been my tormentor on the voyage, and the Admiral's goodness? What thoughts lay beneath the coarse, dark thatch of his hair?

I learned that the Taino took pride in their names, just as we did. The Taino boy told me his was Hutia. He made me laugh by showing me with gestures and movement that a hutia was a small, furry creature of the islands, the name given to him because he could run fast. He had a sister named Anacaona, golden flower. Most of the sailors knew only *caona*, gold, and *chicha*, the villagers' beer, made of corn, which they complained about but drank a good deal of nonetheless.

I had difficulty explaining "Diego," which was the name of a Christian saint. None of the Indians had succeeded in grasping the concept of saints, eager as the Admiral was to convert them. They responded better to images of Jesus on the Cross, but only because they interpreted crucifixion as an effective way of tormenting one's enemies—as indeed it was to the Romans who killed Jesus, or so my father had taught me. Like us, the Christians' God was punished for being a Jew.

While we built the fort, all had a hitherto unknown measure of freedom and privacy. I was happy to complete my Chanukah observance with the loss of only three out of the eight nights of the festival. Not all had a purpose as innocent as mine in venturing beyond the mangrove swamps into the wilderness beyond. On the eve of the New Year, when all had been given several extra measures of strong drink, I witnessed, by pure chance, an act that in pure evil surpassed anything Cabrera had done before.

At twilight, relieved from my post for the whole of the next watch, I stole away. I carried my *tallit*, the fringed shawl we wear when we pray, and my *t'fillin*, the ritual phylacteries, intending to perform my daily prayers. I had already bound the *t'fillin* around my arm and brow when I heard screams of distress coming from some distance away. I crashed through the underbrush, seeking the source of the disturbance. The raucous cry of parrots disturbed by my headlong progress mingled with the human screams, which now held a note of terror.

I burst out into a small clearing and stopped short. On the ground I beheld Cabrera, engaged in a brutal assault on a naked Indian maiden, who writhed and bucked beneath him, clearly an unwilling participant in the proceedings. He laughed as he forced her down. The girl was slight of frame, easy for Cabrera to overpower in spite of his short stature. When I caught a glimpse of her face, I realized she was young, perhaps no older than my twelve-year-old sister Rachel. Her screams grew louder. As I gazed in horror, he silenced her, first with a punch that shattered her jaw, then by seizing her about the neck and choking her until she slumped and fell back against the earth.

To my shame, I failed to act until too late. By the time the paralysis that seized me at the sight let go its hold, the girl was dead.

"Stop!" I croaked, starting forward, though I knew my tardy protest served no purpose.

As he rose from the ground, Cabrera drew a musket from the folds of his cloak and pointed it at my chest.

"It's the Admiral's pet," Cabrera said with an evil grin that bared his rotting teeth. "Well, boy, are you dog enough to take this bitch? You can have my leavings—before I kill you."

"You can't kill me," I said, doing my best to keep my voice from shaking. "As you said, the Admiral will miss me. Besides, a musket shot will bring many running and disclose your crime."

"What crime?" he sneered, kicking the girl's body with a booted foot. "This is but a savage."

"As the cacique Guacanagarí is a savage?" I inquired. "The Admiral won't thank you if you turn the Indians against us and ruin our chance to find the gold of Cibao."

Cabrera snarled, acknowledging the justice of my point. He shrugged and lowered the unfired musket.

"This but delays your death," he said. "Call this moment yet another score we have to settle, you and I."

I held back, for fear of provoking him beyond reason, the words that sprang to my tongue: What is to stop me from reporting this crime? He read them in my eyes.

"You'll say nothing," he declared. "Or I will report your greater crime, which will send you to the Inquisition and a shameful death."

I had forgotten I still wore my *t'fillin*, with the prayer shawl fluttering around my neck and chest. I drew a wavering breath.

"It seems we are at a stand," I said. "What now?"

"First, you help me bury this." He indicated the body with a careless nod. "Then we return to the camp. And we say nothing."

"We say nothing," I repeated. Sick with shame and horror more than fear, I folded my *tallit* carefully and laid it on a bank of moss beneath a tree, the *t'fillin* placed within its folds. Then I turned to help him with the burial.

It took us four more days to complete the building of La Navidad. The fort's walls were made of the *Santa Maria*'s timbers and its cellars stuffed with stores the men would need, including seed. For if we found the mine, Their Majesties would want to establish a settlement. Conquest is for soldiers, not that we had thus far needed arms to cow the Taino. But a settlement requires farmers.

As I worked, the sun beating on my bare back and arms and turning them browner than ever, I had always an uneasy sense of Cabrera's presence. He watched me constantly, alert for me to make some mistake or seek a seclusion that would allow him to kill me with impunity. Knowing this, I stayed close to my fellows at all times, especially Fernando. I did not tell him what was wrong, although he asked me several times. The knowledge I bore was burden enough for me without loading it on another's shoulders. As for Hutia, having seen one of his people so wronged, I could hardly bear to meet his eyes.

The remaining days flew by, yet in my darker moments, they seemed unendurably long. When it came time to choose the forty men who would garrison La Navidad when the rest departed, I was tense and nervous. My palms were damp with sweat and my teeth had a tendency to chatter, despite the scorching tropical heat. I hardly knew what to hope for. Being left behind with Cabrera would prove a certain death sentence. But further voyaging under even more cramped conditions than before would provide opportunities for him to do me harm as well. To my relief, the Admiral chose Cabrera and the other cronies of the treacherous Juan de la Cosa to man the fort. Thus he separated them from de la Cosa himself, whom he naturally wanted to keep under his eye. I would sail on with the Admiral on the *Niña*, there still being no sign of the *Pinta*.

Once the men were chosen, Admiral Columbus entered into negotiations with the cacique for interpreters who spoke the local dialect. The chosen Indians bore little in the way of gear or possessions as they climbed into the ship's boat, in which we would row out to the *Niña*. It seemed to me that in some respects they embodied Christian principles far better than the Spanish Christians. But I reminded myself that I must not criticize, for I was not free of fault myself. Thinking of how I had concealed a murder, however good the reason, I thanked Ha'shem that I did not believe in the Christians' hell.

The new fort's whole garrison and every soul in the village came down to the beach to see the *Niña* sail. I felt both glad and sorry to be leaving as I boarded the boat myself and took an oar. I paid little attention to the Indians until Hutia came running down to the boat. He called out, *"Baba! Baba!"* One of our new interpreters, evidently Hutia's father, stood up and held out his hands, which Hutia grasped. Speaking rapidly in Taino, they embraced. Their hands clung and then parted. Hutia stepped back onto the shore.

In the forefront of the crowd, I could see Cabrera with his arm around a woman. He clutched at her naked body as he leered at me. Still holding her, he raised a gourd of *chicha*, or perhaps a stronger spirit made from the plant that they called yuca. He waved it at me in a jeering salute, then poured the liquor down his throat.

Beside me, Hutia's father called out, "Anacaona?"

"Itá," Hutia replied. I don't know.

The father sighed deeply. Hutia looked grave and sad, with no trace of the twinkle that usually lurked in his black eyes.

I looked from Hutia to his father and then at Cabrera on the shore. Leaping to my feet, I thrust my oar at Fernando on the bench beside me.

"Don't let them leave without me!" I said.

I splashed through the shallows to the beach, where Hutia, looking puzzled, came down to meet me where the water met the sand. A quick glance told me that Cabrera was paying no attention. Another woman had joined the first, and he was busily engaged in nuzzling them both. Ordinarily, this lewd behavior would have caught the Admiral's eye and been stopped at once. But in the excitement of our departure, Cabrera clearly thought he was safe from interference.

I grasped Hutia's shoulders with some urgency. "Anacaona," I said. "I know what happened to her."

I directed his attention toward Cabrera, racking my brain for Taino words to convey my meaning.

"Anacaona! That man killed her!" I could not bring myself to mime the rape, but Hutia's face darkened as I demonstrated with my own hands and body the blow to the jaw and the squeezing of her throat.

"*Anki!*" I said. Evil person. "*Akani!*" Enemy.

"*Bara?*" he said. She is dead?

I nodded, my heart heavy.

"*Bara!*" I will kill him!

He started forward, his face flushed with rage and his hands curling into claws. I held him back.

"Wait," I said, wishing I knew the Taino word for it, if indeed they had one. I put my arms around him from behind and turned him first toward Admiral Columbus, who was watching the ship raise sail from further down the beach, then toward the *Niña* itself.

"Wait until we leave. Once we are gone, you may tell whom you wish and do what you must."

I felt him slump against me. He had understood. He would wait. Only then did I hear Fernando's voice among others bellowing for me to let the savages be and get back to my oar, or there would be no gold left in Cibao by the time we got there.

As our oars raked the water and the sails of the caravel billowed ever greater as they filled with wind, I looked back once more and found Cabrera's eyes upon me.

"I'll see you in hell, boy!" he bellowed, brandishing his gourd.

"If such a place exists, you will surely get there before me," I murmured as the boat pulled into the shadow of the *Niña* and we prepared to climb aboard.

Part Two

SPAIN

Chapter 1

Barcelona, April 17, 1493

"They're gone," the old serving woman called out, "and they won't be coming back." She swept her broom across the doorstep of the neighboring house with vigor.

I stood before my cousins' house. The door hung ajar, half off its hinges, its wooden surface pitted and splintered as if it had been rammed with clubs or soldiers' spears. The ground before the house was littered with broken crockery and clothing that had been trampled into the dirt. One tattered, grimy cloth was a *tallit*.

"Is it bad news, Diego?" Cristobal asked. I had become fond of Hutia's father on the voyage. The little Taino, twice my age and half my height, tugged at my sleeve as he gazed up at the violated building. "This great *caney* looks as if the Canibale had raided."

"Good riddance to them, the swine!" The old woman spat and crossed herself.

"What is that she called them?" Cristobal asked. He had learned much Spanish on the voyage from the Indies, but no one had spoken of the recently banished Jews.

"Marranos." I spoke softly, averting my head from the old serving woman's avid gaze. "Pigs."

"Spain is truly a Christian country now, thanks to our blessed King Ferdinand and Queen Isabella," the old woman said. Piety and malice blended in her tone.

"They owed me money," I lied.

"Your bad luck, young sir." The old woman cackled. "Too bad it wasn't the other way around. No Jews, no need to repay their loans."

Teeth and fists clenched, I strove to keep my face impassive while the spiteful old woman watched. My family in Seville had fled the prospect of the Inquisition's grim tribunal last year, on the very day we sailed to the Indies. But my youngest sister Rachel had been sent to Barcelona for safety months before the expulsion. There had been no time to send for her. I had hoped to find her here. Now dread of what might have happened to her knifed through me.

"Were they arrested?" I asked.

"No, the sly creatures got away," the serving woman said. "They brazened it out, see? We thought they was good Christians. But the swine have one of their heathen parties this time of year. The soldiers came the night of the blood moon."

Two weeks gone, then. On Passover, our most holy festival, the moon had turned red as blood. We had seen it as we made our way across Spain toward Barcelona. The Admiral, ever one to read a marvel as a sign of his greatness, had made much of it.

The old woman leaned on her broom.

"They don't light the fire during their sacrifices and such. Sounds crazy, don't it? But who knows why Jews do anything? The soldiers spotted the cold chimney and figured they'd catch them out. But they must have gotten wind of it somehow. They were already gone."

"Nothing to stay for, then." I shrugged. "I don't suppose they left my gold lying around. Come, Cristobal."

The old woman snorted. "If they did, the soldiers have diced it away by now." Her cackle followed us as we retreated down the street.

Cristobal had to trot to keep up with me. All the people of the Indies were short of stature, with golden skin and thick black hair, coarse as a horse's mane.

"What now?" He wrapped himself more securely in his woolen cloak.

"I must seek out my Aunt Marina. She is a courtier's widow of some influence. I pray she may have news of my sister. But you need not come with me, if you are cold."

"In this wrapping, I am well enough," Cristobal said. "I am but tired of being stared at and pinched by every fool in Spain."

"I am sorry for that and glad of your company."

One might call Cristobal marrano himself. The baptism on which Admiral Columbus had insisted was merely a thin veneer over the true beliefs of all the captive Taino. But only I knew that, having had more interest than the rest in learning the Taino language.

"These are fine dwellings," he said as we turned into a street of stone buildings and heavy oak doors. "They would defy the winds of Juracan, did the god of storms ever visit Spain."

"Indeed."

My aunt had prospered since converting in her youth. At best, she might have taken Rachel in.

"Look!" Cristobal squinted down the street. "Is that the dwelling we seek? Who are those men? They are dressed as if for raiding."

The Taino had no word for war. Nor had they seen metal, except for soft gold, until we reached their shores. But he was right. A band of soldiers, steel helmets glinting in the sun, stood at attention before Doña Marina's door.

The Inquisition! My heart thumped in my chest. How could it be? The family had always believed my aunt a sincere converso and devout Christian, her position unassailable even since her husband's death. We had also been assured, before sending Rachel north to Barcelona, that the Inquisition had as yet no headquarters there, unlike most great Spanish cities, including our own Seville. I saw no hooded priests, but the faces under the helmets seemed grim and pitiless. If Rachel had indeed found shelter here, had they found her out and come to take her away?

I swallowed my fear, straightened my shoulders, and greeted them courteously.

"Good day. I have come to call on my kinswoman, Doña Marina Mendes y Torres. Is this not her home? And may I ask what you do here?"

To my surprise, the soldiers' rigid posture relaxed. Leaning on his lance, the man who seemed to be the captain grinned.

"We are the men at arms of Don Rodrigo Maldonado. This is indeed the home of Doña Marina. Our master is within. He's come a-courting."

Courting? This was no Inquisitorial party, then, but the entourage of some noble suitor of my aunt's.

"Are you one of Admiral Columbus's men, sir, that crossed the Ocean Sea with him?" the captain asked. "Is that fellow not one of the savages?"

With a murmur of interest, the other soldiers surged forward, a few with hands stretched out to touch Cristobal. All Barcelona had seen us at a distance when we entered the city, and as Cristobal had complained, everyone wanted a better look. The captain called them back to order with a sharp command.

"He is a man like you," I said, keeping my tone courteous. "I pray you treat him with respect."

"Of course, of course. Our master takes a special interest in the Admiral's expedition, see. He's got a cousin that sailed with you. One Juan Cabrera. You must know him."

"Indeed." I kept my voice calm, although my stomach turned a somersault, and my pulse pounded in my ears. "He remains in the Indies with the garrison of our fort, La Navidad."

"Don Rodrigo will be most interested to talk with you," the captain said. "His brother too. The elder Maldonado, Don Melchior, plans to join the new expedition as a gentleman volunteer. Will you sail with the Admiral again, sir?"

I could not help grinning back at him. "I would not miss it for a fortune."

"They say all who go will make their fortune in the Indies, sir," another soldier said. "Have you seen the savages' store of gold?"

"I have, though less than Barcelona rumor would have it. I am not acquainted with the Maldonados."

Although Cabrera was merely a coarse sailor given a little power and quick to abuse it, these Maldonados were evidently gentlemen.

"Oh, Don Melchior is a great man, a royal envoy to the Pope. But our master, Don Rodrigo, is an up and coming man." He leaned close enough that I could smell the garlic on his breath and spoke in an undervoice. "He's got friends in the Inquisition, see. He's met that Torquemada, that they say could beat the Pope at chess."

At this point, the door creaked open, and an elderly majordomo appeared, bowing, to escort me into the presence of Doña Marina and her suitor. I had learned much. As one of the Admiral's followers, I appeared to be safe in any company, at least for now, from suspicion regarding my secret faith. But no matter how inclined to help my aunt might prove to be, I could not leave Rachel with her for long.

Chapter 2

Barcelona, April 18, 1493

How hard could it be to be a boy? Rachel shook out the wrinkled shirt and tunic, fraying pair of hose, and oversized woolen cap that her friend Constanza had stuffed in among her petticoats in the flurry of packing. They belonged to Constanza's brother. With her curly brown hair stuffed into the cap and her drab cloak flung over the whole, she would have but to put a swagger in her walk and smear some grime across her face; no one would guess her true identity.

She had been so excited when Diego arrived at the convent where her aunt had placed her for greater safety. She had not been unhappy there, though she had had to remember every second that she was Raquel Mendes, not Rachel Mendoza, and pretend to Christian piety. But to see her brother returned from the dead! Everyone in Barcelona had believed Columbus and his crew were doomed. Instead, Diego had come back a hero. Both of them had cried as they embraced. She had not realized he would make her stay with stuffy old Aunt Marina and plan to send her off to Italy as soon as he could find suitable passage. Surely, if she could pass for one of the ship's boys when the Admiral assembled his new fleet, Diego would *have* to take her with him.

Her window gave onto the rear of the house, above the kitchen garden. Rachel could see the wooden door, so low that a grown person would have to stoop to pass, in the stone wall at the far end of the garden. That door was her gate to freedom.

The inviting branches of an apple tree, just coming into bloom, stretched toward the window. Once dressed, she found that she could squeeze through the narrow opening. She had to stretch to reach a branch sturdy enough to bear her weight. But that was child's play in boy's garb.

Rachel swung and scrambled from branch to crotch to trunk and dropped lightly to the ground. She inched around the gnarled tree trunk to stand with her back pressed up against it on the side away from the house. She peered around it. She must make sure no one observed her. Her heart thumped as she spied a face at the window. It was Pepe, the younger footman. Had he seen her? To her relief, he turned away. She could not be sure if she had seen him wink.

The alcazar was not too far to walk. She had made Diego describe the route the procession would take. Then she had only to gain entrance to the palace. She would pretend she was one of the ship's boys with a message for the Admiral. Better, perhaps, for one of his men. They might deem the Admiral too important to be disturbed. But her errand must be to anyone but Diego. Once she had been admitted, her most crucial task was to keep her brother from seeing her.

Up to a point, all fell out as she had planned. She aroused no interest as she wriggled through the ranks of assembled courtiers. There was not much to see, as the broad backs of halberdiers standing at attention blocked her view of the Taino. She caught a flash of gold and the red of a parrot's wing. The King and Queen, not handsome but richly garbed, sat apart talking in low voices to a white-haired man in a disappointingly drab brown cloak who must be the Admiral. There was Diego, towering over the colorful Taino. She looked away, afraid that even staring at his back would somehow make him aware of her.

Perhaps she could see better from the side. Stone arches formed a shadowed arcade, much like the cloister at the convent, around the sides of the great hall. Ducking her head and murmuring apologies in as gruff a voice as she could muster, she reached the shelter of the colonnade on the side away from Diego. At that moment, the mass of courtiers stirred and shifted. A trumpet sounded a fanfare, and the King and Queen rose to their feet. The whole crowd streamed forward, while Rachel tried to maintain her position, not willing to follow without knowing more.

She caught the arm of a page no older than herself.

"What happens now?" she asked.

"Have you never been to Court before?" the boy said scornfully. "Their Majesties lead the way to the Chapel Royal, where a Te Deum will be sung. Are you coming?"

Rachel shook her head.

"Want an apple? I have two." As Rachel looked up, he added, "Catch."

Rachel caught the apple, thinking with some pride that she would like to see Constanza try to do the same. The boy departed without ceremony. Biting into the apple, Rachel stood watching another young sailor motion to Diego to follow the Taino. Turning back for a moment, Diego caught sight of Rachel. His face went white with shock.

He started toward her, but the other sailor called out to him. He turned back toward the Chapel, clearly reluctant to do so, and was swept out of sight by the crowd.

Rachel looked around for her apple, which she had dropped without realizing it when Diego caught sight of her. It had rolled some distance away, and a hound far more elegantly groomed than

Rachel herself was already sniffing at it. As she shrugged and stood wondering what to do next, fingers like a band of steel clamped down on her arm, while her attacker's other hand seized her roughly by the collar.

"Got you!"

With a cry, she looked up into the triumphant face of Don Rodrigo Maldonado.

"Don't cry out!" He drew her further into the shadows as the courtiers streamed past, intent on crowding into the Chapel Royal with the King and Queen. "No one will pay the slightest attention. I might even beat a page dressed like an urchin without drawing any gentleman's censure. How would you like that, Señorita Mendoza?"

Rachel gasped. Only this morning, her aunt had presented her to him as Raquel Mendes. She twisted and squirmed to no avail.

Don Rodrigo laughed.

"Oh, yes," he said, wrenching her arm cruelly behind her back. "Do you think I am stupid? You cannot escape, little girl. I could have you dragged away in chains right now. If I choose, you might never see sunlight again."

"What do you want of me?" Rachel panted.

She could feel her bowels turn to water and feared she might disgrace herself. If she screamed, would Diego come to her aid? The sound of the Latin chanting, floating out faintly into the audience hall, must fill the ears of everyone listening in the Chapel to the exclusion of all other sound. Even if he heard, he must not try to rescue her, or this evil Maldonado would denounce them both.

Don Rodrigo watched the play of expression across her face as she came to this conclusion with a smile more frightening than his scowl.

"You are no fool either," he observed. "Now, stop fighting me, and I will tell you what I plan for you. Oh, I will not denounce you or your brother—yet."

Rachel managed not to gasp again, but Maldonado felt her tremble.

"Ah, so he is your brother. You have confirmed my guess. See? You are already cooperating with me, and it is not so bad, is it?"

"You cannot touch him!" Rachel said. "He is the Admiral's favorite, as the Admiral is the Queen's."

"Quiet!" He slapped her cheek, not hard, but no one had ever raised a hand to her before. "I can bring down your brother and the upstart Columbus himself if I so choose. There are plenty to take his place. What about the Pinzons of Palos, who brought the *Pinta* safely to harbor and have no love for your Admiral? What about my brother Melchior, who longs to distinguish himself? But never mind. You can know nothing of these matters."

"Then let me go!"

He slapped her cheek again, smiling.

"You will be docile, and your docility will stand surety for your brother's safety. Why should I send such a tender morsel to the auto da fé, when it might be served up as a wedding feast?"

"I have nothing," she croaked, dry-mouthed. "I am worth nothing to you."

"Did you not know?" His tone was silken as a poisoned posset. "It is well known the Jews are shrewd. What interest could your pious Christian aunt have in you, unless she had helped to save your dowry from the wreck of your family's fortunes? I have a lackwit son who could make use of it."

The carved doors of the Chapel Royal opened as a fanfare announced the Sovereigns' return to the great hall. With a sob, Rachel wrenched herself from Don Rodrigo's hands. She caught sight of Diego through a blur of tears. He opened his mouth, willing to betray them both out of concern for her. He must not. She whirled, tucked her head down, and fled.

Chapter 3

Barcelona, April 18, 1493

Until the moment I caught sight of Rachel, I had been fully occupied in a tumult of emotions: enjoyment of the pageantry of the Court, admiration of Admiral Columbus's ability to take the full attention of his Sovereigns in stride, and anxiety lest my charges, which included many brightly colored parrots as well as the Taino, embarrass us through some innocent but unseemly behavior.

When we reached the alcazar, we found the Admiral pacing back and forth in the outer courtyard, his plain brown cloak whipping in the wind. He hurried to greet us as the armored guards uncrossed their halberds and let us pass into the great hall. It was vaulted, with clerestory window panels high in the walls above a colonnade letting in shafts of sunlight that fell at random on the women's headdresses and jewels and glinted off the gentlemen's swords.

King Ferdinand and Queen Isabella were seated on great carved and gilded chairs on a raised dais at the far end of the hall. Any who approached them must do so at a stately pace, bowing low. I had rehearsed the Taino in bowing, but they had difficulty mastering the art and clearly thought it ridiculous, bobbing up and down in quick jerks from the waist like robins pecking the ground.

Admiral Columbus strode forward with no regard for protocol, his white hair flying and cloak billowing with the wind of his passage. Reaching the foot of the dais, he knelt before the Sovereigns. None of us who followed Columbus had ever seen him kneel before, except to God. Rather than bowing his head, he flung his arms wide as if to say, "Here I am! I have done for you what I promised."

"We welcome you, Don Christopher." The Queen held out a plump hand, stiff with rings, for him to kiss.

"It is my honor to serve your Gracious Majesties," the Admiral said, "and Our Savior as well. Then I am indeed confirmed in my honors as Admiral of the Ocean Sea, Viceroy and Governor of the lands I have found and all that I may yet discover?"

There was a rustle among the courtiers at this bold opening. I saw a prelate draped in red, no doubt some great prince of the Church, turn his eyes heavenward.

"Yes, yes, Don Christopher," the King said. "You are confirmed in all your honors and preferments." He added in a deep rumble, "Let us hope that you make as good speed to the Indies on your next voyage as you do in reminding us of our promises."

"I plan to accomplish much more in the future, Majesties," the Admiral said. "My discoveries will extend your realms and bring many souls to Our Savior."

"Your thoughts march with ours." The Queen raised her voice. "Europe needs trade. The Indies promise trade beyond anything Spain has known. And with trade comes prosperity, advancement, and opportunity for those bold enough to take the risk, as our good Columbus has, of leaving the familiar behind."

The courtiers murmured. She raised a hand to silence them, light flashing on her rings.

"We must bring the savages to the love of Jesus Christ Our Savior," the Queen said. "To do so, we must treat them well and lovingly. Further, we must find gold. Our ships will sail the Ocean Sea like winged treasure chests, and other nations will fear our might. Nor will the people of Aragon and Castile suffer in this enterprise. We will settle the new lands with good Christian farmers and artisans as well as soldiers and sailors."

The Queen motioned the Admiral to stand beside her. His face blazed with triumph. This was indeed his moment of glory.

"Now we would see the treasures Don Christopher has brought us and hear more of his travels." She settled herself more comfortably in her chair. "Tell me," she said, "do the rivers really run with gold?"

I grew both weary and restless, standing idly in attendance while the great ones talked. My gaze roamed the crowd. I recognized no one but Don Rodrigo, who acknowledged me with a curt nod but did not approach me. Finally, a trumpet sounded and the Sovereigns rose.

"We will hear a Te Deum in the Chapel Royal," the King announced.

I was wondering whether I could possibly avoid this Christian observance when I caught sight of Rachel, a boyish figure in tunic, hose, and oversized cap balanced like a giant mushroom above a face stamped with alarm and defiance.

The little wretch! Where had Rachel obtained those clothes? If I could have laid hands on her, I would have wrung her neck. But I could not abandon my duty. Nor did I wish to compound Rachel's foolhardiness by calling attention to her in this public place, in the presence of armed men and prelates and royalty itself, not to mention the Admiral.

What would become of my sister? Did the silly girl not realize she might be tortured and killed if she were exposed as a Jew? I must find someone to escort her to Italy. She could not travel alone, especially as we had had no certain news of the family's arrival in Firenze. This was only to be expected, but it worried me. I could not accompany her myself. My destiny lay to the west, under the Admiral's soaring wing. Nor did I wish to confide her to strangers. Could her masquerade have been prompted by some harebrained scheme to travel across Europe as a boy, or worse, to accompany me to the Indies? If so, I must nip that scheme in the bud. I had unwisely told her that she was of an age with some of the gromets. I had underestimated my sister's capacity for seeking trouble.

I looked back once more, but at that moment, a red and green parrot deposited an unwelcome gift upon my head. By the time I had dealt with that, she had vanished.

It was some time before the Indians and I were allowed to depart. I led the Taino toward our lodging through streets thronged with crowds, as all Barcelona wanted to see them. I was glad of the protection of soldiers from the alcazar as well as the sailors assigned to escort duty along with me, without whom I believe the people of the city would have ripped the very ornaments from their arms, ears, and necks. A couple of loose women made as if to strip them of their clouts, demanding to see if they were made the same as European men.

Cristobal, the mildest of men among a people of remarkable peacefulness, entered into a tugging contest with a stout woman who tried to take his cloak, whether for her own use or merely as a memento of the occasion, I could not say. A soldier with a halberd ended the bout before it could be decided and returned the cloak to Cristobal. The Taino hugged it tight around his body, scowling. I started to tease him about Spanish ladies' interest in his person but broke off when I realized that he was shivering. His teeth chattered, and his forehead was beaded with sweat. Although he complained of chill, his skin was burning to the touch.

Our way back led through a busy market. As I herded my charges through the colorful throng, I caught tantalizing glimpses of street jugglers and gleemen plying their trade, woolen shawls, brocaded jackets, and baubles I would have liked to buy for Rachel. I was importuned to give alms to a beggar and bet on a cockfight. I hoped to pass the stall of an herb woman who might have such simples as willow bark and yarrow to ease Cristobal's fever, but saw none. By the time we neared our lodging, all of the Taino were shivering and coughing.

By the time I had all the Taino bedded and breathing more easily, it was too late to call on Doña Marina. I would have to postpone my reckoning with Rachel. In truth, I was exhausted by the long day and relieved to be spared a confrontation with my rebellious young sister till the morning. But I was not to enjoy the full night's sleep I craved. I was dreaming I stood in the crow's nest of the poor, lost *Santa Maria*, my *tallit* whipping in the wind and a *Sh'ma*, a crying out to the Lord, on my lips, when a banging that I at first took for the ship's cannon woke me. I started out of sleep to hear a series of heavy thumps on the wooden door of the chamber.

Chapter 4

Barcelona, April 18–19, 1493

Thanks to the poppy syrup I had doled out, none of the Taino wakened as the banging continued. I thought first of the Inquisition, but as I assembled my scattered wits, I realized the pounding sounded like that of a heavy fist rather than a club or a metal weapon. Perhaps it was not the Inquisition's soldiers, who would surely have kicked in the door by now. As I reached hastily for my breeches and my knife, I heard Rachel's tremulous voice.

"Diego! Diego, wake up! Wake up and let us in!"

I unlatched the door and flung it open. Rachel tumbled into the room. Disheveled and tearstained, she threw herself into my arms. Thanks be to Ha'shem, she was dressed as a girl. Over her head, I regarded a very young man in livery who stood on the threshold, his raised fist still doubled. I raised my eyebrows at him. He lowered his hand, but only to place it on the pommel of his own dagger.

"Who the hell are you?" I demanded.

The boy cleared his throat. His combative stance was clearly borne of bravado rather than confidence. His glance at Rachel betrayed that he was besotted with her. I emitted a low growl. My little sister needed no champion but me, and she was far too young for suitors, especially one so ineligible.

Rachel raised her head from my chest.

"You need not sound so fierce, Diego. This is Javier, one of our aunt's footmen. He insisted on escorting me when he could not dissuade me from going out."

I clutched at my hair with both hands.

"You had better come in, Javier," I said. "Now, Rachel, what is the meaning of this nonsense?"

Rachel bounced onto a wooden stool near the hearth, where coals still glowed.

"It is not nonsense! We must leave Barcelona at once!"

"What are you talking about? We have found you a safe haven with Doña Marina, and as you know, I must attend the Admiral for as long as Their Majesties choose to keep him in Barcelona. And on that subject, what do you think you were doing, appearing at Court in a boy's garb?"

"Never mind about that now! It is *not* safe at Doña Marina's, thanks to that awful man, and I cannot tell if our aunt is hand in glove with him or ignorant as I would have been had he not seized me, so my plan is all for the best."

"Seized you? What man? What plan? Can you not tell a story right end to?"

I remembered now that she could not, and that it was impossible to argue with her. I sighed and sank down cross-legged beside the fire.

"You, boy—Javier, is it? You had better sit as well, for it is evident this tale will take some time in the telling."

"It is all right, Javier," Rachel said. "For all his seeming fierceness, my brother is perfectly harmless. He is merely worried about me."

Giving the boy an encouraging smile that would have pierced his heart like Cupid's arrow were he not already so obviously smitten, she turned back to me.

"Diego, you worry too much!"

"Do I? Then why, pray tell, must we flee Barcelona?"

"I am trying to tell you, if you will only be silent and listen! My dressing as a boy was nothing to worry about. Nobody gave me a second glance, until I had the misfortune to be spied by Don Rodrigo. And he knew me only because he had seen me at our aunt's this morning. He is an evil man who wishes us both harm."

"Are you speaking of Don Rodrigo Maldonado? Our aunt's suitor? Do you say he accosted you at Court?"

"Yes! *Now* will you listen and let me tell you what happened?"

I glanced at Javier, thinking to send the boy to wait outside. Rachel frowned at me.

"We can speak freely before Javier," she said. "He has already heard the story, and without his help, and Pepe's too, I should never have gotten away."

"Pepe?"

"The other footman," she said impatiently.

"They helped you get away from Don Rodrigo?"

"No! From Doña Marina's. I could not with propriety walk through the streets at night without an escort."

"Of course not," I murmured.

"Sarcasm does not become you, brother," she said. "Javier, he is not angry at you, only at me, and you will have his gratitude once he allows me to tell him everything."

Clearly, I had no choice but to loose the reins and give her her head like a mule at the gallop. Accepting that any other course would be futile, I set myself to listen. My horror grew as she told me of Don Rodrigo's schemes and threats. I knew, as she did not, that Papa had anticipated that the Crown would confiscate all Jewish property and possessions. He had saved an ample dowry for Rachel by depositing gold with Doña Marina's bankers well before the royal edict. We were bound to our aunt for this reason. Could we trust her? Would she continue to shield her nephew and niece if it put her in danger? Did she indeed wish to marry Maldonado and count Rachel a price worth paying? Or did she wish to fend off his suit?

Rachel believed that Don Rodrigo was not merely tempted by circumstance, but a villain to the core. I was inclined to believe it. In our brief meeting, the man had claimed kinship with Juan Cabrera, the only truly evil human being I had ever encountered. If his "distant cousin" Don Rodrigo were cut from the same cloth, we were indeed in grave danger.

"That is why I had to come tonight," Rachel concluded. "He could put his wicked plan in motion by tomorrow morning, and if Doña Marina abets him, I would be lost before you reached her door."

"You know her better than I," I said. "Do you think she will?"

"I don't know," she said. "But can we afford to take the chance?"

"I cannot leave Barcelona without the Admiral's permission," I said. "To do so would be to throw away my future as certainly as if the Inquisition took me. What do you propose we do?" I got up to poke at the fire as I spoke, for the coals had grown dim while Rachel spoke.

"Javier has a plan," Rachel said, with an admiring glance at the abashed footman. "Tell him, Javier. You can explain it better than I."

The boy cleared his throat.

"Don't let my brother make you nervous," Rachel said. "It is a good plan."

"My lady owns a farm outside the city," the boy said. "The tenants know me, for I am frequently sent to them with messages. We can obtain mules and provisions there and be on the road by dawn."

"You must not lose your place for us, Javier," Rachel exclaimed. "You need not come with us."

"Indeed not," I said. "Assuming I can square things with the Admiral, I will have enough on my hands without taking charge of a stripling. However, you will lose your place in any case, for you will be hanged for stealing from your mistress."

"I had not thought of that," Rachel said.

Javier evidently had. From his expression he believed, however foolishly, that he would gladly go to the stake for Rachel.

"You cannot return to Doña Marina's, Rachel," I said. "Thus far, we are in accord."

"Then you agree that we must flee," she said, "or you would not have mentioned the Admiral."

"I must get his leave," I said, "or I must stay in Barcelona. There can be no argument about that. If he keeps me here, I will some-how find you another escort. But in the meantime, I will accompany you to this farm. We can certainly concoct some tale that the farmer and his family will believe. Javier must return to Doña Marina's. He must know nothing when it is discovered that Rachel is gone."

"I know the way," the boy said, "and my presence will convince them that you indeed come from my lady. How else will you per-suade them to give you mules and provisions?"

"Gold may be persuasive enough," I said drily. "Surely they will not refuse to sell us food. And I will write to Doña Marina, mak-ing some excuse for borrowing her mules and promising their safe return."

"Then I must come with you that far," Javier said, "so I may carry the message."

Rachel laughed and clapped her hands. Once she knew that I would help her get away, she had thrown off her fear. I confess I was glad to see her eyes sparkle again, even though I hoped she remained on guard against the dangers facing her.

"I cannot approach the Admiral before morning," I said. "That will give us time to get to the farm and confide Rachel to the care of the farmer's wife. I can return swiftly to the city on one of the farmer's mules. The Admiral is always awake at dawn. I must also contrive to leave the Taino in good hands. I don't want them to suffer because of my absence. I believe my friend Fernando will be willing to take my place. He doesn't care for the Indians as I do, but he has a good heart."

I glanced over at the Taino, who still slumbered in their poppy-induced stupor. "You can't imagine how robust and comely they were," I said, "when we first came upon them."

"Perhaps," Rachel said, "being slaves in Spain doesn't agree with them."

Chapter 5

Outside Barcelona, April 19, 1493

It took us till false dawn to reach the farm. Javier led the way, sure-footed even in the dark. Rachel followed, stumbling now and then on the cobbles or tripping on her voluminous cloak. Reaching out a hand to steady her, I hoped that she might grow less ambitious for adventure when faced with the prosaic irritations and tedium of travel.

As a child, she had always been fearless, tumbling out of trees she had insisted on climbing, breaking up a fight between snarling dogs with a stick, and speaking her mind, even to Papa, whenever she perceived injustice. Indeed, it was a measure of how badly Don Rodrigo must have frightened her that she had come to me in such a state of agitation. However, she had far less stomach for boredom than she had for bravery.

We had no reason to believe that Doña Marina's household had missed us yet. If Don Rodrigo were to be believed, he had no intention of denouncing us to the Inquisition as long as he thought that Doña Marina would fall in with his plans regarding Rachel. Nonetheless, we twice turned into a shadowy alley to avoid the white hoods and red crosses of the Hermandad that patrolled the streets. The King and Queen, when they united Spain, had joined their local forces into a single body, the Santa Hermandad, the Sainted Brotherhood, to keep order in the towns and on the roads. To them, even the policing of a street was holy. I had no doubt the *hermanos* were on the alert for heretics as well as cutpurses and footpads.

I wished Papa were here to tell me what to do. But in my heart, I knew. I must remove Rachel from danger. I must persuade the Admiral to allow me to precede him to Seville, where the great work of assembling and equipping the fleet would take place. Once there, on more familiar territory and close to the sea, I would find a way to dispatch Rachel to my parents in Firenze.

We made our way toward the farmhouse between stubbled fields, a few showing the first green fuzz of early crops. The black of night was turning to a hundred shades of gray, and birds were racketing like folk at a festival. Javier doused his lantern.

"Must we rouse them?" Rachel asked, nervous now that we must beg for aid.

Javier laughed.

"You have always lived in a city, have you not? Farm folk are always stirring at this hour. I grew up in the country, and we had cows to milk, chickens to feed, and a dozen other tasks before the sun rose."

As if to confirm his words, a rooster crowed, and cattle lowed as a distant figure drove them out to pasture. The air was fresh and cold, laced with the scent of sweet hay and clean manure, very different from the sharp, salty smell of the sea but pleasant nonetheless.

"What now, sir?" Javier asked.

"We must knock and explain our purpose."

"Do you suppose they will offer us breakfast?" Rachel asked.

A sleepless night had left her with purple shadows under her eyes. I would do well to tell her about shipboard food: wormy biscuit, dried peas, and sour wine in the later stages of a voyage, and irregularly served at any time. But not now.

"If not, we will request it and offer coin. I smell bread baking, do you not? And on a farm such as this, they will have fresh eggs still warm from the laying."

The farmhouse was a low building of wattle and daub. It was roofed with Moorish tile, although the outbuildings surrounding it were thatched with broom. We could hear a rumble of voices from within. I approached the door, while Rachel hung back, looking sick with apprehension, for the success of our whole enterprise depended on our reception here. The mules, in particular, were essential if we were to reach Seville. I motioned for Javier to remain at my side, so the inhabitants might recognize him as one with legitimate reason to be here.

As I raised my hand to knock, the door swung open. Expecting a farmwife in an apron or a plowman in rough garments, I fell back in astonishment when a burly, bearded figure in brigandine and helmet filled the doorway. For a moment, my thoughts whirling, I considered shouting to Rachel to run.

While I stood irresolute, a familiar voice issued from within the farmhouse.

"Step aside, Esteban."

The looming man at arms backed off hastily. With a genteel cough, Doña Marina stepped forward. Like us, she was dressed for travel.

"Good morning, nephew," she said. "You have made indifferent time. We must do better on the road south, for I assume our destination is Seville. Raquel, compose yourself. A lady opens her mouth only to speak courtesies, take her meals, and say her prayers. And straighten your cap, if you please. You will not resemble a gypsy ragamuffin while in my care."

Rachel's mouth snapped shut, and she straightened her cap as directed.

"Javier, don't try to sneak away. You have earned a beating, but I will withhold it, as I know full well who lured you into this adventure. I have left instructions to assign you tasks that I am sure will prove suitable penance. You may ask the goodwife for a bite to eat, but then you must make your way home afoot, since you chose that means of coming here."

Still close to speechless, I stammered, "M-my lady?"

"I am going with you," she said calmly. "I find it convenient to quit Barcelona for a while, and it has been many years since I enjoyed an Andalusian spring."

"How did you know?" Rachel blurted.

"Oh, child," Doña Marina said, "you are foolish indeed if you believed that my faithful old Ernesto would sleep through a disturbance like a gaggle of geese departing through the garden gate or that Pepe could withstand for more than a minute my desire to hear all that he could tell me."

"But Pepe didn't know—"

"I, however, do. Did you think that I remained ignorant of Don Rodrigo's plans? Or that I would collude with him to carry them out? Esteban, saddle the mules, and tell Hernan that we leave within the hour." She turned toward the interior of the house, nodding graciously at the stout farmwife who bobbed in a nervous curtsy, flour rising in clouds from her face and hands. "You might as well come in. Such a long road is best taken on a full stomach."

As we consumed the fresh bread and eggs I had predicted along with ale and a sharp but tasty cheese, I considered the new turn of events. Doña Marina's presence would relieve me of a great part of the burden of responsibility for Rachel. She could chaperone my willful, enthusiastic sister and keep her from running wild, as I could not. And her men at arms would assure our safety. But was her desire to protect us sincere? I would hold my full judgment in reserve. Rachel chattered freely as we ate, taking our aunt's cooperation at face value. With Hernan and Esteban, the men at arms, Rachel was as friendly as a puppy, treating them with the same respect she did me: in short, with none.

"Will Don Rodrigo not pursue us?" I gulped the last mouthful of ale and wiped crumbs from my lips.

"I don't believe so," she said. "He will be very angry that the bird he sought to pluck for his son has flown. As for me, my absence must cool his ardor. As time passes, he will give up and seek easier prey." She stood. "I am ready to depart."

"I will not be easy," I said, "until I have spoken with the Admiral. If I may take one of your mules, I can seek him out now. Once I have his permission, I will rejoin you on the road."

"He was ever very fond of your father," Aunt Marina said.

She led the way around the house, where seven sturdy mules awaited us, five saddled and the other two laden with bulging packs.

"When we heard my brother had drowned at sea," she said, "I cried until I became ill. Then, when we had mourned for months, he showed up at our door, ragged and thin but alive, with Columbus at his side. Each declared he would have been dead if not for the other. He had no kin nearer than Genoa, so he became quite one of the family."

"I cannot imagine the Admiral as a youth," I admitted.

"He had a mop of hair as red as carrots," my aunt said, "though I believe it turned white when he was no more than thirty."

"Will you tell the Admiral about me?" Rachel asked, as I flung a leg over my mule.

"I will tell him," I said, "that I have but now learned of your presence in Barcelona. I shall say that I must escort you to Seville, where family friends have promised to take you in until we can find a way to send you to Firenze to join our parents."

"I don't want—" Rachel began.

My glare silenced her. Now was not the time to argue. I kissed her and bowed over my aunt's hand, kissing the air above it as

Columbus had before the Queen. I turned the mule's head toward the city. As I urged it to a canter that was its most rapid pace, a soft wash of pink, pale gold, and pearl suffused the sky above the wakening city, heralding a new day.

Chapter 6

On the road to Seville, April 19–23, 1493

Once we were on the road, Rachel threw off the oppressive spirits in which Don Rodrigo's attack had left her, trusting to me, Doña Marina, and the two stout men at arms to keep her safe. I too felt more cheerful, having not only the Admiral's blessing on this journey, but his commission to join in the great work beginning in Seville, building a fleet for our next voyage to the Indies. With difficulty, I restrained Rachel from demanding to wear her boy's garments, the better to sit her mule. Our aunt knew nothing of Rachel's masquerade, and I preferred that she never learn of it. Worse, I feared that my sister would repeat to Doña Marina her mad proposal to accompany me to the Indies. While she held her peace on that particular matter, she drove me mad demanding endless details of life on shipboard, the Taino, and the isle of Hispaniola where the Spanish settlement lay.

"It is the only sensible solution," she grumbled when our aunt was out of earshot, no less dignified atop a mule than she would be in a palace or cathedral. "Why should I not wish to follow the fortunes of the man you yourself most admire?"

"It is more work than you imagine to be a seaman, or even a gromet," I said. "Worse, in fact, for the boys must answer to any who choose to give them an order, not only to the ship's master or the pilot. You can't imagine how it is on board a ship, Rachel."

"Then tell me, so I can contrive a way to manage. I can work," Rachel said. "I am strong, and I would much prefer it to becoming a young lady, whether in Spain or in Italy."

"You don't understand."

My sister was an innocent. I could not tell her that the ship's boys held pissing contests over the rails, or that sailors, so often denied the company of women, could quickly become consumed with lust when one was available.

"You would be profoundly uncomfortable," I said.

Rachel snorted and tossed her head. Her mule did the same. She whipped it to a gallop, its hooves sending spurts of dust up from the road. To my chagrin, the fastest of the mules had taken a fancy to her and would allow no other rider on its back. She loved to ride so far ahead that we could not overtake her until we reached the next village. There we would find her, gossiping with the village women at the well, having already made friends with every child, dog, and chicken in the place. Her unreserved trust in all she met made me think of the Taino when we first encountered them: unstinting in their friendliness and expecting nothing but good in return. It troubled me.

Doña Marina, whose mule dared not exceed a sedate trot no matter what the others did, reined in beside me. Knowing I could not catch up with Rachel, I had allowed mine to pause and crop the grass at the side of the road.

"Your father must find a husband for her when she reaches Italy," she said. "That will settle her down."

"She is not yet thirteen years old," I protested. "Rachel is not an infanta, a princess, to be married off as a child." Indeed, by Jewish law, a girl reached womanhood at twelve years and a day. Papa, however, did not approve of the practice of early betrothal. I did not think it wise to make either point to my aunt.

"She will be old enough by the time it is arranged." Doña Marina clucked expertly at her mule, which raised its head and ambled forward.

I gathered up my reins and persuaded my own mount to keep pace with hers. We were passing a grove of cherry trees in full bloom, and the balky creature had decided they were good to munch. No doubt we would find Rachel garlanded with pink blossoms when we reached the next village.

"Aunt," I said on impulse, "why did you leave your ordered life to keep us company?"

Doña Marina sniffed. "It is evident you have never had sole charge of a girl of Raquel's age."

"I am already aware of my deficiencies in the matter," I said. "But why?"

"I was growing weary of the sameness of my days," she said. "Raquel is an enlivening companion."

I dared to laugh at that, and she permitted herself a rusty smile.

"Too much so, as I know too well," I said. "Had you no intention of accepting Don Rodrigo's suit, had the complication of our presence not arisen?"

"Never," she said. "I don't mean for him or any other man to take my inheritance from Torres—or my liberty. A widow can be her own woman as a wife or maiden cannot."

"That is what galls Rachel so," I said. "She has an independent spirit."

"She reminds me of myself in my youth," Doña Marina said.

I tried to conceal my astonishment, evidently without success.

"Do you not think," she said, "that I must have been a rebellious girl? How else could I have turned my back on my father's faith and the life of a good Jewish wife that he intended for me?"

I said nothing, hoping to hear more.

"I was lucky," she said. "I married an old man. He was both kind and generous, and he didn't live long. Does that seem cold to you?" Her lips curved in a humorless smile. "Women have few choices in this life, and neither maiden nor wife has the freedom that even the most miserable man takes for granted. Since becoming a widow, I have lived as I wanted." This time, her smile reached her eyes. "Except for a regrettable absence of adventure until now."

"And Don Rodrigo?" I ventured.

"Soon enough," she said, "his fancy will light on another rich widow."

"The cousin Don Rodrigo mentioned," I said, "he who sailed with us on the *Santa Maria* and yet remains in the Indies, was reputed to be an informer for the Inquisition."

"I had not heard of him before," she said. "It doesn't seem as if they were close companions. Has he influence?"

"At Court, you mean?" I shook my head. "None at all. He is a low fellow and not what one would expect of a family like the Maldonados."

"Every family has at least one relative to embarrass them," she said. "I myself was an embarrassment to the Mendozas when I chose to embrace Christ."

"Papa did the same."

"But in his heart, he didn't mean it. He never understood my choice."

At that moment, a sow wandering across the road signaled our arrival in the village. Hairy, brown as dirt, and of an impressive size, she ignored us as she grunted encouragement to the half dozen piglets that followed her. The men at arms, who had followed us all day at a discreet distance so as not to intrude on our talk, caught up with us as we waited for the porcine procession to pass.

Rachel was not at the well, though all the village women gathered there were crowned with cherry blossoms. They laughed and pointed toward the biggest cottage at the end of the dusty street.

"The alcalde's wife invited her to dinner." Evidently, no one refused the mayor's wife. "They await your arrival."

We found Rachel sitting in the doorway of the cottage, shelling peas. She held the bowl in her lap, knees wide to make a net of her long skirt. The posture was disgraceful, but considering she had spent hours astride a mule every day for the past week, I decided it would do no good to scold her. Doña Marina's snort signified more amusement than disapproval, if I was not mistaken.

"What took you so long?" Rachel shouted as we approached. Her braids were coming down, and her cheeks were as rosy as her crown of blossoms, which sat askew so that she looked like a tipsy wood nymph. "They have killed a kid for our dinner, and I was allowed to milk the nanny goat. Watch out for the billy, though. He doesn't like mules."

Chapter 7

Cordoba, April 26, 1493

As the journey continued, we did not always feast on roasted kid. Nor were we always offered the mayor's own bed, with his children turned out to sleep on hay in a shed alongside my aunt's men at arms. In the towns along the way, Doña Marina would lay out gold for a chamber in a well-kept inn for herself and Rachel, though the guards and I made do with benches in the common room. I didn't mind, except that I never had enough privacy to don my *tallit* and *t'fillin* for prayer. Ha'shem's hand had certainly been under us so far, and He deserved my thanks.

Rachel's Jewish observance was neglected too. She wore a silver cross to reassure the curious and deflect suspicion. My mother had done the same, although I could remember her grimace of distaste each morning as she put it on before going to the market. Rachel had no such qualms. As we rode along, she chattered freely about the sisters in the convent, the daily round of worship, and her friends among the other girls, some there to become nuns in time and others to be schooled to piety and virtue before their marriages. Rachel showed no sign of applying either the Christian religion or the piety and virtue to herself.

As we traveled deeper into my native Andalusia, the air grew warmer. The season progressed almost before our eyes from the pale shoots and plowed earth of early spring to spring at its height, lush with a thousand shades of green. We passed orchards of apple, plum, and apricot, trees heavy with clouds of pink and white blossom, as well as the deep, brilliant rose of quince and starlike orange and lemon blossoms that lent the air as sweet a scent as that of Hispaniola. Kestrels and falcons circled above. The songs of thrushes and warblers rose all around us, above them the high, liquid tones of larks. It seemed to me that the very manure on the fields smelled sweet, as if the cows that supplied it grazed on flowers.

Now, even with another perilous voyage ahead, I remembered that Andalusia was home. My spirits rose higher every day until they almost matched Rachel's. How could I, who had crossed the uncharted Ocean Sea on a frail cockleshell of a boat and reached the Indies, fail to believe that anything was possible?

And so we came to Cordoba. The city, once ruled by the Moors, now harbored a tribunal of the Inquisition. I would have preferred to skirt it for that reason. I could not call attention to our private adherence to Judaism. To Esteban and Hernan, my aunt's men at arms, I hoped we passed as Christians. Furthermore, Rachel clamored to see the sights of Cordoba, which she had never visited. These included the magnificent cathedral, once a mosque, with its forest of columns topped with arches composed of broad stripes of red and golden-white stone.

In Moorish times, Cordoba had been a great center of learning, where Muslims, Jews, and Christians lived at peace. Our own philosopher Maimonides had been born there, as had his fellow, the Arab Averroes. But the Reconquista had changed that. Cordoba's alcazar was renamed the Palace of Christian Kings, and the sights available to travelers included the abandoned Jewish quarter and a slave market. This last I passed with eyes averted, fearing to see Jewish slaves among the wretched Africans and Moors.

Having risen early and broken our fast with nothing more than water and some elderly lumps of bread, we decided to visit the great market in the arcades of the Plaza de la Corredera before seeking lodging. The plaza was thronged with people and animals. Produce spilled out of carts and baskets ranged beneath cloth awnings rigged to offer shade as the day grew hotter. Bawling calves, chickens squawking, and vendors crying out wares of indescribable variety made speech impossible. From the baking earth underfoot rose the smells of rotting vegetables, frying meat, fresh dung, jasmine and orange blossom, and the garlic breath and sour sweat of many human bodies crushed together.

I helped the men at arms rope all seven mules together so that we could lead them in a string. Hernan and Esteban strode beside the two pack mules, eyes alert and hands on the hilts of their sheathed swords. Not only would pickpockets and cutpurses abound in such a crowd, but gypsies or seeming beggars might seek to distract us while their fellows made off with our packs, if not the mules themselves.

"Don't let go of Rosa's bridle," I admonished Rachel, for so she had named her mule. "If you get lost in this crowd, we will be hard put to find you."

"I itch!" Rachel said. "Can we not rest in the shade before going on? My skin is prickling with the heat." She tugged at the neck of her gown. Her cheeks were flushed dark red, and damp tendrils of hair lay plastered against her brow.

"Where would you have us rest?" I gestured at the packed plaza, in which it would have been hard to insert so much as a wooden staff between one person and the next.

"We must find a well," Doña Marina said. Even she had dismounted. She picked her way through the crowd with dignity, one hand raising her skirts above the dust and the other resting lightly on her mule's neck. "We must refill our water skins, or we will find ourselves fainting in this heat." She patted delicately at her neck, cheeks, and forehead with a handkerchief trimmed with Flemish lace.

"Oh, yes!" Rachel said. "Water is what I wish for most, although I am hungry as well. Hernan, you are the tallest of us. Can you see a well? Look, over there. Is that not a fountain? I am sure I see the glint of spray rising in the sun."

As all of us stopped and craned our necks, Rachel gave a cry of excitement, let go her mule's bridle, and darted away from us into the crowd.

"Raquel!"

"Rachel, stop!"

As I started forward, meaning to run after her, something glittered at my feet. I bent and picked it up. It was Rachel's silver cross, its chain broken. When I looked up, she had disappeared.

Chapter 8

Cordoba, April 26, 1493

Rachel plunged forward, forgetting everything but her thirst. A plaza this big must surely have a great stone fountain built atop a well from which folk could draw water at any time. She was almost certain that she had seen the sparkle of spray. But when she had pushed past a multitude of people, none of them inclined to give way to her, she could see nothing resembling a fountain, only a vast sea of heads bobbing like ocean waves, interspersed with the canvas awnings of market carts like sails upon the sea. She must tell the others she had been mistaken. But when she turned, ready to retrace her steps, she could see no sign of Diego, Doña Marina, or the men.

To her right, a mule brayed and another answered. But when she elbowed her way through to them, she saw that they belonged to strangers. Then the sunlight glittered on a pair of metal helmets, but her hope that their wearers would prove to be Hernan and Esteban was dashed when she got close enough to see their faces. She stood still while the crowd eddied around her, biting her lip and trying not to cry. Diego would be so angry! She would endure any scolding he might give her for the sight of his face. How would he ever find her? There must be hundreds of people in the market. She didn't know her way around Cordoba, not even in what direction the road to Seville lay. In any case, they would surely not continue their journey without making every effort to find her. If only they had chosen an inn first! She could have found someone to tell her how to get there. But they had not.

Perhaps she would spy the hoods and tunics of the Hermandad. Surely a city as big as Cordoba maintained a company of the brothers to keep order. With luck, they had a central station where she could ask for help. Or a troop of soldiers, at least one with a respectable captain, might be kind to a Christian girl. Rachel's hand reached up to finger the silver cross she always wore. It was gone! She had dropped it somewhere in this teeming place, and she would never find it. That meant she could not ask a soldier for assistance, as he might serve the Inquisition. With it, she appeared a Christian, not worth a second glance. Without it, her olive skin, dark hair, and long, slender nose proclaimed her a Jew. And to be a Jew in Spain meant death. Neither youth nor pleading would save her.

She heard shouts and the tramp of booted feet. A troop of soldiers marched directly toward her, helmets flashing with a blinding brilliance, lances held high, their fluttering pennons snapping in the breeze. The crowd parted readily, many, in fact, diving out of their way so as not to be trampled. She stared, paralyzed by fear like a hunted creature. A commotion arose, both men and women shouting.

"Stop!"

"Don't let her get away!"

In too great a panic to wonder how either soldiers or mob could have identified her as their quarry, she stood frozen until she saw a short figure hurtle toward her in a confusion of jingling chains and bracelets and colorful, ragged skirts. The little girl cannoned into her so hard that she nearly lost her footing. Reflexively, she threw her arms around the child to keep her balance. The girl, in turn, wrapped her skinny brown arms around Rachel and clung to her, whimpering damply into Rachel's skirt as the soldiers came pounding up and ground to a halt surrounding them.

A stout market woman in apron and kerchief pushed past the soldiers. Two hulking youths followed her, shouting and brandishing cudgels. Rachel panted like an animal at bay.

"That's her!" the market woman cried. "She stole an orange and knocked over my cart, the dirty little gypsy!"

"We don't need her kind," yelled one of the youths, "stealing from respectable folk."

"Beat them and lock them up!" shouted the other. "Or drive them out of town! We don't want them here!"

At this, the child, who looked to be no more than six or seven, lifted her tearstained face from Rachel's skirt.

"I didn't steal!" Her black eyes flashed, and her small hands formed claws as if to fly at her accusers and scratch them.

The leader of the soldiers dipped the tip of his lance toward her. The child shrank back against Rachel.

"Liar!" screamed the woman. "We know them gypsies' thieving ways! And who knocked over my cart?"

"It was an accident!" the little girl screamed back. "I didn't steal your fruit, you fat, cross-eyed *gadji*!"

"Then what's this?" the woman cried. She plunged her hand into the neck of the child's ragged bodice and held up an orange, her eyes glittering with triumph.

"I offered to pay!" the child cried.

"With lies!" the woman countered. "Search her well," she challenged the soldiers, "and you'll find not a coin upon her, unless she's been thieving from others than me this day."

The little girl tugged at Rachel's sleeve. When Rachel bent down, she said in a low voice, "I offered to read her palm. It was a fair trade, and I was hungry and thirsty, but she would have none of it. You must believe me!"

Rachel patted her shoulder.

"I will help you explain to the soldiers. Surely we can make them understand." She caught the leader's eye and opened her mouth to speak.

"They're in it together!" the market woman bawled. "Look at them, two dirty gypsies, alike as two peas. Arrest them both! My sons and I will bear witness."

"But I am not—" Rachel began.

The soldier nodded, and four of his men stepped forward and clapped an iron grip on Rachel's arms and the little girl's.

"You can tell it to my captain at the guardhouse," he said. "I'm just the sergeant. It's my job to bring in anyone who makes a disturbance, and you've done that all right."

"But I didn't—"

"Save it for the captain. Forward, march!"

Rachel looked around wildly. This would be a good time for Doña Marina, with her unfailing air of authority, to appear. The little girl appeared to be more angry than cowed, kicking and spitting. The two soldiers who held her had to carry her at arm's length, with her body twisting to get free and her feet still kicking well above the ground.

The child caught Rachel's eye. Her lips moved silently.

"Wait. Be ready," she mouthed. Her gaze darted around the crowd, scanning it in all directions, then returning to Rachel.

Rachel cast a puzzled look about. All the faces she could see looked hostile: some angry, some gleeful to see gypsies taken into custody.

The child hissed at her and repeated, "Wait. Be ready."

The daggers seemed to fly out of nowhere, one hitting the steel helmet of one of Rachel's captors with a loud ping, another piercing the leather corselet of one of the child's jailors high in the shoulder.

Yet another dagger grazed the cheek of the third, while a volley of stones rattled against the helmet of the fourth, two or three striking him in the face so that he cursed. All of them dropped their prisoners' arms, while the rest of the soldiers whirled and drew their swords, though their enemy remained invisible. The onlookers, who had crowded close to enjoy the spectacle of somebody else in trouble, now started screaming and trampling one another in their haste to get away from a fracas in which they might actually get hurt.

The little girl landed neatly on her feet and grabbed Rachel's hand as tightly as the soldiers had held her arms.

"Run!" she said.

The child pulled Rachel along at a pace that left her gasping. As they fled through the panicked crowd, the girl gave a piercing whistle, followed by a stream of words in a language Rachel didn't recognize. A man's voice responded in the same language, and the child changed course to pull Rachel toward it, zigzagging to throw off pursuit. When Rachel threw a quick look over her shoulder, the uproar seemed no more than the normal hubbub of the market, and the soldiers had been swallowed up in the sea of folk going about their business.

Chapter 9

Cordoba, April 26, 1493

We combed the market for over an hour without finding Rachel. We did find a well, in the opposite direction from where Rachel had claimed to see water spouting. But even filling a water skin and pouring its entire contents over my head didn't refresh me. Imagining what might have happened to her made sweat break out on my forehead again a moment later.

"We must inquire of both the soldiers and the Hermandad," Doña Marina said. We had seen small bands of these bodies going about their business. The men at arms took up this idea with enthusiasm.

"It stands to reason she would seek their help," Esteban said.

"If not, they might at least have seen her," Hernan said.

Their broad, kind faces looked worried, for they had grown fond of Rachel, who treated them like indulgent uncles. I could not tell them that it would be folly for Rachel to attract the attention of either the civil guards or the military, especially without a cross about her neck. Doña Marina intervened.

"Esteban, can you find a station to which these men must return?"

"That will be the guardhouse, my lady. It's easily found, for they are usually located near the quarter where—"

He broke off, red-faced, by which I deduced that he would search first in the quarter where men might seek the company of loose women. That brought to my mind another horror to add to my dire imaginings of what might befall Rachel if we failed to find her.

"Do so, then," Doña Marina said. "Make inquiries there. You, Hernan, must seek out a decent inn, for we will not leave Cordoba until Raquel is found. You and I, Diego, will remain here in the shade until they return." She cast a sharp but not unkind look at me. "Don't despair: it accomplishes nothing. If Raquel is wandering lost, it is likely she will think to seek us here, where she last saw us."

I could not deny the good sense of her words, though the knowledge that worrying would not help didn't prevent me from doing it. The men at arms departed on their errands. Doña Marina sat straight-backed on a saddlebag and took out her embroidery, plying her needle as if she took her ease in her own home. I slumped against a column, too dejected to move my legs out of the sun's heat as it rode across the sky, changing the pattern of shadow in the arcade.

I must have drowsed, for I jumped at the sound of Esteban's rough voice.

"No luck, my lady. They said they'd taken up no damsel in distress today, nor even any miscreants or heretics, save for two dirty gypsy girls."

I stood, shaking sleep out of my eyes and wrinkles out of my garments in an attempt to face whatever came next like a man and not a sloven. If we removed ourselves from the great plaza, how would Rachel ever find us? I wished Papa were here. I would gladly face his wrath at me for losing Rachel for the sake of his strength and wisdom.

A shout heralded Hernan's arrival. No doubt he had secured lodging where we might rest. As if I could! Doña Marina laid her hand on Esteban's arm, and they went to meet him.

"Ssst! *Gadjo*, boy!"

I looked around, but saw no one. The sharp hiss came again.

"Ssst! Come!"

Now I saw him, a wiry figure crouching in the shadow of a pillar. He grinned at me, his teeth stained and broken, but his black eyes bright in a swarthy face. His clothes were dingy and tattered, like a sailor's after a month at sea. But the pair of steel daggers at his waist were bright, not new, but carefully tended.

"Come," he repeated. "I take you to your sister."

"What! Where is she?" I crossed the distance between us at a single bound and clutched at his arms. "What have you done with her?"

I could feel his muscles harden, but he made no attempt to free himself.

"She is with the Roma. Safe. She save our *chavi*, we save yours."

"You must take us to her at once!"

With gritted teeth, I refrained from shaking him as Doña Marina bore down on us, Hernan and Esteban in her wake. Each kept a hand on his sword, but neither drew, though their posture betrayed their readiness to spring forward if need be.

"Who have we here?" Doña Marina demanded. "Have you news of my niece?"

She waved the men at arms back a pace. I stood close enough to tackle the gypsy if he attempted to flee. But he didn't. He gave my imposing aunt the same impudent grin he had given me.

"She is safe with the Roma."

Behind her, Esteban exclaimed, "The two gypsy girls!"

"What happened?" My fingers itched to shake the story out of him. "Did the soldiers have her?"

"I told you. She save our Drina, we save her. You and you," he nodded to me and to my aunt, "come get her. No *churara*, no swords." He flicked a hand at the men at arms. "Too many *gadjo*."

Doña Marina remained calm. She would have made a good ship's master.

"My nephew and I will accompany you. Diego, you will lead Raquel's mule. Hernan, you will take the remaining mules to the inn."

She nodded at the heavily laden pack mules. If the gypsy led us someplace where he and his fellows could rob us, they would not get our gold.

"Esteban will come with us," she said.

The gypsy scowled and shook his head vigorously.

"He will leave his sword behind," Doña Marina said.

"My lady!" Esteban protested.

I regarded her with admiration. I had not known my uncompromising aunt could be such a fine negotiator. She would have made an admiral. The gypsy shrugged. He turned and motioned to us to follow.

"You have knives, Esteban," she said. "So has he. But he will not betray us."

The gypsy grinned again. "I bring you to your *chavi*," he said. "Rachel. Our Drina call her sparkling girl."

That didn't sound as if Rachel were a frightened prisoner.

"*Chavi?*" I said. "Drina?"

I had heard the gypsy language in snatches on market days. They worked as itinerant farm laborers during spring planting and at the harvest, but did not settle in towns or stay anywhere for long. They made baskets for sale and were said to read one's destiny in the fall of cards or the lines in one's palm, if one were credulous enough to believe they could foretell the future.

"*Chavi* is girl in our tongue, Romani. Drina the name of your sister's new friend."

"Drina," I repeated. "Are you her brother?"

He laughed. "Her *nano*, uncle. I am Shandor." He cocked his head in inquiry.

"Diego," I said. "Are you taking us to the gypsy camp?"

"Not gypsy!" Shandor spat. "We are Roma!" He struck his chest with his fist. "I am Rom. We are an ancient people."

"Roma, then," I said. "Rachel is at your camp? You take us there now? If you don't let my sister go, I will fight you all. If she has been harmed, I will kill you."

Shandor laughed. "With what?" He gestured contemptuously at my knife. "I am best knife thrower of us all, except Marko, father of Drina. Four soldiers have Drina and Rachel. We get them back, soldiers never even see us. But have no fear for Rachel, she has honor among us." He laughed again. "Your sister say you worry too much."

Chapter 10

The gypsies were encamped in a sunny meadow, their gaily painted wagons grouped like dwellings in a village. Women stirred bubbling pots over several open fires ringed with stones, and the air smelled pleasantly of wood smoke and stewed rabbit. A man seated on a nearby log was mending a tin pot. Mothers called out to infants and toddlers who crawled, rolled, and chased each other through the grass. Older children curried mules that, while not as well bred as ours, looked sturdy enough to pull the wagons. The women and girls all wore long, full, brightly colored skirts, and both men and women were bedecked with jewelry that flashed in the sun.

The whole encampment hummed with music. One woman, gnarled and squat as an olive stump, with long iron-gray hair streaming down her back, carried herself like a beauty as she stretched out her arms and sang in a husky, plaintive wail that reminded me of Moorish music. A dancer who looked even older faced her. He strutted and stamped, arms upraised, back as straight as a soldier's and the pride of a grandee in his bearing. Several musicians accompanied them. Three of the men played small lute-like instruments whose pairs of strings they struck with their fingers to create a bold flurry of sound. Women shook jingling tambourines or snapped a pair of wooden shells in either hand to create a clacking rhythm. Others, both men and women, clapped in rhythmic patterns, occasionally contributing a line, delivered with great passion, to the song.

During our circuitous journey from Cordoba to the camp, through woods and along winding tracks off the main road, I had learned that the Roma regarded what they called *gadjo*, anyone not a Rom, much as we Jews did gentiles: folk of whom one did well to be wary. They would never understand our ways and might turn on us at any moment. When the Roma in the camp caught sight of us emerging from the trees at Shandor's back, all activity stopped. But their stillness lasted only a moment. Then they surged forward, curious and even welcoming.

I took a young woman stirring something in a great black iron kettle, with a little girl crouching at her side and chattering at her, to be a Rom mother—until she whirled and revealed herself as Rachel. Dropping the long-handled spoon she held, she ran toward us with outstretched arms, her face indeed sparkling with excitement and enthusiasm. A small, disheveled dog bounded at her heels, barking loudly.

"Diego, Diego! Is it not splendid? The Roma saved me, and I am learning to speak Romani and make rabbit stew. Come and meet my friend Drina, she is little but very quick and bright. You know Shandor, but you must greet Drina's father, Marko, and her mother, Tshilaba. Tshilaba is not much older than you, but she has Drina and two babies and another coming, and when she heard what happened, she kissed my hand and said, *'Gestena!'* That is 'thank you' in Romani, and you must say it to all of them, to Shandor and Marko and Tshilaba, for she skinned the rabbits, and Drina too, for I would never have run in time if she had not taken my hand. Oh, and Marko snared the rabbits, and here is Drina's dog. His name is Baxtalo, it means Lucky, and I *wish* I could have a dog of my own, but I know you would say no."

I caught her up in my arms, laughing and shedding a tear or two that I hoped nobody noticed, even as I scolded her.

"Rachel, you are *never* to run off in a crowd like that! You must promise to be more mindful. I could never have faced Papa and Mama again if I had lost you, as I feared I had."

"I am perfectly safe," she said, hugging me fiercely before she sprang down and danced lightly around me, too excited to stand still. "All the Roma have been very kind to me. You worry too much."

"So I gather you have told the whole tribe," I said drily.

I let her lead me off to meet Drina and eat wild strawberries the two girls had picked themselves, as the scarlet stains on their mouths and fingers attested. I was dizzy with relief at getting Rachel back. We spent the rest of the day with the Roma in feasting and much needed rest. Doña Marina was ceremoniously greeted by an old woman, wrinkled and bent but radiating authority, who Rachel whispered was their queen and Drina's great-grandmother. Esteban, of whom the men were at first exceedingly wary, won them over by almost matching them at knife throwing, beating them at archery, and losing a pocketful of coin to them at dice. He laughingly refused to wager on whether he could guess the location of a dried pea under three shells, which disappointed them but won their further respect.

As I would surely have lost, I did not compete, but instead spent some time talking with Drina's father.

"You *gadjo* think all Roma are thieves," Marko said. "How can we earn when they will not let us work, but drive us away if we seek to settle among them and learn new trades?"

"Thus the Jews became bankers," I told him, "for they would not allow us in their guilds. And so we grew rich and aroused their greed and envy."

"That fate, at least, will not befall the Roma," Marko said. "And I do not need the gift of foretelling to say so."

The children, both boys and girls, were not restrained by Jewish or Christian notions of manners. They had already adopted Rachel as one of themselves, chattering to her and Drina as they converged on me and patted every part of me they could reach. Their curious hands explored my skin, my garments, and my hair. The young women, equally interested, hovered nearby and giggled.

"They look as if they would like to pat you too," Rachel said, giggling herself.

"Women don't touch a young man!" Drina said, scandalized.

As evening fell, more and more of the Roma took to dancing around the fire, their movements both fierce and fluid. They beckoned to me to join them. As I shook my head, a stick tapped my shoulder. I looked up to find the old queen of the Roma regarding me. I leaped up from the log on which I had perched and bowed low, which amused her.

"Sit," she said.

When I had done so, she settled herself beside me, leaning lightly on her knotty wooden walking stick. She sat the log with as straight a back as Doña Marina on her mule.

"Why do you wander?" I asked. "Why do you not settle in towns and villages like other folk and make a home there?"

"The rabbit who has only one hole is soon caught," she said. "A saying of the Roma."

"My people would have done well to remember that," I said. "We allowed ourselves to believe Spain was our home. Now they have driven us out and taken all our possessions. They may do the same to you."

"All you can see, you possess. Another saying of the Roma." She lifted her face to the sky, then flung her arms wide in an expansive gesture that took in the meadow, the woods beyond, and the ground at our feet. "You see the earth, the sky. Who can take these from you? Who can steal from you the lark on the wing, the flower in the meadow, the rabbit in the grass, the strawberry hiding under the leaf, the open road?"

I thought Cristobal would like her.

"I read your hand," she said.

"You wish to tell my fortune?" I could not entirely keep my skepticism out of my voice.

She spat on the ground.

"The cards, lines in the palm, they reveal wisdom to those who know how to read," she said. "No man or woman can tell the future. Give me your hand."

She held out her hand, palm up. At her nod, I laid mine upon it. She squinted over my palm and traced its lines and creases with one finger.

"Ha! Like us, you are a wanderer."

"We Jews have been wandering for close to fifteen hundred years," I said.

"Then is it not time to make the best of it?" she asked. "Learn from the Roma. Every home is no home. Family is the heart, not the hearth alone."

"The Jews are the people of the Book," I said.

"As Roma people of the road," she replied.

"We also name ourselves the Chosen People," I said, not sure why I told her this.

"Chosen? By whom?"

To that, I knew the answer.

"By God."

"Ha! And for what?"

"Truly," I said, "it often seems that we are chosen but for misfortune and death." I had not dared admit as much to another soul since I bade my parents farewell a year ago.

She leaned forward and patted my shoulder. Then she seized a bundle of dry sticks from a stack lying ready for the fire. With a quick, wringing motion, she snapped the fagot in two and tossed it into the flames. She raised her hands, fingers fluttering, and followed the path of the sparks upward. I felt a chill prickle my neck.

"You *gadjo*, but a good boy," she said. "You find another way. You and your sister green wood—bend, not snap."

I wished I could ask her how to find that way, but I doubted she would or could have told me. As she said, her art was not fortune-telling, but wisdom.

Chapter 11

After spending one night with the Roma, we bade them farewell and made our way as quickly as possible to the inn where Hernan awaited us, fretting with anxiety as he wondered whether to set out in search of us. Since we had to reenter Cordoba to reach the inn, Doña Marina made Rachel put on her best dress, sadly wrinkled from the pack in which it had lain since our departure from Barcelona. Further, she lent her a lace veil to cover her hair and mask her face from anyone who might have witnessed the previous day's altercation with the soldiers.

We slept at the inn that night. The long week's travel had left Doña Marina with a fierce desire for a hot bath. Between her commanding presence and a quantity of silver coin, she persuaded the innkeeper's wife to carry many buckets of boiling water to the chamber she shared with Rachel. She offered to make the woman fill a tub for me, but I declined, as did the men at arms. We made do with cold water at the pump in the inn yard. Indeed, the men at arms professed themselves amazed when I stripped off my clothing and poured a bucket over my whole body.

"I bathe my body at Christmas and Easter," Hernan declared, "and that's good enough for me."

"Do you not have fleas?" I asked.

"What has that to say in the matter?" Hernan scratched beneath his tunic, looking puzzled by my question. "So does every Christian man in Spain."

Thus he confirmed my mother's opinion of the gentiles. I said no more.

The next day, we moved on. Through the heat of the day I dozed, slumped in the saddle. My mule clopped along, head hanging and nose brushing the earth as if it too would be glad of a siesta. As always, Doña Marina's straight back and her mule's gliding walk gave credence to the claim of a muleteer at the inn in Cordoba that mules had a smoother gait than many a horse. Or perhaps, given my aunt's strength of will, her mount simply knew better than to jounce or bob with her aboard.

That evening, rather than squandering more of our coin in a town or even a village inn, we stopped to camp in the ruins of a castle, most likely destroyed in the centuries of warfare against the Moors. The men at arms were disappointed. Predictably, they favored the towns, which offered strong drink and female companionship. I didn't mind camping. I still felt safer away from people. The broken stone, with a remaining arch or carving here and there, was beautiful in its wild way. We saw not a soul and heard no sound but the twittering of birds preparing to sleep and the homely lowing of cattle in a nearby field.

"The sunset promises to be well worth seeing," Doña Marina said, "painted on such a vast open sky. I seldom see the like within the walls of Barcelona. I shall take a walk and enjoy the evening air. You need not worry for my safety, for the men will accompany me with a lantern. If you need more light before my return, there are candles in the second pack mule's left-hand saddlebag."

From our perch on big stones that had tumbled from the main arch of the castle gateway, Rachel and I watched them out of sight.

"Have you kept count of the days?" I asked. "It is Friday night. She is giving us an opportunity to celebrate Shabbat."

"Shh, I know." Rachel spoke more softly than was her wont. She took my hand and laced her fingers through mine. "Let us watch the sun go down."

Only quiet fields lay before us. Even the mules seemed to sense the peace of the moment. The fiery ball of the sun, more brilliant than the largest of Queen Isabella's rubies, sank below the horizon, then flared up into clouds that appeared in a clear sky as if for no other purpose than to reflect back the dying rays in pink, gold, and lavender splendor. As the display faded to a deep red and then to the dark blue of evening, Rachel leaned over and kissed my cheek.

"Shabbat shalom," she said. May the peace of the Sabbath be upon you.

"Shabbat shalom."

As I drew her toward me and kissed her cheek in turn, she giggled.

"Your beard is scratchy. You have truly become a man, my brother." She gave me an impulsive hug.

"And you are still not quite a woman, my sister," I retorted. "But in this place, you are the woman of the house. Do you remember the *b'rucha* over the candles?"

"Of course!" she said. "Wait, I have a clean kerchief for my head in my pack. I will get it while you find the candles. And I must take this thing off." She tugged the silver cross on its chain, which I had mended, over her head.

"Remember to put it back on, after," I said.

"I will not make that mistake twice," she said. "Although I didn't remove it, Diego. You know the chain broke—"

"Hush," I said. "Let us light the candles."

I lit one candle from the small fire the men had built in the stone hearth of a hall that still had most of its walls. I dripped wax onto the paving stones.

"Let me, let me," Rachel cried. "It is my task to light the candles."

I handed her the candles. Though her braid swung close to the flame, I refrained from criticizing as she lit the second candle with the first, then pressed both candles into the wax so they would stand upright. The white kerchief tied around her hair, much like those my mother wore on Shabbat, made her look older. She cupped her hands around the two small, brave flames and closed her eyes.

"Baruch atah Adonai Eloheinu melech ha'olam . . ."

Chapter 12

Seville, May 4–June 1, 1493

We entered Seville at dusk, Rachel drooping with fatigue, the pack mules limping, and even Doña Marina's face showing the strain of keeping her back erect. As night fell, we made our way along the Calle Sierpes, still bustling even at that hour. We avoided the Jewish quarter. Although a few conversos remained in Seville, we were bound for the home of Christian friends of Doña Marina.

The Espinosas lived not far from the Plaza de San Francisco in a mansion so fine that I wondered what these grand folk would make of such unprepossessing travelers. But I need not have worried. When the massive wooden door opened to Esteban's knock, light spilled out and what seemed like dozens of people drew us in with cries of welcome.

The hospitable Espinosas quickly made us feel at home. Don Francisco, the head of the family, had a jutting chin, a mane of silver hair, and a commanding presence that was mitigated by the twinkle in his eye. His wife, Doña Beatriz, doted on her four daughters: Adelina, Graciela, Eulalia, and Aldonza. The household included four sons too: Paquito, named for his father, Horacio, Faustino, and Leon. A fifth, Valerio, was a soldier. He had taken part in the fighting at Arras between Duke Maximilian of Burgundy and the French the year before. Our Sovereigns were allies of the Duke, and Valerio's company were among the troops that occupied the town. The family had not received news of him in some time, but as far as they knew, he was still there, making sure the townspeople didn't help the French to take it back.

The girls fell on Rachel with cries of delight, insisted on replenishing her wardrobe from their own abundant stores of gowns, shawls, ribbons, and lace, and immediately took to calling her "little sister." Within the first ten minutes, she was made privy to all their secrets. Eulalia had recently become betrothed and went about looking like a cat that had fallen into the cream bucket. Aldonza, the youngest, was sickly, subject to occasional shortness of breath and easily fatigued.

The sons welcomed me with equal enthusiasm. The Espinosas talked incessantly of soap. Like many of the lesser nobles of Seville, they had mercantile interests as well. These included a manufactory devoted to this lucrative product, and Don Francisco had made sure that all his sons had a grasp of how it was made and sold. My head whirled with the constant discussion of saponification, the virtue of various woods to produce the wood ash that yielded lye, the superiority of pure olive oil in providing the finest grade of soap for merchants' ladies as well as the nobility, and whether the cultivation of flowers to add fragrance to their soaps might not allow them to seize more of the market not only from their rivals in Seville but also from the masters of the art in faraway Marseille.

The brothers' cheerful company suited me. With them, I visited their manufactory across the river in Triana. Believing me a newcomer to Seville, they insisted I must at least once cross the wooden bridge that floated on a string of bobbing boats. I came back laden with fragrant soaps that they had pressed on me, saying I might present them as gifts to Rachel and Doña Marina or, if I preferred, save them to win some young lady's favor. The excursion was marred for me only by the proximity of the fortress where the Holy Inquisition had its headquarters.

"That is where we burn the heretics," Horacio said, with a wave of his hand as we passed the grim gray tower.

"You lie, brother," Paquito said, cuffing him playfully on the ear. "The interrogations take place here, but the burnings are in the Plaza, in front of the Cathedral."

Then they turned the conversation once again to soap. But as we passed, I imagined I could hear the cries of innocents tortured for keeping faith with Adonai and see their tears running from the dank stone walls.

The only shadow on the Espinosas' sunny family life was their Moorish slave, Amir. A slim, brown-skinned boy with delicate features, he said little and kept his eyes cast down as he poured coffee, the bracing beverage that the Moors had brought to Andalusia, held the horses' bridles when the men prepared to ride out, and swept up leaves in the pretty courtyard, set about with orange and lemon trees in tubs and graced in its center by a fine fountain. We had seen many of his kind since the fall of Granada. Seville had no central slave market, but cried such wretched creatures through the streets as if they were melons or artichokes.

Rachel lost no time in befriending him.

"I hear him crying in the night, Diego," she said. "His father was a scholar and a man of means, but he died in the fighting last year. Amir saw his brothers killed and his mother and sisters stripped naked and sold to strangers before they brought him to Seville in chains and sold him."

"He could have fallen to a far worse master than Don Francisco," I said. "At least he is not beaten or ill used."

"That is not worthy of you!" Rachel cried. "Would the absence of such ill use reconcile you to the loss of your own freedom?"

"I did not mean to say that I condone it, Rachel. Papa once said to me, 'In the tent of Abraham, there were both slave and free—but we have progressed a little since then.'"

"That is what I meant," she said.

Besides the manufactory, the Espinosas held lands, both farmlands leased for their revenue and groves devoted to the growing of olives, both for use in soap production and for trade. I rode out with them to see the rows of sturdy trees with their gnarled trunks, silvery leaves tossing in the wind, and taste both the useful fruit itself and various grades of oil. All the sons were knowledgeable, their upbringing having combined the industry of merchants with the courtesy of nobles.

I asked many questions, for I did not mean to be a sailor all my life and wanted to learn all I could. Whether I made my home in Italy or in Hispaniola, should our settlements there take hold, I meant to have a trade that I could carry anywhere, whether as a farmer, an artisan, or a merchant. I had seen no olives in the Indies, but neither had I seen much gold, yet all swore it was there in abundance. Besides, the climate was so mild and the lands we had discovered so fertile that surely no plant would refuse to grow there.

"The olive tree doesn't like wet feet," Paquito warned me.

"Then I shall not situate my groves in the *mangue* swamps," I said.

They plied me with questions about these curious trees of the Indies that lived in water, their roots forming thickets that rose into the air and entwined so closely that even the Taino's smallest canoa or dugout boat had difficulty passing through them.

"Don't any of you wish to visit the Indies?" I asked. "There will be work aplenty for both merchants and farmers, as well as gold for all, and surely the settlers will be in need of soap."

But they laughed and said that they were well content with their ancestral lands and their existing trade routes, save only for

Valerio, who had been mad for fighting since earliest childhood and was now getting his fill.

The Espinosas insisted on lending me a horse, a fine gray mare whose gait varied from a shambling walk to a bone-jarring trot to a reckless gallop. The Espinosas laughed at me and swore that I must show her who was master, and then she would go as sweetly as any other mount in their stables. I offered instead to accompany them on the mule on which I had arrived in Seville, but they laughed and said it would shame their horses to be seen with such a companion. There was no malice in their teasing, so I kicked the mare a little harder and made the most of more congenial companionship than I had enjoyed since leaving my boyhood home.

Rachel declared herself affronted not to be invited to view either the olive groves or the soap manufactory. Nor was she offered a horse. Nonetheless, she was well entertained. In the company of the Espinosa daughters, she enjoyed many excursions within the city, bringing home ribbons and trinkets from the fairs and markets, for the sisters had full purses and constantly pressed gifts on her which she was bound by politeness as well as inclination to accept. In return, she sang, told stories by the hour, and sought any occasion she could find to run errands for Doña Beatriz. She spent much time with young Aldonza, the pet of the whole family, whose fits of wheezing sometimes kept her from joining in their walks or forced her to return early to the house. Rachel found she could persuade the others to continue if she offered to accompany Aldonza home, after sitting in the shade with her until she recovered enough to walk.

"Truly, Diego," Rachel told me, "I am happy to do so, and not only because they are all so kind to me that I long to repay them in any way I can. Aldonza is so sweet, and her illness is so frightening. Today at the market she could scarce draw a breath, and when she did, she wheezed like a poorly made bellows. She was drenched in sweat too. Yet she fretted only that her sisters and I would lose our pleasure through her falling ill. When the fit passed, I sang to her, for she loves music and cannot sing herself, since she so easily becomes short of breath."

"You are a good soul, Rachel," I said, tucking an errant curl back under her cap.

"The Espinosas' is a happy house, is it not, Diego?"

"Yes, indeed. Matters could not have fallen out any better. Once the Admiral arrives, I will not be able to spend much time with you, but I will be easy in my mind, knowing you are not only well cared for, but loved."

"Ours was a happy house, was it not, Diego?" she said wistfully.

"It was indeed." I put my arm around her and squeezed her shoulders. "And you shall have a happy home again in Italy, once you are restored to Papa and Mama."

"I don't want to go to Italy!" I felt her stiffen within the curve of my arm. "I want to go with you."

"Rachel, you cannot." It distressed me to hear that she had still had not given up her wild notion of shipping with us. "It is impossible. Besides, do you not wish to see Mama and Papa and relieve their anxiety?"

"I long to see Mama and Papa, and the girls too," she said. "But surely they know I am with you by now. You have sent so many messages!"

Indeed, I had sent messages from Barcelona to Firenze, in care of prominent Jews. I had sent another letter off by an Espinosa caravan that departed for Italy two days after our arrival in Seville. I hoped by the same means to dispatch Rachel herself before the Admiral's fleet sailed, if I could not find her a sure means of transport by sea.

"They will not be content," I said, "until they can see you with their own eyes and hold you in their arms."

"Why have we not heard from them, Diego?" Rachel asked. "I had one letter at the convent, while you were gone, but nothing since. They assured me they were well, but they had not yet reached Firenze."

I was uneasy at the lack of news myself, but I did not wish to worry Rachel.

"We must assume they arrived safely," I said. "Things are always turbulent in Italy, which is divided into a host of little states, and France is not much better. Even such news as the death of kings or the Admiral's safe return from the Indies can take months to arrive at its destination. If their messages were delayed or lost along the way, that does not mean they are not well settled by now. Our aunt assures me that she is making inquiries through her bankers, whose direction Papa also has. The Medici of Firenze, a great banking family themselves, are known to be kindly toward the Jews. Our family's most pressing anxiety is your safety, which you can allay by joining them."

Rachel primmed her lips up in a pout. "I am certain they worry about you too. That did not stop you from sailing with Admiral Columbus."

"That was different!" I said. "You cannot wish to cause Mama and Papa pain."

"Of course I don't!" she said. "How can you think it? They have suffered enough. But I long to see the world before I settle down."

I had to laugh to hear her talk of settling down. Her thirteenth birthday took place during our first week in Seville, and the Espinosas made a great occasion of it, with feasting and presents.

"You will see more of the world on the journey to Firenze," I said, "than if we had never left Seville."

"You chose to sail with Admiral Columbus rather than accompany the others to Italy," she said. "Why can you not understand?"

"It is you who doesn't understand," I said. "I have my way to make in the world. Papa no longer has his fortune, so it is up to me to restore our family to prosperity. Your work has already been set, to be a good wife and mother when the time comes."

"Dull work indeed!" She jerked her shoulders away and presented her hunched back to me. "Would it content you to do the same, with no other occupation or adventure?"

I deemed it time to change the subject.

"Where do you and the other girls go this afternoon?"

"To the Cathedral, to confession." She made a face. "I wish I had not to pretend with them. Do you think they guess?"

"I cannot say. They surely must know that Doña Marina is converso, but they treat her like any other Christian."

"And so she is," Rachel said. "She has been truly happy to be able to attend Mass with the family. I would like to think they like us for ourselves, and that knowing we are Jews would make no difference."

"We cannot put it to the test," I said. "It is too dangerous."

"We have had no danger since we arrived here." Rachel sighed. "I might as well be back at the convent."

I had to laugh. But it was a great relief to see Rachel well guarded, for a servant armed with a stout cudgel escorted them. They usually went no farther than the great Plaza de San Francisco, around which the Cathedral, the Alcázar, and the Archbishop's Palace were clustered. Most beautiful of these was the Alcázar. Now the royal palace, it had been built by the Moors as a fort. Its slender bell tower, La Giralda, had been a minaret, from which their muezzins, not so different from our Jewish cantors, called the Muslims to prayer. The great building was rich with marble, soaring arches, and stone so lacy it might have been living vines and flowers. But in the shadow of these great buildings, unsavory folk loitered: beggars, thieves armed with knives, tricksters with marked cards and loaded dice with which they hoped to gull the unwary, and peddlers of produce who could be counted on to give short weight or rotten fruit to any foolish enough to offer them coin.

"I am to wear Graciela's farthingale to church," Rachel said. "We had better take only the widest streets, or I will be sure to get stuck. The hoop is so wide that the skirts above it catch the wind, like the sails of a ship."

"It is well that you don't mind when the girls dress you like a lady and call you a little princess."

"Oh, they love to dress me up," she said. "It gives them pleasure."

"Will you deny it gives you pleasure too? I heard the gales of laughter coming from your chamber this morning."

"Of course it is pleasant to wear ribbons and lace and look one's best," she said. "But it is not my *life*."

Chapter 13

I looked daily for Admiral Columbus's arrival in Seville. But the Queen took such keen interest in the preparations for the voyage and the planning of the trading colony in Hispaniola that she would not part with him before going over every detail a dozen times with the Admiral himself.

In the meantime, the Sovereigns appointed the Archdeacon of Seville, Don Juan de Fonseca, to be responsible along with the Admiral for the preparations for our departure. The appointment was the talk of the streets and taverns. Fonseca, who was the Archbishop's nephew, had set up his headquarters in his uncle's palace on the Plaza de San Francisco. Once I had seen Rachel settled and spent enough time with the Espinosa brothers to feel guilty about remaining idle, I reported to him, certain that he could find a use for me and eager for fresh news about the Admiral and our progress.

Don Juan greeted me without surprise, having already heard of me. Royal couriers traveled constantly between Barcelona and Seville. Admiral Columbus himself had suggested the Archdeacon employ me. Fonseca was a small, wiry man with a high forehead and thin lips that were always moving slightly, as if he never ceased calculating sums or reviewing lists of provisions. Or perhaps he was praying, although he didn't seem to devote much of his time to religious duties. Having already made the voyage and seen the unknown lands, the Admiral would provide the required experience. Fonseca would supply the organization necessary to equip the fleet. He had a herculean task before him. No less than seventeen ships must be outfitted to carry a thousand men or more, along with horses, domestic animals, and implements of all kinds for both farming and mining, when the settlement should be established and the gold mine found.

The Archdeacon was pleased to learn I wrote a fair hand and put me at once to copying lists, invoices, and agreements with the local merchants. We needed great quantities of biscuit, oil, and wine, salt pork and beef, metal breastplates, muskets, crossbows, and a host of other necessities. Don Juan wished every item accounted for in triplicate. His passionate pride in his gift for provisioning matched the Admiral's pride in his skill at navigation. If he didn't personally inspect every cask and barrel, it was only because even a prince of the Church could not cram more than twenty-four hours into a day. He had to purchase the ships themselves, at a price that would not beggar the expedition, as well as hire all the sailors, soldiers, craftsmen, and farmers and calculate their wages. These were the Admiral's tasks as well, but Fonseca said many times a day that if he waited for Columbus to finish dallying with Their Majesties, the fleet would not be ready to sail before next spring.

As the Archdeacon demanded more and more of my time, the Espinosas declared themselves sorry to lose my company. They never ceased trying, half in jest, to persuade me to shirk my duties and join in their pleasures. To console them, I offered to approach Fonseca on their behalf. They ended in getting a substantial contract for oil, which pleased them greatly, although the Archdeacon

drove such a shrewd bargain that I was left uncertain whether I
had after all done them a favor.

Applicants for places in the expedition began to gather in
Seville and in Cadiz, the port city at the mouth of the Guadalquivir,
some fifty miles away. There was no shortage of volunteers. The
year before, we had sailed into the unknown with hearts as filled
with dread as with hope, knowing we might never see land again,
much less make our way home. But now the case was very different. In the end, two hundred gentlemen volunteers took ship
with us, along with priests and even a physician. I could have done
without the priests, who would surely make it harder for me to say
my prayers up in the crow's nest, as I had done on the first voyage.
Their mission was to convert the Taino, but I had no doubt their
zeal for sniffing out heresy would make the journey with them.

Every day I brought the Espinosas a budget of news and fresh
tales. Some I shared with the family at large, others only with
Rachel.

"Fifty caballeros on fine horses arrived today, sent by the
Queen," I told them one day. "Did you not see them parading in
the Plaza?"

"Why, that is sixteen for each of us," Graciela exclaimed.
"Eulalia doesn't need one, as she already has a *novio*."

"Adelina and Graciela may divide my caballeros between
them," Aldonza said. "I don't wish for a *novio*."

"A convent, then, sweet one?" Paquito tweaked one of her
auburn curls. "Your sisters are not good enough, but you may be
our little saint if you wish."

"No convent either," Aldonza said. "I wish to stay with Mama
and Papa always."

"And so you may, pet," Adelina said, kissing her cheek, and all
regarded Aldonza with affection.

Another day, I told them that weapons, armor, powder, and
shot were coming in from as far away as Malaga and Granada, as

well as from the royal artillery in Seville. The Espinosas thought
nothing of it, except to remark that I would be well protected. But
when Rachel and I were alone, I expressed my reservations.

"The Queen has said we are to treat the Taino well," I said.
"And none deny that they are a gentle and peace-loving people.
Why, then, must we carry so many crossbows and muskets across
the Ocean Sea? Why must every soldier wear a metal cuirass?"

"It may be," Rachel said, "from fear that you may encounter
fiercer tribes. We have heard the Caribe are more warlike and that
the Canibale are disposed to eat their own kind."

"Rachel, none of them have a shred of metal beyond the soft
gold ornaments they wear and nuggets such as those they gave us,
which they keep as trinkets. They have no iron, no steel. When
shown our swords, they took hold of them by the blade and cut
themselves sorely, so ignorant are they of weapons. When they
hunt, they use sharpened spears of wood and arrows tipped with
sharpened fish bones. Besides, any man will speak ill of his enemies. My friend Hutia admitted to me that the Caribe and the
Taino are equally gentle, or equally warlike, in each other's eyes,
and that it is a common insult, a kind of jest, to say one's neighbor
eats people."

"Against wild animals, then," Rachel suggested. "A musket or
crossbow would be protection against, let us say, a wild boar."

"There are none," I said. "Neither boar nor any other animal
larger than a manatee."

"What is a manatee?"

"A gentle creature like a porpoise, but bigger and less shapely.
The Taino hunt the manatee for food and also the hutia, which is a
kind of rodent, larger than the biggest rat."

"Why is your friend called Hutia?"

"He is quick. The hutia runs very fast, as it must if it is to escape
the cooking pot."

Another day, I returned late from Jerez de la Frontera, not far from Cadiz. I had started out before dawn, and I expected to find all asleep on my return, but Rachel had waited up for me.

"The Inquisition is everywhere!" I said, flinging my weary body onto a bench and tearing into a loaf of bread I found on the table, for I had eaten nothing all day.

"Diego!" Rachel wrung her hands. "What happened? Were you questioned?"

"No, no, I didn't mean to alarm you. My tale would be amusing, were the Inquisition a fit subject for jokes." Recovering from her fright, Rachel poured ale into a tankard and handed it to me, then set before me a fist-sized lump of golden cheese. "Thank you, I am indeed hungry and thirsty."

Rachel sat down beside me on the bench and leaned her elbows on the table.

"Tell me."

"You know I was sent to Jerez today to see about the wheat that Don Juan has ordered from two dozen different sources and also to visit the many bakers who are charged with making biscuit for the voyage." I wiped my mouth and cut off a piece of cheese with my dagger. "Fonseca fears that we will be cheated if a close eye is not kept on all these folk, from farmers to millers to bakers. But I was not needed. The Archdeacon told me that he already had a man in place, and that I must present myself first to him. He didn't tell me that his overseer is a Holy Inquisitor! This Fray Alonso has all well in hand, and he seemed very confident that none would dare lie to him or offer him short measure or weevily flour. Considering his office, he is probably right."

"Why did he choose such a person to be in charge of flour and biscuit?" Rachel asked.

I shrugged. "Don Juan is a churchman himself. I suppose he naturally thinks of colleagues in his own trade, as would Papa or Don Francisco in the same position. This Fray Alonso was pleasant enough to me, knowing me only as the Archdeacon's emissary. But I am glad he stays in Jerez and not Seville. Having marked me once, he might take a second look and start to wonder."

Once the search for likely ships began, I was sent often to Cadiz. I refrained from requesting the Espinosas' horse for these excursions. But when I told Don Juan that I had access to a mule, he at once recruited it.

"It shall be returned to its owner once the fleet has sailed."

He regarded me benignly, as if certain I would appreciate his generosity. I reflected that if he had ever met Doña Marina, he would know that without a doubt the mule would end up in its own stall in the Espinosa stables.

So I rode my old companion back and forth between Seville and Cadiz, sleeping on the floor of the expedition's quarters on the docks as often as in my comfortable bed at the Espinosas'.

In the first week of July, Admiral Columbus arrived at last. He expressed pleasure at seeing me, praised my industry, and promptly commandeered me, leaving Fonseca short a secretary. Nor would he tolerate any but himself passing judgment on the vessels to be selected.

"Ships are not like beans," he grumbled to me after an acrimonious meeting with Don Juan. "They are not all alike, with as many as possible to be crammed into a barrel. Equipping a fleet is no job for a bishop!"

Then he must inspect every inch of rope that Fonseca had acquired and pace the deck of every vessel already assembled, with me scurrying, like as not, at his heels, making note at his command of every seam in need of caulking or bit of brass that wanted polishing.

The Admiral also allowed me, at my request, to return to my task of tending the Indians. I was eager to see how they had fared since my departure. To my dismay, some had died, and I found the rest weaker and more discouraged than I had left them. Cristobal still coughed, the worse for the Admiral insisting on taking a more mountainous route to Seville so that he could pause at the monastery of Guadalupe and fulfill his vow to pray before an image of the Virgin there, in exchange for safe passage home on our previous voyage.

"I did all I could for them," Fernando told me. "But once their novelty had worn off, most lost interest in them. I believe Her Gracious Majesty cared only to see them baptized and thus deemed their purpose served."

He cast a quick glance around him. We lived in an age when all knew it was best not to be heard criticizing the Sovereigns, however mildly. I had invited him to drink at my expense in a pleasant tavern off the Calle Sierpes, to thank him for taking on my task at short notice, without even my sense of personal connection with the Taino to lighten it. He believed that the Admiral had sent me ahead to serve as his eyes and ears in Seville. He knew nothing of Rachel.

We soon fell to talking of the ships, as we had a keen interest in both their seaworthiness and their comfort.

"The chief vessels are bigger than last time," I told him, "for we carry many men and more cargo than you can readily imagine. But the Admiral has also insisted that some be of shallow draft so that they can sail close along the shore without running aground like the poor *Santa Maria*. Most are caravels, but the few small barques are very light indeed."

"What of the flagship?"

"A beauty. She is called the *Santa Maria* like our old ship, but the seamen already call her *Mariagalante*. I hope we will both draw berths on her, for if we do, I don't think we will have to sleep on coils of rope again. Also, the Admiral has hired a cook."

Fernando laughed. "We may expect to see little enough of the dishes served to the Admiral."

"We can hope." I smiled. "Guess what vessel will be found among the caravels."

"Not the *Niña*?"

I nodded, grinning. "It is she who should be named *Galante*."

"She brought us safely home through terrible gales," he said.

"May whatever ship carries us this time do the same," I said, "and all the fleet as well."

"God willing."

Fernando crossed himself, and I made a vague gesture that I hoped appeared the same to him without offending Ha'shem. He had kept His hand under me so far, and Rachel too, and I hoped it would please Him to continue to do so.

Chapter 14

Seville, July 16, 1493

"No, Mama!" Aldonza said. "I will go. I am well enough."

"You were short of breath again this morning, my angel," Doña Beatriz said, casting an anxious look at her youngest child. "And please don't try to tell me that you slept well last night, for I see blue shadows under your eyes."

"She didn't," said Graciela, who shared a bed with her. "She tossed and turned all night, trying to catch her breath, and this morning the bedclothes were damp with sweat."

"I have recovered now," Aldonza protested. "It is my duty to attend."

"Our standing is high enough," Don Francisco declared, "that no one will take it amiss if you are not well enough to be there."

"But all must witness it," Aldonza argued, "even the King, if he should happen to be in Seville. I would not be remiss or appear less devout than the rest of you."

"Let her come, Mama," Paquito said. "If she feels unwell, one of us can take her home."

"I will be glad to do so," Rachel said.

The entire family was assembled in the courtyard, where all habitually gathered for a morning repast of bread, fruit, and coffee. The golden morning sun fell on the animated faces of the Espinosas, grouped lovingly around Aldonza. Rachel and I sat apart, in the shadows. Since the present discussion had started, she had gripped my hand hard enough to make it ache, but I did not remove it from her grasp. Her distress was no greater than mine.

"There, it is settled," Aldonza said triumphantly. "We shall all set out together, and if I feel unwell, Rachel will escort me home."

"The crowd may get boisterous," Doña Beatriz fretted. "Two girls alone might be accosted."

"I will accompany them if need be, Beatriz," Doña Marina said. She sat straight-backed on a stone bench in the lacy shade of a lemon tree with some fine embroidery in her lap, though she had not put needle to cloth since the beginning of the conversation. "You need have no fear for them."

The younger boys, excited by the prospect of the day's pageantry, were feigning swordplay with only air for swords. Faustino, pursuing Leon around the fountain, paused and turned to us.

"Have you ever seen an auto da fé, Rachel?"

"No," she said, poking my thigh with our joined hands in a covert plea for help.

"There is no tribunal in Barcelona," I said. "Nor on the Ocean Sea."

This raised a laugh. Rachel released my cramped hand. I rubbed at it to get the blood flowing again, glad to have diverted their attention.

Although it was the law that all attend the ceremonial burnings of so-called heretics, my parents had always found an excuse to spare Rachel this terrible sight. Being older and a boy, I was not so lucky. I did not look forward to the screams of the victims as the flames consumed them, nor the smell of burning flesh. The victims were likely to be marranos like us. Above all, I feared to learn that one of the poor souls tied to the stake with quick-burning fagots heaped around his feet was a friend.

I remembered my first burning, at the age of ten. My father stood beside me, not flinching or turning away, though the penitents, as they were called, had visited our home and broken bread with us on Shabbat. His big hand, warm and steady as the kiss of God, had never left my shoulder.

"Look, Diego," he had said. "Look and remember."

I had been ready to vomit at the sight of their agonized faces and the smell of roasting meat, but had managed not to, determined not to shame my father or my people.

"Papa," I had whispered, "is it for this that we were Chosen?"

"No, son," he had replied. "We are Chosen to be steadfast in our faith in God, no matter what evil befalls us, even this."

The Espinosas, Doña Marina, Rachel, and I set out in a body, joining the throng flowing along the Calle Sierpes toward the Plaza like a river of bright colors and cheerful cries, for to the Christians, the auto da fé was a festival. Having made up their minds that heretics and Jews were evil, indeed hardly human, they were not troubled at the prospect of watching them die in agony. Even the Espinosas, kindest of people, perceived it as a holy rite, like the sprinkling of babies in baptism or the anointing of the dying. It never occurred to them to wonder whether their own souls were damaged by finding entertainment in the pain of others.

The fire lay ready for lighting before the great doors of the Cathedral. The victims were forced to walk in procession to their doom. We could hear the deep chanting of the monks before they came into sight. The buzz of the crowd grew louder as eight unfortunates appeared, each flanked by two black-clad priests. The penitents were swathed in yellow robes with pointed caps. Their faces were hidden under hoods, cloths stuffed into their mouths so that none could be moved to pity by the spark of humanity in their eyes or to horror by their cries.

The priests screamed at them, "Repent! Repent! You may still be saved!" above the cries of vilification from the crowd. The priests didn't mean that if they repented, they would be spared, but only that if they accepted the *fuego resuelto*, they would be strangled first and thus avoid the cruel pain of death by fire. I imagined the terror they must feel, alone in misery and dread. They could not even see the sky as they stumbled or were dragged toward death, feeling, perhaps, abandoned even by God. I felt a grim satisfaction in remembering, from my studies of Christianity at the time of our feigned conversion, that their Jesus had had such a moment of doubt while nailed to the Romans' cross. The priests claimed that he had suffered it so that mankind would be spared such suffering in the future. This didn't seem to be borne out by today's festivities.

Behind us, I heard a woman say, "These heretic Jews were foolish not to have left when they could."

"Marranos are easily detected," a man replied. "Their neighbors have only to observe that their chimneys don't smoke on a Saturday."

"They shun pork," the woman said. "It is comical, when one remembers that we call them swine."

"If they don't like the smell of roasting pork," another man said, "they will be most unhappy a short while from now."

They all laughed heartily, as my gorge rose and I feared I would be unable to refrain from retching.

The victims were bound to the stake. The fire was lit. The crowd fell silent, so all could hear its crackling breath as the flames leaped upward. I heard Rachel's gasp and turned to look at her. She was white as a sheet.

"Don't look," I said.

I put one arm around her shoulders, and with the other, pressed her head against my chest. She wept, her shoulders shaking and the damp of her tears soaking into my shirt. As the first screams of pain burst through the gags, Rachel cried out.

"No! No! Stop them! It is wicked, wicked!"

"Hush, Rachel," I murmured in her ear. "You must be silent. Do you want us to join them in the fire?"

I held her, striving to muffle her words against my chest, as she twisted in my arms. My horror at the burning turned to terror for Rachel. Her distress was beginning to attract attention.

Luckily, a commotion arose behind us. I turned, seeking the source of the disturbance, without letting go my hold on Rachel. The Espinosas were no longer watching my people burn. Doña Beatriz sat on the ground, holding Aldonza in her arms. Doña Marina knelt beside her. Ever provident, she had produced a small flask of water and a kerchief. She dampened the cloth and mopped Aldonza's brow, which was beaded with sweat. The girl's breath was no more than a fitful, ragged wheeze that labored to emerge between her white lips. The rest of the Espinosas hovered over them, the girls fluttering like pigeons as they uttered cries and exclamations of distress.

"We must get her home," Paquito said. "Let me, Mama, I will carry her."

"Give her to me," Don Francisco said. He scooped Aldonza up in his arms.

Paquito assisted Doña Beatriz to rise, and I leaped to help Doña Marina, still keeping one arm around Rachel. I gave the other to my aunt. Along with my concern for Aldonza, I felt great relief. This catastrophe would get us out of here.

Don Francisco led the way, forcing a path through the mob. All the Espinosas followed. The crowd was howling now, caught up in a bloodlust that they no doubt believed was religious ecstasy, as the flames leaped higher than the Cathedral door. Rachel still trembled, her own breath shaky and her face white with shock. Doña Marina, on my other side, reached out and patted Rachel's forehead with her still damp kerchief. My aunt and I exchanged a glance. Her lips tightened. True Christian she might be, but the auto da fé was no pleasure to her. She had been Jewish as a child. The Espinosas had been taught that this cruelty was a form of grace. We had not.

It took twice as long as usual to reach the Espinosas' house, pushing our way against the frenzied crowd. Don Francisco didn't wait for a servant to open the door. Indeed, all were most likely in the Plaza, bound to this civic and religious duty. Don Francisco put his back against the heavy oak and swung Aldonza inside as it opened. Murmuring endearments, he carried her not to her own chamber but to the one he shared with Doña Beatriz. He laid her gently on the great bed. Doña Beatriz flew to his side as the others crowded around. Rachel, Doña Marina, and I remained close to the door, not wanting to intrude unless our help was needed.

"There, my darling," Doña Beatriz crooned, "you are home now. Rest, and presently you shall feel better."

"She is no longer wheezing, Mama," Adelina said. "Her breathing must be easier."

I could hear Doña Marina's quick intake of breath. Doña Beatriz looked up at Don Francisco, her eyes wild with alarm. Don Francisco once more bent over the bed. The others crowded close, so we could no longer see Aldonza lying small and still among the bedclothes. After a minute, he stood up, his face raw with grief.

"She is dead."

Chapter 15

Seville, July 17–August 1, 1493

When we returned to the Cathedral for Aldonza's funeral rites, all signs of the auto da fé had been swept away. The great vault was filled with the light of thousands of candles. The scent of flowers and the sound of sobbing filled the air, for everyone who knew her had loved Aldonza. Doña Beatriz, racked with grief, could not have followed her daughter's coffin had Don Francisco not supported her on one side and Doña Marina on the other.

The Espinosas' house was now an unhappy one. The distraught mother begged my aunt to postpone her planned visit to friends in Malaga. Her daughters could not console her, for sight of them invariably reminded her of Aldonza and set her weeping once again. She exclaimed over and over that they should not have allowed her to attend the burning, that they should have remembered that smoke upon the air, even from a homely hearth, had always made Aldonza's breathing worse.

Don Francisco's sorrow took the form of silence, an increased attentiveness to his work, and a tendency to avoid the company of his wife and children. I too could escape to work. As many hours as I chose to spend within sight of the Admiral or Archdeacon

Fonseca, so many could they fill with tasks for me. The fleet in the harbor at Cadiz was growing, while the nearby shipyards were busy day and night, building, at a feverish pace, the smaller vessels that were required to accommodate our explorations among the islands.

Rachel had a harder time than Doña Marina or I. Still shocked by the horror of the auto da fé as much as by Aldonza's sudden death, she did all she could to serve and cheer the sisters. But without the outings and entertainments of the previous weeks, she longed for distraction, even work like mine.

"Oh, Diego," she exclaimed, "can I not offer my services to Admiral Columbus as a scribe? For you have said yourself that he could give you twice the writing if you had twice the time. You may present me as a lady, albeit an industrious one. I will even wear my farthingale. Surely I could come to no harm simply sitting at a desk putting quill to paper."

"The Admiral is so pressed as to daunt a lesser man," I said. "He must be conversant with every detail, especially of the ships they are building in Cadiz. And his humor is choleric, for he quarrels constantly with Don Juan. The Queen—" Here I lowered my voice and looked around to make sure none overheard us. "The Queen must have been mad to give the task of fitting out the expedition to two such incompatible men. At any rate, I don't want to trouble him with such an odd request."

Rachel sighed. "To me, it doesn't seem so odd," she said.

Over the following weeks, the pall of mourning over the formerly merry household did not lighten. Doña Beatriz sought consolation in her prayers and resisted every effort to distract her mind from the loss of her dearest child. Paquito and his brothers spent a week in lugubrious idleness. Then they could bear no more and turned to galloping their horses into a lather outside the city on the pretext that the soap manufactory must not be neglected or that those who tended the olive groves must be kept up to the mark. But they came home smelling of strong drink, and none reproached them.

Rachel confided that she found the sisters' company increasingly difficult.

"They can think of nothing but their grief," she said. "I cannot fault them for that. Surely we would feel the same if one of our sisters died." She paused, frowning.

"What is it?" I asked. "You know you can tell me anything. What troubles you?"

"Each day they must recount several times their story of that horrible day: Aldonza's insistence on going to the Plaza with the others, how she was taken short of breath just as the flames started to rise, and what happened after. They spoke as if the unfortunates who also lost their lives that day offended chiefly in allowing the smoke of their burning to interfere with Aldonza's breathing."

"That is hard to bear in silence."

"This morning, Eulalia said, 'It is all the fault of the Jews! They must envy Christian families, especially happy ones like ours before we lost Aldonza. We had no misfortune until they were punished.' Punished!" Rachel repeated, outraged. "She said, 'Perhaps they ill-wished us as they burned.'"

I drew her close, and she leaned her head upon my shoulder.

"What did the others say?"

"They laughed," Rachel said. "It was hard for me not to speak, and I cannot feel as fond of Eulalia as I did before."

"Nor should you have to," I said, kissing her cheek.

"Besides," she said, "she becomes tiresome on the subject of her betrothed and his many virtues: how strong he is, how kind, and how well he sits a horse."

I laughed. "You will say the same of some young man one day."

"I will not! You are strong and kind enough for me. And I can sit a horse myself, when anyone will let me have one."

"One day," I said, "you will not be content with only a brother."

"I don't believe it," she said.

"Take courage, love. We will not stay here forever. In fact, we must be wearing out our welcome rapidly, now that they have no good fortune to share with guests."

"Has the Admiral named a date for your departure?" Rachel asked.

"He talks as if all may be ready the first week in September," I said, "and the Archdeacon sneers like a camel each time he mentions it. You must prepare yourself for our parting, Rachel, for both are determined to be off before October. The season's favorable winds will not last forever."

Doña Marina departed for Malaga, after commending me as a good boy growing into a fine man. This gratified me but disgusted Rachel, for our aunt admonished her to obey me and fall in cheerfully with whatever plan I settled on to dispatch her to Firenze. Except for this unwelcome advice, Rachel agreed that Doña Marina had proved a surprisingly pleasant companion and a rock in times of trouble. We would miss her.

After her departure, we hoped the family's passionate desire to blame the Jews for Aldonza's death would subside. But their conviction, especially the girls', that the *penitentes* had all but murdered Aldonza instead grew with time. Rachel and I had to dissemble so that the family did not suspect that we were Jewish ourselves, or even overly sympathetic to Jews.

"Why would anybody wish to be a Jew?" Graciela asked one morning as we lingered over coffee in the courtyard.

"It is a mystery," Adelina said. "They must be taught from birth to believe that evil is good."

"They smell," Eulalia said.

"True," Adelina said, "and they care for nothing but gold."

If that were true, I thought, then surely not only the Admiral and the thousand-odd Spaniards who clamored to join his expedition but also the King and Queen themselves must be Jewish.

"It is said they kill babies in their rituals," Graciela said.

I had heard enough. "Ladies, you must excuse us," I said. "I must be about my duties. Raquel, will you walk with me? If you don't think it tedious to watch me count and write up lists of barrels of seed for planting, dried peas, molasses, vinegar, oil, and wine, you may spend the day as my companion."

Rachel leaped up, throwing down her needlework in such haste that she pricked her finger.

"Oh, yes! If you will spare me a quill, I can help." She turned to Adelina. "If you don't need me here?"

"No, dear, you must go," Adelina said kindly. "We are poor company lately, I fear. Please don't feel that you must share every moment of our gloom."

We made our escape, heaving simultaneous sighs of relief when the great door of the house swung closed behind us.

"It is unbearable," Rachel declared. "How much longer must we stay?"

"We cannot leave abruptly," I said. "They must not be allowed to think we are offended by their accusations of the Jews."

"I cannot tell which is worse," she said, "their mad notions about us or never being able to correct them. Forever hiding what I feel is exhausting."

"I know, little sister. I will take you away the moment I find a ship or caravan for Italy."

"Must I wait so long?"

"Have patience. I will do my best to keep you diverted."

"Then take me to visit Cristobal! I long to meet him."

Thinking it over, I could see no harm in it. I had told her much of him and of Hutia. It would divert Cristobal too, as he had not yet been offered the opportunity to have a rational conversation with a European lady.

"Very well," I said. "You will like Cristobal, and he you. Don't tire him, however, for he has been ill."

We found Cristobal sitting cross-legged in the sunny courtyard of the inn where they were lodged, the clout between his legs
his only garment. Rachel's mouth dropped open, for although she
had seen the Taino in their scant garb at Court, this close view
startled her.

"He is more clothed than his people were when first I met
them," I murmured. "If you are to become acquainted with the
Taino, you must respect their customs."

Among the most bitter of the laws against the Jews had been
the forbidding of our *tallit* and *t'fillin*, the symbols of our worship.
Perhaps the Taino felt similarly about covering their bodies, I told
her.

"Cristobal, good morning! I have brought you a visitor."

In the sunlight, I could see how pale and yellow his golden
skin had become. He was as thin as a skeleton, for our food sat
uneasily in his stomach. His eyes were sunken and his flesh wasted.
Nonetheless, I told him he looked well and introduced my sister.

"I am very glad to meet you, Señor Cristobal." Rachel bobbed
in a quick curtsy, which made Cristobal grin with pleasure. "I hope
that you will tell me of your home."

"My home is what you Christians call paradise," Cristobal said,
"and I long to see it again, though I fear I will die before I see
the cave on the mountain where our people were born or eat the
sacred bread again. The *cemi* cannot hear my words from here, so
far across the great water."

"We are not Christians," Rachel said.

"Ah, yes, your brother has told me. You are of the people your
caciques have sent away or killed, as they will the Taino before
long."

"Why do you say the King and Queen will kill the Taino?"
Rachel asked. "How do you know?"

"I have seen it, little sister," Cristobal said. "As you can see, they have already started." He held out his arms so we could see how the skin fell away from his bones.

"They think our religion is evil," Rachel said, "because it is not theirs."

"They think we have none," Cristobal said, "no matter what we tell them. What will happen if they learn that Yucahu and Atabey remain in our hearts? Will they nail us to a dead tree like their God?"

"They give us to the fire," I said, "if they learn we are faithful to Adonai." So there would be no misunderstanding the gravity of our position, I added, "*Barbacoa*," their word for grilling meat.

"While still we live?" Cristobal looked horrified.

"We have seen it," Rachel said.

"Who are your *cemi*," Cristobal asked, "apart from Adonai?"

"We have only one God," Rachel said, "but He is all-powerful."

"In what land does he rule?" Cristobal inquired.

Rachel looked blank, then said, "He is everywhere."

Cristobal's raised brows and crooked smile betrayed his skepticism.

It was time to put an end to this theological discussion. "We must bid you good day, Cristobal. I have work to do, and Rachel comes with me."

"I have enjoyed your company." Cristobal looked sad.

Rachel stepped forward and gave him an impulsive kiss on the cheek.

"I shall return and talk to you whenever I can," she told him.

"That will make me happy," he said as I led her away.

We found Archdeacon Fonseca conferring with a gentleman I had not met before.

"Ah, young Mendoza!" the Archdeacon greeted me. "I must present you to Don Melchior Maldonado, who will join the expedition as a volunteer."

I bowed with a great flourish to cover my start of surprise. I could feel Rachel trembling as she stood close behind me, as if my body were all that stood between her and being seized at once by Don Rodrigo's brother.

"And who is this young lady?" the Archdeacon inquired jovially as Don Melchior returned my bow.

I had no choice but to present her as my sister Raquel, hoping that Don Melchior was not party to his brother's schemes. His expression remained courteous and no more.

"The Queen permits two hundred gentlemen volunteers to sail with us," I told Rachel, desperate to prevent silence enough for any of us to think.

"At our own expense!" Don Melchior added, smiling for the first time. "We have a noble mission."

He seemed kindly enough. But what if he dissembled? What story had Don Rodrigo told him? Even if he were misguided rather than evil, he could still be a great danger to us.

"Indeed, sir," I said, "for you will bear arms in our defense, should we have need of greater numbers than the soldiers the fleet will carry."

"I should like to hear your account of the voyage of discovery one day," he said, "perhaps over a flagon of ale. I have a distant cousin, one Juan Cabrera, at La Navidad," he said.

"We expect great things of those who had the honor to remain," I said.

Privately, I meant not that Cabrera and his mates might have found the fabled gold mine of Cibao, but that I hoped the villain would refrain from raping and killing any more Taino maidens. Surely, with our ships gone and only the garrison to back him up, he would manage to behave himself.

After this, Don Melchior excused himself, having affairs of his own to attend to. At parting, he said he looked forward to my company on the voyage. As I bowed, I prayed devoutly that our paths would not cross before we sailed and that we would be assigned to different ships. What would happen when he and Cabrera met remained in Ha'shem's hands.

"He was courteous enough," Rachel said, once we were alone. "Do you think he recognized our names?"

"We will know when the Inquisitors come knocking at the Espinosas' door."

Chapter 16

Every day, the fleet grew closer to readiness for departure, prodded by messages to the Admiral from the King and Queen, who were as impatient for us to set sail as Columbus himself. Rachel visited Cristobal almost daily, bringing him sustaining broths and soft bread to cosset his rotting teeth. They had long conversations in a mixture of Castilian and Taino, which Rachel picked up quickly as she plied him with questions about his people's beliefs and way of life.

"I fear that he is dying," Rachel confessed to me one day. "No matter what I do, he grows steadily weaker. And his teeth become ever looser in his mouth. His gums are puffy and cause him great pain when he tries to chew."

"I wish the Admiral had not taken him," I said. "He was not forced aboard the ship. Indeed, he volunteered. But he had no idea how different Spain would be from Hispaniola."

"You have shown him much kindness," Rachel said. "He told me himself how that has eased his longing for home, if not his pain and illness."

"It may be too late for Cristobal," I said, "but we would do well to eat lemons and oranges so as not to suffer the tooth rot ourselves. If only all who sail with the fleet would do the same! Some fruit of a similar virtue must grow in Hispaniola, because in the Indies, Taino teeth are whole and white. It is the sailors, who eat nothing but salt pork and biscuit while at sea, who suffer as Cristobal does."

"How did you manage last time?" Rachel asked.

"I brought a few lemons aboard the *Santa Maria*," I said, "and acquired more in the Canaries, where I believe we will stop again before setting a course westward across the Ocean Sea."

"This time you must save the seeds," she said, "to plant at La Navidad when you are settled there. Even better, can you not obtain a sapling lemon tree? It would yield fruit much sooner."

"I don't think we sailors will stay long in La Navidad," I said, "although if things have gone well, as the Admiral hopes, at least some of the settlers will disembark there and begin the task of building a colony. Much depends on whether those who remained have found an abundant source of gold. In either case, we will continue to explore. The heart of the Spanish settlement must be in whatever spot best lends itself to trade."

"Still," Rachel said, "even if the gold mine has already been found, all that will take time. Until then, it is likely that the Admiral will use La Navidad as his headquarters ashore, so wherever you are sent, you will have to report back and harvest your lemons."

I laughed. "You have an admirable command of logistics, little sister. It is a pity that we cannot persuade Archdeacon Fonseca to take you on as his assistant. Very well, if you insist, I will try to find an appropriate sapling to carry on board, either in Cadiz or in the Canaries."

I had not yet found a berth for Rachel, as I had hoped, on a ship trading around the Mediterranean coast. For myself, I felt increasing excitement about the fleet's departure. I would have more responsibility this time as an able seaman and higher pay as well, though I would hold no coin in my hand until our return. Indeed, as the Indians used no coin and gave us freely whatever we asked for, the principal use of such coin as the sailors carried would be for gambling, which my father called a fool's road to poverty.

On a bright, cloudless day in early September, my mule and I took the road to Jerez. The Archdeacon sent me to ask Fray Alonso, whom Rachel called the bakery inquisitor, for the latest tallies of our supply of wheat, flour, and biscuit. Once that was done, I had errands for Admiral Columbus in Cadiz. I would spend the night there and return the next day, unless one of the ships' masters had further tasks for me. I also wished to pay visits to the two ships I most wished to sail on, my favorite being the new flagship, *Mariagalante*, and my second choice the brave little *Niña*.

As I passed through the gate of Jerez, I thought of the time, not so long in the past, when the town had marked the border between the dominion of the Moors and that of the Christians. The Moors had been a proud people, skilled in the arts of building and healing. Now most of those who remained were slaves like young Amir.

I found Fray Alonso at the chief mill where flour was being ground for the voyage and made my request. Greeting me warmly, he sent a servant for the documents I wanted and invited me to join him in the shade while I waited. He offered me a cup of the rich wine for which the town was famous. How his demeanor would change if he knew I was marrano! It would always puzzle me how a man could hold both kindness and cruelty in his heart.

I was sipping the last of my wine when Fray Alonso called a genial greeting to Don Melchior Maldonado, who bowed to me as courteously as before. Once my heartbeat quieted, I realized I had no reason to believe he knew of our connection with his brother. My companions knew of no reason to guard their tongues in my presence. I regretted the wine, which caused a certain lightheadedness, and set myself to keep my expression politely impassive as they spoke of Rome, where Don Melchior had been the royal ambassador to the Holy See. Luckily, neither Fray Alonso nor Don Melchior was looking at me when Don Melchior said, "I expect my brother to arrive in Seville in a day or two. He wishes to bid me farewell before I embark."

"You must bring Don Rodrigo here," Fray Alonso said. "We will share a bottle of the finest Jerez wine and drink to your health and the success of the voyage."

"I thank you," Don Melchior said. "Rodrigo will be happy to renew your acquaintance. We can easily pause here on our way from Seville to Cadiz, for my brother wishes to see the fleet. He met Admiral Columbus and saw the painted savages at Court in Barcelona some months ago and thus takes a keen interest in all having to do with the expedition."

Don Rodrigo Maldonado in Seville! And worse, in Cadiz, where it was impossible that two people spending any time on the docks could avoid coming face to face. Apart from the ships themselves, the expedition's affairs in Seville were concentrated in a single quarter: the Archbishop's Palace and the area surrounding the Plaza de San Francisco, which Rachel crossed daily to visit the ailing Cristobal. I must get her away!

"And how does your higher business prosper, Fray Alonso?" Don Melchior asked.

"The Holy Inquisition never sleeps," Fray Alonso said. "If we believed our task was done when we expelled the swine from Spain, we underestimated their greed. Many would not be parted from their gold, but chose to remain, thinking they could deceive us. Their lust for gold knows no bounds, but they are no match for us in our holy purpose."

"So your mission prospers," Don Melchior said. "I am glad to hear it."

"We have been ordered to redouble our efforts," Fray Alonso said. "We hope to establish tribunals in such cities as still lack means of ferreting out the heretics. The Moors, too, must be dealt with. They are less sly than the Jews, in that they refuse outright to embrace Our Savior. But enslaving them is not enough. Sooner or later, Their Majesties will see they must be driven out."

"His Holiness is of a mind with you," Don Melchior said. "Being Spanish born himself, Pope Alexander would rejoice to see an untainted Christian Spain."

Glad they did not seek my opinion, I took my leave of Fray Alonso and Don Melchior as quickly as I could and urged my mule toward Cadiz, earning a reproachful bray every time I dug my heels into its flanks. My business there could not be concluded until the next day. I spent a sleepless night. Next morning, after discharging the last of the Admiral's commissions, I sought out a quiet lodging house at some distance from the docks and rented a room from its incurious proprietor. I said it would be needed for no more than three weeks and that the chief tenant would be a young relative of mine. When the landlord shrugged and took my gold without asking any further questions, I heaved a sigh of relief.

On the road back to Seville, my desperate haste overmatched the mule's stubbornness. The beast nearly achieved a gallop over the last few miles. As I neared the Espinosa home, I turned over in my mind ways to explain the need for our immediate departure that would neither arouse suspicion nor insult their hospitality.

I need not have fretted on that account. The Espinosas had a new tragedy to bear. In my absence, the family had received word that their soldier son, Valerio, had been killed at Arras. Although the battle was long won, the Spanish occupying the town engaged in periodic skirmishes. During one of these, Valerio's musket had exploded. These modern weapons were known to prove as danger-ous on occasion to those who wielded them as to those who faced them. So it had been in poor Valerio's case. The news, brought by a disabled soldier returning home, was several months old. This increased rather than diminished the distraught family's horror and grief.

Doña Beatriz had taken to her bed, where she wept without cease, refusing to sleep or be comforted. She must have at least one of her remaining daughters at hand night and day, as if they might be snatched away if she relaxed her vigilance. Don Francisco had overnight become an old man who crept ghostlike through the house. The boys, too wretched to escape to their former distractions, clung to one another. In their black garments, they seemed like a flock of awkward crows in too small a cage as they fidgeted from room to room.

Rachel, white of face with eyes and nose swollen red from weeping, flung herself into my arms when I arrived.

"Diego, you must take me away *now*! We are only in the way."

"Don't worry, I have come to do just that. Dry your eyes. Pack what you can that is warm and small and valuable. Leave the farthingale and the fine laces behind. You will not need them."

"Shall I dress in my travel garb?" Rachel asked. "The garments I wore on the road from Barcelona?"

"No, though you may bring them along. You may wear the disgraceful shirt and breeches you acquired in Barcelona and your cloak over that."

Rachel's wan face lit up at that.

"Diego! You are going to let me dress as a boy."

"I can see no other choice," I said, "since I cannot provide a chaperone for you in Cadiz. But this doesn't mean you will have a boy's freedom. Don Rodrigo comes south. Remember that he is the only person in all of Spain who knows you in those garments as a girl."

"He has seen me in a dress as well," she said.

"He must not see you at all," I said. "Our lives depend on it. And I cannot mount guard over you. I must go about my duties as if nothing has changed."

"I will be careful, I promise!"

"Ha'shem grant that this doesn't prove to be the worst decision I have ever made."

"It will not! It will not!" Rachel squeezed my waist in a bone-crushing hug. "How many mules may we take to Cadiz?"

"Two for us to ride and a single pack mule. But they must end in the Espinosas' stables to await our aunt's return. Why do you ask?"

"No reason. Will you take me on board *Mariagalante* while we stay in Cadiz? Surely I may at least *see* the Admiral's flagship."

Rachel always had a plan, however harebrained it might be. Leaving in the cold, damp gray of early morning, we had hardly rounded the first bend when she insisted we halt at the edge of an olive grove, where we found Amir, the Moorish boy, awaiting us.

"We must help him reach the coast, Diego."

Rachel regarded me with clasped hands, sparkling eyes, and a determined chin while the boy, head bowed, awaited my reaction. Judging by his demeanor, he expected my wrath, perhaps a blow. I knew that he was not the ringleader of this plot.

"He can ride behind me on Rosa," she said. "He will pass as my servant when we enter Cadiz."

"And then what?"

Hearing my tone, ironic rather than furious in spite of myself, Amir looked up, his face brightening.

"I will slip away as soon as we enter the city, master, and you need trouble yourself no more about me. I will find a fishing boat to take me east along the coast and thence to Gibraltar. From there, I will take passage to the Maghreb, where many of my people have fled. Or I may be fortunate to find a skiff that I can row myself."

"And steal it?"

"If I must."

Fierce pride warred with shame on his face, which had already lost the impassive expression of a slave. I could not blame him for seeking any means to free himself. No one growing up in Seville, as I had, could avoid observing the traffic in human flesh and breathing its stench of misery and despair. Coffles of Moors from all the great Andalusian cities, made captive by successive conquests, were herded naked through the streets, chained to even blacker Africans, while auctioneers cried out their price. I feared that the golden-skinned Taino would one day meet the same fate. I refused to contemplate the possibility that Jews might so suffer.

"Very well," I said. "You may come."

Rachel had already extended her hand to help Amir mount the mule behind her.

"I told you he would agree." She flung me an impish grin and drove her heels into Rosa's flanks. The mule belched and broke into a trot. "At heart, Diego, you are still Papa's son."

Chapter 17

Cadiz, September 6, 1493

We entered Cadiz as the sun rose. The early light tinted the tumble of white houses that fell in tiers from the mountains to the harbor in a dozen pearly shades of rose and gold. In the market, stalls had already opened. We breakfasted on fresh bread and coffee before making our way to the lodging house I had secured.

Rachel was in high spirits, trusting me to conquer any obstacles in our path. I suspected that because I had allowed her to don boys' garments, she believed she would be permitted to join the fleet as well. I, on the contrary, had confidence that the Admiral would oppose any such outlandish venture. If she would not take no from me, she would be obliged to accept it from him.

"What do we do now?" Rachel asked when she had bounced on the narrow bed and approved the view from the small window with its glimpse of the harbor.

"First, we must cut your hair," I said. "Then we must see Admiral Columbus."

"Diego!" Rachel squealed. She flew at me and flung her arms around my waist, squeezing hard enough to leave me gasping.

"You are going to let me come to the Indies! Oh, you are the best of brothers!"

"The most foolish of brothers to the point of madness," I said, loosening her grip so that I could breathe. "But that doesn't mean I consent to this folly. If Admiral Columbus agrees to take you on board, you may come with us. But don't count your passage assured. He will refuse to lend himself to this deception, even if he thinks it may be done."

"Must we tell him I am not a boy?" Rachel asked as I took my knife to her thick braid. "Can I not simply sign on as a gromet?"

"Impossible. We do nothing without the Admiral's consent."

If we practiced such a ruse without his knowledge and were discovered, she would suffer imprisonment and scorn. But I might lose my life at the rope's end for having permitted it. I didn't tell her that.

"There, it is done." I handed her the severed braid.

She regarded it without regret. "Let us burn it," she said. "We don't wish the landlord to grow curious. The Admiral will not report me to the Inquisition, will he? Or you for harboring me?"

"I am glad to know you have that much appreciation of the risks we face," I said. "But no, I don't think so. Admiral Columbus is a good man. I believe his old loyalty to Papa will outweigh his devotion to his faith. But don't underestimate that devotion. He sees his mission to convert the Taino and bring Christianity to the Indies as a sacred one. You must never show any doubt of that unless we are alone."

"I have that much sense," Rachel said. "Don't forget I was schooled in a convent. I can play the Christian as well as you, if not better. Besides, we will not discuss religion with the Admiral. We will simply ask him to allow me to accompany you to the Indies."

"In a fleet of seventeen ships and more than twelve hundred men with not a single woman."

"I will not be a woman," Rachel said.

I groaned. "You cannot be a gromet," I said. "The ship's boys are too rough. You could not hold your own while maintaining your disguise."

"Then I will be the Admiral's page."

"Are you willing to perform such duties as emptying his chamber pot each morning?"

"If I have charge of it," Rachel pointed out, "I will be able to use it myself. You cannot say that I am not practical."

"What about your courses?" Had I not older sisters, I would not have known enough to ask such a question.

"I don't bleed yet," she said, "and am not likely to begin on the voyage. Once we are ashore, I will contrive something when the moment arrives that I must. The Taino women must solve this problem every month."

"The Taino women go naked," I retorted, "and are no example for a well brought up Jewish girl." How had she lured me into an extended debate about the details of a plan that would surely never be realized?

"You worry too much." She tossed her head and adjusted her breeches. "Let us go see Admiral Columbus."

"Very well," I said. I wished to get her away from the docks and out of sight well before Don Rodrigo's arrival in Cadiz. The fewer who saw her in my company before then, the better. Besides, the sooner the Admiral refused to let her sail with us, the sooner I could address the greater worry of finding passage for her to Italy on a ship I thought seaworthy and well manned enough to carry her without excessive danger.

We found the Admiral conversing with two gentlemen I had not met before. The elder of these he introduced as Don Antonio de Torres, master and owner of *Mariagalante*. The other, who was almost as tall as the Admiral and thatched with a shock of bright red hair, I took by his plain brown robe to be a cleric. The Admiral presented him as Don Diego Columbus. Once I knew, I could see the resemblance. I had heard of the Admiral's brothers, though I had not before met either of them.

"Young Diego," he told his brother and Don Antonio, "sailed with us on the *Santa Maria* and by his diligence both at sea and ashore has earned a place on our flagship."

My heart leaped. I was to sail on *Mariagalante* with the Admiral!

"My poor brother," he added, smiling, "will have to make do with a lesser caravel."

So Don Diego would join the expedition. He seemed pleasant and mild mannered. In any case, I would not have much to do with him until we reached the Indies, if then.

The Admiral took Torres by the arm and led him away, leaving his brother, Rachel, and me to follow.

"You will like *Mariagalante*, Diego," the Admiral said. "She is both spacious and seaworthy, and I assure you that my quarters are three times the size of my cabin on our former vessel." To the others, he said, "This lad writes the clearest hand of any in my company and has been of great service during our preparations."

"Better you than I," Don Diego remarked with a grin. "In my younger days, my brother tried to turn me into his scribe, but he had to leave off in despair, for he used to compare my hand to chicken tracks."

"I will lose this fellow's skill once we embark," the Admiral said, "as I have even greater need of able seamen. How do you plan to compensate me for this loss, young Diego?"

As I opened my mouth to say that I didn't know, Rachel dug her elbow in my ribs and cleared her throat loudly.

"Excellency!" she said, bobbing in a neat bow. "May I offer myself as a replacement? If it is not too forward of me to say so, I am adept with a quill, quick at languages, and not given to pranks or drunkenness."

Forward! She would neither drown nor hang, for I would kill her first!

"May I present my young cousin—" I stopped short, for I had not considered the need to supply Rachel with a boy's name.

Rachel bowed again, one hand over her heart.

"Rafael Mendes, Excellency," she said, "at your service and hoping greatly for your favor."

The Admiral cast a piercing glance at her and another at me. Don Antonio looked bored, which I considered fortunate. Don Diego's face remained tranquil. I risked a look of entreaty at the Admiral.

"Let us speak of this further," Admiral Columbus said. "Gentlemen, will you excuse me? I must secure, if not this paragon, then another of the same ilk. If I do not, Their Majesties will be most displeased with my reports, for they will be unable to decipher them. Come with me, lads."

The Admiral led the way to a room that had been set aside for him in the Alcázar so that he and Archdeacon Fonseca need not work under the same roof during their frequent disputes. He closed the door, bolted it, and turned to face us, his face stern but not yet angry.

"Now, Diego, this is no time to play tricks. We must get the fleet under way before the season for favorable winds is past. Explain yourself and this young lady, who I surmise is closely related to you."

"Oh!" Rachel said, crestfallen. "You have guessed that I am not a boy." She brightened as she added, "But the two gentlemen noticed nothing out of the ordinary."

"Excellency, I must apologize for my sister Raquel's boldness."

"Excellency," Rachel cut in, "our case is desperate. I must leave Spain. My parents have told me that you knew me as an infant. For their sake, I—we hoped that you would stand our friend."

"*I* would not so presume, Excellency," I said. "But I prefer that my sister not appear publicly in her own guise at this time. And when we came upon you—"

"He promised I could make my own petition," Rachel said.

I groaned inwardly. I didn't wish him to think that I claimed influence with him as a kind of coin. Neither did I think he would be impressed by childish exclamations of "I did not!" from me and "You did so!" from Rachel.

"What gave us away, Excellency?" I asked. "Does she so resemble me? For if she does, we are lost, as none must know who she is."

The Admiral smiled, his eyes at their most kindly, to my great relief. "No, but she greatly resembles your mother."

Rachel fell to her knees and clasped her hands, her brown eyes huge and pleading. "Oh, please, Excellency, let me serve you. Indeed I write a fair hand, and I will do any task you set me. I am not afraid of rough work or dirt."

"Nor the unknown dangers of the Ocean Sea?" he asked.

"Not while you are with us, Excellency," she said. "For you have navigated to the other side and know the way."

The Admiral laughed aloud. "I am tempted to offer you passage," he said, "if only to have at hand one soul whose confidence in me is absolute."

"Then you agree?" Rachel glowed with satisfaction until she saw that the Admiral was shaking his head.

"I am sorry, child," he said, still kindly. "I cannot."

"Oh, Excellency, are you *sure*?" Rachel's eyes filled with tears.

My own heart sank, even though I had desired this refusal and was relieved that the request had not earned us the Admiral's ill will. However, now I had no alternative but to find Rachel passage to Italy, and speedily too. In truth, the best ships and captains had already signed on to sail with the Admiral.

"Come, Raquel," I said, grasping her hand. She let me draw her away, but continued to look back over her shoulder. "We must not take up any more of the Admiral's time."

"Believe me, my dear," he said, meeting her eyes, "it is for the best. You will see."

"It is *not*. I will *not*." She had just enough propriety to mutter it under her breath.

None of us had mentioned the Inquisition.

Chapter 18

Cadiz, September 25, 1493

All Andalusia, it seemed, flocked to the docks to witness our departure. It was a sparkling day, sea and sky competing to win the palm for bravest shade of blue. Pennons fluttered and sails bellied in the breeze, flashing colors as bright as parrots in the forests of the Indies. Along with my fellows, I was kept so busy hauling sheets, taking my turn at the capstan to weigh anchor, and otherwise playing my part in the complex dance that getting a great ship under way entailed that I hardly heard the boom of cannon, the blare of trumpets, or the excited shouts of the spectators that accompanied our departure.

At least I no longer had to worry about Rachel. For three weeks, while I sought passage to Italy for her not only in Cadiz but in Palos and the surrounding seaside hamlets, she had stayed mostly out of sight. If she had slipped out to explore Cadiz on her own once or twice, I had not caught her at it. She assured me she was working hard to perfect her performance as a boy so that no one would be able to penetrate her disguise as Don Rodrigo and the Admiral had. Indeed, she had not sulked for more than a day or two after the Admiral's refusal and always showed a cheerful face when I came back tired and hungry from another long day's toil in preparation for the fleet's departure.

The Admiral, the Archdeacon, and all those charged with out-fitting the ships had become increasingly frenzied as our sailing day approached. It seemed that they had requisitioned every coil of rope and square yard of sail for twenty miles up and down the coast. I made many such requests myself and became skilled at smoothing the ruffled feathers of the shipmasters and chandlers so importuned with silver and promises of vicarious glory.

Between my duties and my private mission, I inspected every unseaworthy tub and interviewed every old salt too crippled by arthritis to be tempted by the lure of the Indies. The few sound vessels and competent seamen who chose to ply the Mediterranean as they always had all told me that they would not embark on their own ventures until the Admiral's fleet was well away. So I was much relieved to strike a bargain with a Genoese captain who declared he was ready to sail at once, but preferred not to risk his little vessel on the Ocean Sea. The *Strega* rode at anchor off a hamlet five miles east of where the fleet lay. The captain planned to catch the same tide as the fleet, then make for Livorno via Marseille and Genoa. My young brother, Captain Olivero assured me, would dine at the captain's table. For the fee I offered, he would not have to share a berth nor turn a hand to any work, and at Livorno he could hire a mule to carry him inland to Firenze.

I was not so foolish as to pay Captain Olivero in advance, nor did I allow him to meet Rachel until our common sailing day dawned. Mist still clung to the docks when we arrived, and the air was cool, although those who remained ashore would be sweating under a scorching sun by midday. The captain looked less than prepossessing in the morning light, with his blue-stubbled chin, broken teeth, and food-stained jacket trimmed in tarnished gilt. But Rachel squared her jaw and shook his hand firmly when I introduced her as Rafael Mendes.

I could not embrace her under the captain's eye. I clapped her on the shoulder with what words of cheer I could muster and bade her kiss my parents and sisters for me when she reached Firenze. I watched as she marched up the gangplank, looking small and forlorn with her knobby bundle over her shoulder. When she reached the deck she turned to give me a smile and raise her hand in farewell. I waved back, turning away before I dashed a tear from my eye. Then I mounted my mule, slapped Rachel's mule so it would follow apace, and rode hell for leather back to Cadiz, where I was lucky to arrive on the deck of *Mariagalante* before anyone had a chance to miss me. I had duties aplenty waiting for me aloft and below.

The Admiral, to his own disgust and the disappointment of the crowd, had taken ill the night before and remained in his cabin. He was attended by Dr. Chanca, a physician who had attended Their Majesties and had joined the expedition to care for the company's health. We had sailed without a physician on the first voyage but had been blessed with general good health throughout and a minimum of wounds. I wondered if we would be so lucky this time. If not, we would see how effective Dr. Chanca's remedies proved to be.

So neither the Admiral nor I was on deck when, as seamen prepared to raise the gangplank, a slender boy with a knobby bundle bouncing on his back came pelting toward *Mariagalante*, shouting at them to stop. When he introduced himself as Rafael Mendes, hired on by the Admiral himself to serve as his page, the sailors shrugged and pulled him aboard, their burly arms making the task no harder than pulling on the sheets to bring the great mainsail a point or two further into the wind.

Rachel, as she told me later, kept demanding to be taken to the Admiral until someone pointed the way. Dr. Chanca at once pressed her into service, pleased with an intelligent, biddable servant who comprehended orders quickly, obeyed them cheerfully, and was not too squeamish to scurry back and forth between the Admiral's cabin and the lee rail bearing basins of blood and vomitus. By the time the Admiral, slightly revived after being bled, caught sight of her face, the ship had passed Gibraltar.

The gromets looked askance at her, suspicious of her cheerful self-confidence. They were wary of each other on this first day, no doubt wondering who would be the leaders, the bullies, and the scapegoats of their company. Yet for the moment, they left Rachel in peace, perhaps deterred by the fact that she was armed with bodily fluids that might be used as an impromptu and very unpleasant weapon.

Despite the basin of vomitus, I was sorely tempted to grab her shoulders and shake her hard when, not long before sunset, I caught sight of the self-assured young page's face. As she rinsed the basin in the spray that splashed constantly on the bow, I got hold of her and demanded an explanation, keeping my voice low with an effort. "What happened? What were you thinking?"

Rachel's chin jutted out, and her eyes filled with tears, which disconcerted me as she knew it would. "What were *you* thinking? That horrible man was a pirate!"

"What!" I forgot to be quiet, which gave Rachel the opportunity to shush me and put me even more in the wrong.

"Don't worry," she said, "he didn't have a chance to harm me. Once you were gone, he bade me stay in what he called a cabin. It smelled vile, and a good-sized mule would not have room to lie down. So I crept out and overheard him laughing about me with the pilot. They planned to take my gold, which they knew I must have to get from Livorno to Firenze, and throw me overboard to drown."

"The villains!"

"Yes, and at first I thought they would seize my bundle and be thwarted, for you know I carry the gold on my person." She patted her waist, around which she had wrapped a sash that she had stitched into a hidden purse during those last days of waiting in the lodging in Cadiz. "But they had thought of that. They said that as long as they must search my body for coin, they might as well use me for a bum boy. What is a bum boy?"

"Never mind that. I am sorry, Rachel, indeed I am. I thought it would be all right, but I was mistaken. What did the Admiral say?"

"Very little, for he was throwing up when I arrived." Rachel grinned. "When he realized it was I, he tried to be stern, but I believe he wanted to laugh. He said I am to sleep on the floor in his cabin, work hard, and not make trouble even for you." She paused to consider her words. "To be honest, he said, 'You are not to make trouble for anyone on board, your brother least of all.'"

I clutched my hair in my hands and tugged on it. My hair would grow long enough on the voyage to express any amount of frustration. But I would prefer that Rachel obeyed the Admiral's command.

"I sent a letter to Aunt Marina's bankers in Firenze by the Archdeacon's own courier bound for Rome," I said, "telling Papa and Mama to expect you. Papa might even travel to Livorno to meet the *Strega*. They will think you drowned when you don't arrive. And don't say that I worry too much!"

"Truly, I am sorry, Diego," Rachel said. "I paid a boy to deliver a note to Doña Marina at the Espinosas' when she returns from Malaga. A *nice* boy, not a pirate, who thanked me for the silver coin I gave him and swore he would not fail me. Doña Marina's bankers will get word to Papa and Mama. It will be all right. It *must* be. I am glad that I am with you."

Night had fallen. I glanced all around to make sure no eyes were upon us. Then I put my arms around her and hugged her close to my heart. She clung to me. After a moment, she let go, nodding to show me that, like me, she understood our need for discretion.

"Oh, Rachel, it is hard not to be afraid, but I am glad you are with me too."

"Would you like to see what I wrote? I copied it out in a fair hand and kept the draft." She pressed it into my hand. "You can keep it if you like. I must go now. The Admiral needs me."

To Doña Marina Mendes y Torres
My dear Aunt,
I have gone with Admiral Columbus and Diego. Diego did his best to send me to Italy, but it didn't work. We thank you with all our hearts for your great kindness to us.

Please send word to Papa and Mama so they will know I am not lost at sea. Please give them all my love and Diego's too. He and Admiral Columbus will keep me safe.

Your dutiful and affectionate niece,
Raquel (Rachel Mendoza)

Part Three

THE INDIES

Chapter 19

San Sebastian, Gomera, Canary Isles, October 5–6, 1493

By the time we reached the Canaries, Rachel had won over almost all on board. None suspected she was not a boy, although on first impression a prissy one, as she was always neatly groomed and, unlike the gromets, did not attempt to emulate the coarse language of the older sailors. They soon saw, however, that when not attending the Admiral, she took her turn on watch and never shirked the endless tasks of mending, scrubbing, and bailing. Moreover, she expected no one, including the Admiral and me, to fight her battles.

The ship's boys learned that what she lacked in strength, she made up for in agility and wit. Once she had beaten the lot of them in a race up the rigging to the crow's nest and reduced the biggest bully to tears with a scathing assessment of his behavior, motives, and probable end, they accepted her as a sort of mascot, whose eccentricities were to be tolerated. These included cleaning her teeth daily with a frayed length of rope, as I did myself, and frequently sucking on a lemon. She always offered to share, though all refused and no doubt would one day suffer from swollen, toothless gums in consequence.

The only shipmate she failed to beguile was the Taino known as Diego Columbus, the Admiral's interpreter since the earliest days of the first voyage. He and Cristobal were the only Taino still alive to make the return journey to their homeland. Unlike Cristobal and those who had died of fevers, the flux, the cold, the unaccustomed food, and perhaps homesickness and despair, the interpreter was unaccountably robust and accustomed to being the Admiral's favorite. Once or twice he tried to do Rachel an ill turn, such as setting a full bucket in her way to trip over or rolling her spare shirt in fish guts. I offered to intervene and teach him a lesson he would not soon forget, for the Indian was no fighter. But Rachel scorned my assistance. She washed out the stinking shirt with soap, then she gave him such a dressing down in front of the grinning crew that he slunk away without a word and confined himself to sulks and baleful looks thereafter.

The Canaries were a string of fertile isles with mountains rising above crescent curves of sand. As the Admiral had found the year before, winds originating here would carry us westward across the Ocean Sea to landfall in the Indies. The conquest of these isles had begun long before. Some of them were still held by the native Guanche. But Gomera, where we dropped anchor, was held for Spain by Doña Beatriz de Peraza, who had been a maid of honor to Queen Isabella in her girlhood and was said to have attracted the attentions of King Ferdinand. The Admiral himself was said to be in love with her. Neither Rachel nor I were invited to her castle to behold her purported beauty, though to Rachel's delight, the lady ordered dazzling bursts of fireworks and a salute of cannons to celebrate our arrival in San Sebastian, the principal town.

While the Admiral exchanged courtesies with Doña Beatriz and reviewed his charts, we sailors labored to provision the fleet anew and herd cattle, sheep, and pigs aboard to join the horses we already carried, for the new colony in Hispaniola must have livestock. When not on duty, we had leave to wander where we would. Most of the men went no farther than the nearest tavern. But Rachel insisted on a brisk walk to the outskirts of the town, where farms and groves of oranges and lemons began. We came away with a sack of tangy fruit, along with a lemon sapling that had a root ball the size of my fist. With her usual persuasiveness, Rachel assured me that she would assume full care of it once on board *Mariagalante*, would I but carry it back to the ship. She had already won permission from the Admiral to keep it in his cabin, thus demonstrating that he was no more proof than I against her blandishments.

"It will need sun as well as water," I said.

"Then I will give it a daily airing on the deck," she said, "and we will plant it at La Navidad in honor of our arrival there."

"I suppose you will want me to dig the hole," I grumbled.

Rachel merely laughed. Linking her arm through mine, she skipped along, bobbing like a dinghy in the wake of a caravel.

"You had better not skip nor cling to my arm," I warned her, "where any can see us."

"I won't," she promised, "but there is not a soul in sight. It is a beautiful day, and we have such a great adventure before us."

"Not every adventure is kissed by the sun," I said, thinking of storms at sea and man's capacity for greed and cruelty.

"You worry too much," she said. "Give me an orange. We must not be remiss in preserving our teeth."

I drew an orange, which the ancients called a golden apple of the Hesperides, from the sack. I cut the glowing sphere, still warm from the sun, in two and handed half to Rachel. We ate the orange as we went, juice dripping down our chins.

"Look, there is Cristobal," Rachel said as we approached the ship. "He must be feeling better, to have come up on deck."

We clambered aboard and joined him at the rail. The scene below us was one of purposeful chaos, as always on the docks in any port. Sweating men in shirtsleeves barked orders. Boys drove lowing cattle and bleating sheep and goats toward the ships. Women hawked cooked meat and fruit. Heavy wooden crates and barrels swung over the side and onto the deck with rope and hook, like a giant's fishing pole. Everywhere we saw Guanche slaves at work, their golden skins grimed with dirt and sweat and their muscles bunched with effort.

"I am glad to see you in the sun, Cristobal," Rachel exclaimed. "Do you feel stronger today?"

"A little."

His face lightened as he looked at her tenderly. Indifferent to clothing, Cristobal had not been deceived for a minute when Rachel was transformed into a boy. We trusted him to say nothing, and he did not. In turn, I studied him. In truth, he looked worse: his skin jaundiced, eyes bloodshot, and wasted frame shivering in spite of the blistering sun.

"Do you not want to go ashore?" she asked him. "There is much to see."

Cristobal spat over the side. "I see well enough from here."

The noise and color made the lively scene seem cheerful, but Cristobal's eye rested on the laboring Guanche, whom their overseers kept at work with shouts and the occasional crack of a whip.

"What do you see?" I asked.

"I see dead men walking," he said. "I see the future of the Taino."

Chapter **20**

On the Ocean Sea, October 13–November 3, 1493

The Canaries being known for their tranquil air, we had to wait for the wind. But once it came, it filled our sails and sent us scudding westward. The blue dome of the heavens arched above us, and the sea, with its hundred shifting shades of blue and green, stretched out before us. The voyage passed quickly, and not only because the weather favored us. On our first voyage, we had constantly to fight back fear. If the Ocean Sea proved to stretch far beyond our reckoning, we should be dead of thirst, starvation, or the destruction of our ships by storm long before we reached the Indies. This time, we knew our destination.

All were eager to see the Indies, those who had shipped with us in 1492 no less than those for whom this was the first voyage. As we worked, ate our dried peas and biscuit, and lay looking at the brilliance of the stars at night, our conversation often turned to speculation as to how the men left at La Navidad fared and how soon we ourselves would lay our hands on gold.

Now and then, I found myself joining in the dreams of the others, wishing for wealth sufficient to restore my family's shattered fortunes. I longed to lay gold enough before them that my mother would not go shabby, my sisters without husbands, or my father old before his time.

Of the missions with which the King and Queen had charged us, only the Admiral and the priests seemed to care about the conversion of the Taino. The leading cleric, Fray Buil, was haughty and intolerant. I made sure to avoid him. Of the others, only young Fray Pane was unassuming and humble. He often sat with Cristobal when neither Rachel nor I nor occasionally Fernando could be spared from our duties. Once we had left land behind, Cristobal grew steadily weaker, till he could barely sip a posset or a little wine and could not hold down solid food at all. When Fray Pane said his rosary and murmured prayers for the saving of the Taino's soul for Jesus, he also wiped his brow and held the basin while Cristobal retched and shuddered. The priest seemed to understand that baptism in Spain had meant little to him. But rather than recoiling in horror or crying heresy, Fray Pane patiently put his point of view over and over again, hoping to make a deeper impression before the Indian died.

"It grieves me," the little cleric said to me, "that he should die without the comforts of religion."

As he understood none of the Taino tongue, Fray Pane didn't know how often Cristobal called out to Yucahu and Atabey, his gods of father sky and mother earth, and to Maketaori Guayaba, ruler of the underworld where the Taino believed their souls went when they died. At night, Cristobal told us, the souls of the dead turned into bats, which flew abroad and feasted on the guayaba, or guava. This fruit had a tangy savor similar to that of lemon.

"If I do not live to reach my own land," Cristobal told us in the ghost of a whisper, "my bat soul will have to make do with your lemon tree. So tell it to make haste to grow and bear fruit, for a soul that cannot feed will starve and fade away."

Rachel wiped away a tear. I took his skeletal hand in mine as if I could pass to him some of my own strength.

"You will see your village again," Rachel said. "You must!"

"I pray to Ha'shem," I added, "that you will be reunited with your family. Hutia must long to see you, and it would not be right to disappoint him." I hoped to fan in him the spark of a will to live. But I was not hopeful, though I tried not to infect Rachel with my gloom.

"Do bats have teeth?" Rachel asked. When Cristobal nodded, she said, "They must have healthy teeth even in the afterlife, from feeding on such fruit." This won a smile from Cristobal, as she had hoped.

Except for us, none on board regarded him or took any care to make sure he was fed, clean, and resting as comfortably as he could. The Admiral would have left him in Spain, had I not requested that he be allowed to return to his homeland, promising truthfully that he would not take up much room or consume more than the smallest quantity of the ship's provisions.

The Admiral's indifference to Cristobal's fate did not surprise me, although it shocked Rachel. When he had decided to carry some of the Taino to Spain, he was not yet committed to enslaving them all. I believed he held that plan in reserve, should the gold we amassed in the Indies prove too little to enrich the Crown beyond its previous prosperity. He had brought Cristobal and the others to display to the King and Queen as marvels, herding them like prime cattle. But the Taino proved a disappointment to him, becoming ill and dying rather than remaining handsome and strong. So being a man of vision whose favorite cry was *Adelante!* Go forward! he set his sights on the horizon and moved on.

Diego Columbus might have helped and comforted his compatriot, understanding better even than we the conflict between Spanish and Taino ways. Instead, he felt so jealous of his fellow Taino that he had tried to persuade the Admiral to leave him behind in Spain. He certainly loved the Admiral for elevating his status from that of slave to valued interpreter and was reluctant to share this distinction, which protected him from death or mal-treatment, for fear of losing it. He had apparently decided from the beginning that the God of the Christians, perhaps embodied in his mind by the Admiral, was more powerful than the Taino gods and changed his cloth accordingly.

Once aboard, Diego Columbus found in Rachel a new and more dangerous competitor. So both of us were in the interpreter's bad graces and kept an eye out lest he do us some truly damaging disservice. Rachel especially could not avoid him, because he still served the Admiral. Illiterate, he could not act as a scribe, and thus eyed paper and quill itself with loathing.

Several times when Rachel came into the Admiral's cabin, she found spilled ink and spoiled paper on the Admiral's desk, or quills she had painstakingly sharpened snapped in two. These things were precious, for our supply was limited. Other than Rachel, the interpreter was the one most often in the cabin. While he took care not to get caught, neither of us doubted he was responsible.

"He is sly and mean-spirited," Rachel said, in a fury. "I thought the Taino were great of heart and generous, like Cristobal."

"No race consists only of good men," I told her, "not even the Jews. But I have met no other Taino with such jealousy and envy in his heart. Perhaps it is we Europeans who have infected him with our fear that if others enjoy plenty, he will not have enough."

"Enough what?" she asked. "Quills and ink?"

"Enough of whatever such men covet because they see that others value it," I said. "Gold, land, rank, but also love, esteem, and even friendship. Will you tell the Admiral of this? Or would you like me to take the man aside and convince him to fear my wrath? I will do it if you say the word."

"You have become a man, my brother," Rachel said. She wrinkled her nose at me, and the fire died out of her eyes. "I would quake before you myself, did I seek to oppose you in any way. No, let us leave it. The Admiral is still fond of the fellow. It would pain him to know him so vindictive and untrustworthy. I can clean up the ink and sharpen more quills."

"As you wish," I said, noting that, like me, Rachel avoided the interpreter's name, wishing to call him neither "Diego" nor "Columbus." "But let us not turn our backs on him, especially if he finds us alone at the rail on a moonless night."

Chapter 21

Dominica, November 3, 1493

The wind continued steady and the weather fair. We sighted drifting grasses and birds that we knew nested ashore. Pelicans, which I had considered birds of good omen since our first voyage, visited us on deck. Comical and ungainly once they folded their wings, they were eager to contest the catch of fish with which we varied our diet of salt beef and the tiresome and by this time wormy biscuit. We made landfall three weeks to the day from our departure from the Canaries.

At the cry of "Land!" from the lookout in the crow's nest, all those not on watch roused from slumber and stumbled toward the rail, scratching at their bodies and rubbing sleep from their eyes. Rachel, barefoot and tousled, emerged from the Admiral's cabin, where she slept on a pallet near the door. The Admiral overtook her in a couple of eager strides. The men who clustered around the rail made way for him.

Dawn was breaking. A high mountain pierced the bank of steel gray cloud before us. The peak was little more than a black bulk, as the sun was rising behind us in the east. As we watched, its slopes were touched with pearl and then gold until those with keen eyes could discern the green of forests.

We sailors had much to do before we could land. We scurried about our work, hardly needing the orders of master and pilot to ready the ship with speed and efficiency. The Admiral returned to his cabin, taking Rachel with him to assist in writing the great news not only in his logbook but also in the letters he was preparing for the Sovereigns. When he returned to the deck, he summoned Fray Buil and the other priests to lead prayers of thanksgiving for our safe arrival, exclaiming on the omen of our making landfall on the Christian Sabbath.

"I will name this island Dominica," the Admiral declared, then bowed his head in devotion as the company began to sing.

Rachel slipped away, whispering to me that she would tell Cristobal, too weak to rise from his pallet below, that he was home. I didn't know how much the news would please him. We were still far from Hispaniola, where my friend Hutia and the rest of his family awaited him, surely praying to their gods that he still lived. His village lay near our fort of La Navidad. My enemy Cabrera waited too, and I remembered with a shudder of apprehension how he had cursed me as our boat pulled away from shore. But I was no longer a boy to be intimidated. I trusted that when the time came to face him, Ha'shem would be with me. As the company sang their Latin Hail Mary and Praise to God, I murmured under my breath the words of the Psalm of David: "The Lord is my shepherd, I shall not want . . . I shall fear no evil . . ."

A hand fell on my shoulder. My eyes flew open. It was only my friend Fernando, who whispered, "Rafael asks you to come quickly. Cristobal is dying."

I found Rachel kneeling with Cristobal's head in her lap, tears falling unheeded down her cheeks. A small candle illuminated the dark enough to see the labored rise and fall of the Taino's chest, his breath harsh with his approaching death.

She raised her face to mine.

"He is too weak to rise and go above. I cannot bear it that he may not see the land with his own eyes. It is so close, so close!"

"I can carry you," I offered. "Do you wish to see the island?" He weighed so little by now that I could do it without even breathing hard.

"It is not my home," he whispered, each word costing more than he could spare from his small store of remaining breath. "It is enough that I have crossed the water. The *cemi* can hear my voice again. I will rest in the arms of Atabey, and my soul will reach Coaybay before the sun is high."

"What can I do for you, my friend?" I asked. My eyes stung, and I had to force the words past a lump in my throat.

"Tell my son," he gasped, "tell Hutia he must be a brother to you and the little one. Tell him he is Taino and I am proud of him."

"I will miss you, my father," Rachel said in Taino. She kissed his forehead gently.

He touched her cheek, his hand trembling with the effort to raise it as she bent over him.

"My soul will fly tonight and seek to feed. If it cannot reach the shore and find the guayaba, I will come to your little lemon tree tonight. Look for me."

"I will, my father."

His head fell back, the death rattle rose in his throat, and he moved no more.

I found kaddish, the Hebrew prayer of mourning, rising to my lips: *"Yit'gadal v'yit'kadash sh'mei raba . . ."*

The fleet made no attempt to land until the evening, passing through still channels past several islands. Then the Admiral ordered all ships to drop anchor on the lee side of a flat island he named *Santa Maria* la Galante for our flagship. He took a party ashore to plant the royal standard and raise a cross. Against my advice, Rachel had requested that we be allowed to bury Cristobal.

As I expected, with all that must be done to make this first landing a success, the Admiral had no time or thought to spare for such a request. Diego Columbus said loudly that the Taino had no prohibition against burial at sea. I knew this for a lie, but it would have been foolish to debate it once the Admiral had ordered it done.

So Cristobal went overboard, wrapped in a sail, and Rachel refused the opportunity to set foot ashore, as she meant to wait for Cristobal's soul to come as a bat to the little lemon tree. The sapling, which had been in bloom when we acquired it and delighted Rachel by setting tiny green lemons during the voyage, had spent the day tucked out of the way on deck near the bow, where it would not be mishandled during the commotion of making landfall.

"Do you wish me to wait with you?" I asked. From the stubborn set of her jaw, I deemed it useless to point out that the chances of a bat making its way to the ship were small, whether it was in truth the Taino's soul or an ordinary fruit bat.

"No," Rachel said, "you need not hold back on my account. You must be eager to set foot on land. Unless you wish to avoid having to help raise the cross?"

"I can join the party that will go in search of dry wood and fresh water," I said. "I will come to you as soon as I return."

When we boarded the ship again near midnight, I found her crouched in the bow, sobbing. The little lemon tree was gone. Although we could not prove it, both of us believed that Diego Columbus had thrown it overboard.

Chapter 22

Once having set foot onshore, all were eager to reach La Navidad. We longed to know what progress had been made there toward a colony and, of greater interest to most, the finding of gold. Even I, who had reason to dread the reunion with our former shipmates, felt my pulse quicken at the prospect of beholding the fabled mine of Cibao. The Taino of Hispaniola all assured us it lay in the nearby mountains, but we had failed to find it the year before. There would be riches enough for all if its location had been revealed in our absence.

We did not linger on Dominica or its neighboring isles, although the Admiral named each one and sent a party ashore to set up the royal flag and claim it for the Crown. We passed island after island, many mountainous with densely forested slopes, all set like jewels in seas of astonishing colors from palest aqua, in which fish painted like gypsy wagons in green, yellow, orange, red, and black darted to and fro, to the dark turquoise of the deeper waters between the isles.

On one island, which the Admiral named *Santa Maria* de Guadalupe, we stayed almost a week. This island was one of the most beautiful we saw, one of its marvels a waterfall that fell from the clouds down the slopes of the highest peak. A party of ten men that the Admiral sent to investigate the interior became lost in the forest. Search parties failed to find them. Instead, they were guided back to the shore by twenty Taino who Diego Columbus declared had been captives of the Caribe and that their captors ate human flesh. Remembering my friend Hutia's words on the subject, I was skeptical, but the Admiral ever afterward considered the Caribe to be foul and wicked. Yet his admiration for the Taino did not prevent him from enslaving them.

Leaving Guadalupe behind, we bore northwest toward Hispaniola, passing more than half a dozen isles of varying size and terrain. The greatest of these was not only populated but well cultivated, for we could see the mounds on which the Taino planted yuca and rows of the spiky topknots of the heavy fruit, brown and prickly without but golden green, juicy, and intensely sweet within, that the Taino called *yayama*. We sailed as close to the lee shore as we could, seeking a harbor. Finally we anchored at the mouth of an estuary whose waters the Admiral believed must be sweet further inland. According to his custom, the Admiral declared that henceforth the island would be known as Santa Cruz. He sent an armed party of twenty-five up the river in one of our boats.

I can report but not explain what happened when our party suddenly came upon four men, two women, and a boy in a dugout canoa. On our first voyage, the Indians we met had greeted us with joy and been eager to press gifts upon us. That these didn't might be attributed, as the Admiral believed, to the fact that they were Caribe, our enemies and not our friends. Or it may be that our reputation had gone before us, and these folk believed that if they didn't fight, they would be carried off. They had good reason, whether or not they had already heard of the men with metal weapons in their winged boats, for our ship's boat moved to block their escape as they still stared, surprised and uncertain of what to do.

Seeing they were blocked and could not flee, the Caribe prepared to fight. Battle was joined. Since they had only bows and arrows to counter the Spanish swords and muskets, the outcome was a foregone conclusion. Rachel, watching beside me from the deck, caught her breath as they carried to the ship an Indian who had been wounded in the gut. Biting her lip, she refused to turn away as they laid him on the deck, bloody intestines spilling out of his belly in a slimy tangle. Dr. Chanca bent over him and shook his head.

"This one will not live to make a slave," he said.

Rachel cried out in horror as two sailors seized him by his arms and legs, swung him back and forth to gain momentum, and heaved him overboard. But worse was yet to come. The wounded Carib, clutching his belly with one hand, dog-paddled with the other toward shore. The Taino captives whom we had already taken crowded to the rail to watch, Diego Columbus beside them.

"They say we must kill him," the interpreter said. "If not, he will bring a host of Caribe down on us."

Rachel clutched the rail so hard her knuckles turned white.

"That is not what they said," she said between gritted teeth.

"I know," I said softly, for though not as adept at languages as Rachel, I too had learned much from Cristobal. "But we can do nothing. Close your eyes if you cannot bear to look."

But Rachel watched steadily as some of the shore party recaptured the gutshot Carib and tossed him back on board. Close to fainting with pain and loss of blood, the man was trussed securely with rope and thrown back into the sea.

"If he can endure it, I can watch it," she said.

I longed to put my arm around her, but although no one was paying us any attention, I could not embrace the Admiral's page boy.

"There is more than one kind of auto da fé," I murmured.

There was a great shout from the shore, and from the woods a host of Caribe came running, shaking spears and launching arrows toward the ships, for the shore party's boat, having rammed and sunk the Caribe canoe and killed or captured all aboard it, had speedily returned to the safety of deeper water. The Caribe, painted for battle in red, white, and ochre and screaming with rage and frustration, could not reach us. Our better-armed men, however, could wound and make captives of those who swam out to the ship. Diego Columbus declared that these were Taino slaves who preferred us to the flesh-eating Caribe. In any case, they were doomed to regret their choice.

Among the gentleman volunteers was a childhood friend of the Admiral's, Michele de Cuneo of Savona. A bigheaded, boisterous fellow much given to boasting and coarse remarks, he had been in the thick of the battle, bellowing as he swung his sword, even laughing, as if killing itself were a joy. He returned to the ship with a screaming naked maiden under his arm, kicking and squirming in her efforts to get free. He paid no attention until she managed to scratch his face and attempted to bite his arm. Then he swatted her on her bare buttocks with the flat of his still bloody sword, which made her scream louder than ever.

Cuneo looked up, laughing, at the Admiral, who stood above the fray where he could survey the battle in its entirety.

"Eh! Colombo!" he called, surely the only man who dared to address him thus. "Can I keep this one for myself?"

I heard Rachel's sharp intake of breath as the Admiral nodded, raising his hand in assent and quirking one side of his mouth in a brief smile.

"Do you hear that, girl?" Cuneo cried, though of course she could not understand him. "You belong to me now, and I shall use you as I please."

He got a better grip on the girl by seizing a handful of her hair, which made her cry out in pain, and thrusting his arm between her legs from behind so he could bunch the flesh of her naked belly in his fist. Her cries rose to a scream as he carried her below.

Much of the noise on deck died away as the rest of the captives were subdued and the Caribe on the shore fled. The gromets, with bucket and scrubbing brush, began to clean the deck of blood and other detritus of the battle. I remained with Rachel. We could hear the screams continue from below. The rhythmic slap of a length of rope on bare flesh punctuated the girl's cries.

"Diego!" Rachel cried. "What is he doing to her?"

I took her hand and pulled her down beside me on a coil of rope.

"Do you know what is meant to happen between a man and a woman?"

"Yes," she said. "Elvira told me."

"What did she tell you?" I asked. Our eldest sister loved to hoard information and spring it on us at the moment when it would most devastate or embarrass us, and she did not always pause to verify her facts.

"She said that a man and a woman do the same as when a bull is set to a cow, so she will bear a calf and furnish milk. And that is how human folk make a baby. And I know it is true, for I asked Mama. She said there is pleasure in it too, when it is done correctly."

Papa had said the same. I would not admit to Rachel that I had had no opportunity yet to investigate the matter for myself. So I simply nodded, hoping my little sister thought me wiser than I was.

"Mama told me about rape too," Rachel said. "That is what Cuneo is doing, is it not?"

"Yes, but—Mama told you?"

"She said I must have this knowledge," Rachel said, "so that if I were taken by the Inquisition, at least I would not be taken by surprise."

At that moment a series of piercing screams came from below. Cuneo would not heed the Taino girl's plea for mercy. But Rachel and I understood. The girl begged for freedom, threatened to kill him if he did not stop, then cried hopelessly for her mother.

"Cuneo is a beast!" Rachel said, her voice trembling.

"He is, but few of our shipmates would agree with us."

As if to prove me right, a burst of lewd remarks and cheers greeted Cuneo as he appeared on deck. He wiped at a thin line of blood trickling down his cheek where the desperate girl's nails had found their mark.

"The *puta* is shameless," he said, grinning as he adjusted his breeches. "Once I had thrashed her well, she served me as if she had been brought up in a school for harlots."

I could not hold my tongue. "So would your wife," I snapped, "did you beat her as soundly as you did that wretched maiden."

Cuneo swung his massive head from side to side like a bull considering whether to charge. Below, the girl could be heard sobbing. I waited with my hand on my dagger, ready to fight if I had to. But Cuneo, pleased with himself for successfully concluding his sport, as he would no doubt call it, decided not to be offended. He gave a shout of laughter and turned his back on me.

As the others dispersed with a final jest or two, Fernando sauntered over and leaned against the rail. "You have made an enemy," he said.

"Cuneo had best be my enemy," I retorted, "as I would be shamed to count such a turd as my friend."

Ordinarily, I tried to guard my language, which could turn as rough as any other sailor's, in front of Rachel. But when I searched my mind for a gentler epithet for Cuneo, I could not find one.

Chapter 23

La Navidad, Hispaniola, November 27–28, 1493

"The fort itself may not impress you," I told Rachel as our vessel sailed along the coast of Hispaniola, "for we built it in a hurry and without preparation or proper materials. But it is more interesting than it looks, for its walls are made of the timbers of the *Santa Maria*. She was as gallant a ship as this one, though the sailors called her an old tub."

"You have yourself become a sailor to the core," Rachel said, laughing, "waxing sentimental over a broken wreck."

I smiled, but said, "Believe me, her loss was a tragedy. It is only thanks to Ha'shem that we made it ashore and then back across the Ocean Sea with only the *Niña* and the *Pinta* to carry us."

A fiery sunset was fading in the sky, and I was due to go on watch soon. But we lingered at the rail, watching the gulls, pelicans, and other diving birds and admiring the sweep of forest and mountain scalloped by beaches of pristine sand, rosy in the reflected light. When it grew dark, Rachel hurried below to attend to her chores for the Admiral, and I reported to the pilot for duty. For the time being, I was ordered to remain at the rail, scanning the darkness, by ear as well as by sight, for the shoal water that had destroyed the *Santa Maria*.

"Keep a sharp eye out for any sign of the savages as well," the pilot warned me. "For we don't know how they may be disposed toward us, and it is best to be prepared."

This unease was born not only of our experience with the Caribe of Santa Cruz, for we found signs that all was not well here in Hispaniola. Last year, Guacanagarí, the cacique whose village lay closest to La Navidad, had given us a warm welcome. This time, no villagers appeared to greet us, but one of the parties we sent ashore found on a riverbank the decomposed remains of two men bound with ropes. No one wished to believe that these were Spaniards. But the men who had seen the remains reported that they included scraps of tangled hair that might have been a European beard rather than the thick black thatch that grew on Taino heads.

Peering into the darkness with all my senses alert, I heard a barely perceptible splashing that I thought might be either the dipping of paddles or some sea creature going about its business. I held up a lantern, but it failed to pierce the blackness before me. I saw nothing until I heard a shout from below, close to the ship.

"Guamikeni! Guamikeni!" This was what the Taino called the Admiral.

I held the lantern high. The light fell on a pair of round, dark faces and gleaming smiles. The Taino held up two golden masks of such magnificence that I gasped.

When I demanded that they declare themselves, they indicated by signs that they wished to come aboard.

The pilot appeared at my elbow, and the rest of the watch began to gather.

"Are they hostile?" the pilot asked.

"I don't believe so, sir," I said. "They call for the Admiral, and they bear gifts."

"Throw down a rope, then," he said, "and send for His Excellency."

By the time the visitors had climbed aboard, securing their canoe, the Admiral had come up on deck. Diego Columbus trotted at his side.

"We come from your friend Guacanagarí," they said. "Our cacique welcomes you and gives you these as a token of his love and loyalty." They held out the masks.

The Admiral took one of the masks in his hand, nodding to a sailor to bring his lantern closer and turning it this way and that. A buzz of excitement arose from those close enough to see.

"Gold! They bring gold! Our fellows must have found the mine!"

The Admiral's eyes lit up, but then his lips tightened, as if he struggled to restrain his eagerness to ask the source of such a quantity of gold.

"What of my men?" he asked. "Do they prosper?"

"Oh, yes, great Admiral. The *arijua*, the foreigners, are well. Our cacique has been their loyal friend."

"Loyal?" I muttered to Fernando, who stood by me. "When a man speaks of loyalty, he generally measures it against some betrayal."

The Admiral heard me.

"What has happened in our absence?" he demanded. "Do you swear that all my men are well?"

I noticed that Diego Columbus did not translate "swear," since there is no such concept in the Taino language. Indeed, I thought the Taino had told us less of truth than of what they deemed it expedient for us to hear from the day we first encountered them in 1492. Nor could I fault them for it. They had no cause save the generosity of their nature to trust us or to offer us their friendship.

"Yes, yes," the Taino said. "A few were sick, and some died in a fight. But otherwise the friends of Guacanagarí are as you left them."

"A few? How many? What kind of fight?"

"The *akani*, the enemies of Guacanagarí, don't like the *arijua*. When they came to attack our village, they fought Guamikeni's men as well."

"How many?"

The Taino looked at each other, smiled, and did not answer.

"Why does Guacanagarí not come himself to greet me? Where is your cacique?"

The Admiral looked at the ship's master, Don Antonio de Torres, who stood close by, and asked him, "Why don't our men come to greet us? If these Indians know that we have arrived, so must they."

"Our cacique Guacanagarí was wounded by the *akani*. He sends you his love, for he cannot walk to come himself. This was the doing of the *anki* Caonabo, the evil person who attacked our village."

"It sounds to me like a pack of lies," Fernando muttered in my ear.

Guacanagarí's ambassadors were given food and drink, and much was made of them. Everybody wanted to examine the golden masks. I stayed close by throughout their visit, hoping to hear them talk more candidly between themselves in Taino. When they left, I sought out the Admiral, who had retired to his quarters. Rachel opened the door, looking mussed and sleepy. Over her shoulder, I could see the Admiral seated at his writing desk, the masks propped up before him. They glittered in the flickering light of a candle.

"Diego! Have you seen the golden masks?" Rachel burst out in an excited whisper. "And tomorrow we shall go ashore!"

Evidently, the Admiral had not confided in her, for she obviously knew of nothing amiss.

"Excellency, may I have a word?" I said.

He rose and came to meet me with a nod to Rachel. She slipped outside the door, no doubt to stand guard. I knew she would have preferred to put her ear to the keyhole, had the oak door not had a massive iron bolt instead.

I reminded him that I had learned a fair amount of the Taino language.

"I listened to the talk between the two," I said, "and I fear that more is amiss than they care to tell us."

"What did they say, then?"

"They said nothing clearly," I admitted. "It was all hinting. But I greatly fear that more of our men may be dead than we believe. I wonder, too, if Guacanagarí is truly as steadfast a friend as he would have us think."

"Nonsense!" the Admiral said. "I don't believe it. Perhaps they have all fallen sick with a flux and are too weak to make their way out to our anchorage in the dark. We will go ashore in the morning and see for ourselves. Dr. Chanca will come with us and Fray Buil as well, so if their bodies or their souls need tending, we will be prepared. If it is past your watch, get some sleep, for we will need our wits about us."

"Then I may be one of the shore party, Excellency?"

"Certainly," he said. "You have done well on this voyage, young Diego, and so has little 'Rafael.'"

Warmed by his praise, I bade Rachel good night and lay down in a dry, quiet corner of the deck. But sleep would not come. I watched the stars wheel slowly in their great dance until they began to pale and the sky to lighten. From the shore, I could hear parrots scream as they woke and stirred to meet the approaching day.

Word of last night's events had been sent to the other vessels. Gentlemen and soldiers from the other ships, as well as ship's officers and all the clerics, met us on the shore before the dawn had faded from pink to blue. I was not surprised to see Don Melchior Maldonado among them. Like me, he wished to know if Juan Cabrera lived. I was glad Rachel had remained on *Mariagalante*, though I myself was not afraid of Cabrera's genius for evil. I had proved myself beyond all doubt on this voyage, and I was no longer under his command.

I realized with some surprise that I no longer feared the Inquisition either, at least as long as we remained in the Indies. I had kept Cabrera's secret, saying nothing of Anacaona's murder, because he knew my secret too. I had no wish to return to Spain in chains to be given to the fire, if not hanged on the spot. For it was a capital crime to be a Jew in Spain, and was not the Admiral's fleet an outpost of Spain? So, too, were the islands he had claimed, now flying the Green Cross banner. But even Fray Buil and his fellow clerics were talking eagerly of gold as we marched toward La Navidad. Their minds were not bent on sniffing out heresy.

I had forgotten how like paradise Hispaniola was: the whisper of the breeze tossing the verdant canopy above us and clicketing the great fans of foliage that grew at our feet; the jewel colors not only of parrots with their raucous cry but of small birds that sipped nectar from flowers as colorful as themselves or perched, singing sweetly, on leaf or branch; the myriad butterflies that lent the very air not only color but gaiety. Even the nakedness of the Taino seemed to me, this morning, not an ignorant absence of shame but the embodiment of innocence, as it had been in Eden.

It was hard to remain cautious and apprehensive on such a morning. As we marched, our weapons slackened in our hands. Our gaze softened, feasting on beauty wherever we looked, rather than scanning for danger. A cheerful hubbub arose, as if we were marching straight to the gates of the gold mine of Cibao.

"At any rate," I heard one soldier tell another, "they'll have a bite of fresh bread for us to eat, instead of that infernal biscuit. I don't know how sailors stand it for months at a time."

"They'll likely have stronger drink than sour wine," his comrade said, grinning. In spite of all Archdeacon Fonseca's care, the merchants had sold us wine in rotting casks, which had let much of it seep away and turned the rest to near vinegar. "And some of those *yayama* we had on Dominica. I've never tasted the like."

"And women," another soldier said. "I'd like to get me one of them naked women for myself. Or maybe two."

"These lads at the fort have had near a year to pick them over," the first man said.

"Don't worry, there are plenty in the woods," the second said, and all of them laughed heartily.

I was not pleased to hear them speak so. When the Queen commanded that the Taino be treated lovingly, she had not meant that her soldiers and sailors were to emulate Cuneo of Savona. But before I could say something sharp, the rank of men in front of us stopped short. Walking some way back among the company, I could not see at first what had halted them. But cries of dismay from those in the vanguard soon reached us. In spite of the officers' orders, the men broke ranks and shoved one another in their haste to reach the front. I confess I did the same.

The charred and abandoned ruins of La Navidad lay before us. The little fort had been burned to the ground.

Chapter 24

La Navidad, November 29, 1493

Although none could deny that the fort had been destroyed, the Admiral was reluctant to believe that all forty of the Christians could be dead. He had cannon fired again and again, hoping to hear an answering shot that would confirm, as he wished, that the survivors had withdrawn into the woods, taking at least some of their artillery with them. But no answer came. And most of the Taino, rather than flocking to see us as they had in the past, ran away when we caught sight of them. A few bold fellows risked our wrath to barter with us. Since they offered us gold in exchange for hawk's bells and red caps, the Admiral did not refuse to treat with them. Now realizing that I too was a competent interpreter, he set Diego Columbus and me to questioning each of them over and over. But we could not get a satisfactory answer out of them.

That at least some of the garrison were dead became ever more plain. The Taino who came to barter showed us the decaying bodies of eleven Spaniards hidden in the grass. Dr. Chanca, who knew such things, declared that their condition showed they had been dead only a month or two. Their features could no longer be discerned, but I recognized the ornament that Juan Cabrera had worn in his ear, not a ring but a bit of gold fashioned into a skull, with two chips of ruby for its eyes. My last words to Cabrera the year before had been a true prediction. If a hell existed, he was surely there now. I could not be sorry that he was dead.

I saw Don Melchior Maldonado surveying the bodies. To my relief, he did not recognize the tiny jewel, for as he had said, Cabrera was only a distant cousin. His face, however, grew grimmer as it became more evident that we might never know what had become of those whose bodies were missing. The soldiers buried what remains we had, and Fray Buil said a mass for the repose of their souls.

Not all the Taino could maintain their silence indefinitely, for they were a naturally friendly and loquacious people. They claimed that Guacanagarí's enemy, Caonabo, had attacked their village as well as the fort, and that his people's poisoned darts and fishbone arrows were responsible for all the Christian deaths. The Admiral demanded that the cacique come to him, if he wished to prove his friendship. They said he had been wounded by Caonabo and could not leave his *hamaca*, the woven hanging beds in which the Taino slept.

Several of the Taino, while denying any responsibility for the Spaniards' murder, complained that each of these men had kept several women in their quarters in the fort.

"They were jealous, Excellency," Diego Columbus told the Admiral, "for so many women preferred to live in your warriors' huts that they had not enough for themselves."

I thought it far more likely that the Spaniards had assaulted and subdued the Taino women. Each of the men, we were told often enough that I believed it, had kept five women in his private hut. My opinion was confirmed a few days later when half a score of Taino women from the isle of Boriquen, whom we had "rescued" from the Caribe, jumped overboard, swimming half a league to escape us. Worse, we made every effort to recapture them and succeeded in bringing four of them back to the ships.

No one but I, and of course Rachel, found anything odd or contradictory in this. I believe that the Spaniards' and even the Admiral's blindness to the wrong in how they treated the Taino lay in the simple fact that the Taino were not Christian. Thus what the Spaniards called Christian virtues, such as charity, fair dealing, and decency, need not be applied to their relations with the Taino. This was no different, in the end, than their attitude toward the Jews.

Don Melchior, who still had not given up hope that his cousin had somehow survived, volunteered to lead an advance party to visit Guacanagarí and get to the bottom of the matter. In the end, the Admiral gave him a caravel so that in addition to questioning the cacique, he could scout a possible location for a new settlement. I accompanied him as interpreter, while Diego Columbus stayed with the Admiral to help deal with those Taino who came to trade or were captured. If the Admiral had ever doubted the merit of enslaving them, he did so no longer after discovering the Christian dead and the blackened remains of the fort.

We had sailed no more than three leagues along the coast when a canoa paddled out to us, those within it saying that we would find Guacanagarí in a nearby village. Don Melchior led the shore party himself, requesting that I accompany him, along with Dr. Chanca, who would be able to ascertain the truth about the cacique's wound. We found him lying with a bandaged thigh on a *hamaca* in a dark hut crowded with attendants and relatives. The men wrinkled their noses at the stench of sweat and damp, though I didn't think the smell half as unpleasant as that of a cabin full of Christians after a month at sea.

"I must see what lies under that bandage," Dr. Chanca said. "Let us get him out into the light. If he is indeed wounded, I must sniff at the wound to ascertain if it has become infected."

At Don Melchior's command, I translated this request, using language far more polite than the doctor's.

Guacanagarí, as cooperative as he had been on our first meeting in 1492, dismissed his entourage and allowed an attendant to help him outside and seat him on a log. As Dr. Chanca began to unwrap the bandages, he moaned and winced.

"*Guay*! It hurts! The pain is terrible!"

"What weapon wounded you?" I asked, not waiting for Don Melchior or Dr. Chanca to prompt me. "An arrow? A spear?"

"A stone."

When I translated this, Dr. Chanca stripped off the remaining bandage without the care he had shown at first.

"There is no wound!" he exclaimed.

"But it hurts!" Guacanagarí insisted. "Do you not see the terrible bruise?"

Don Melchior seized him by the shoulders as if to shake him. At this, the Taino cried out in protest and drew closer around us.

"Better not, sir," I said softly.

Maldonado growled and backed off.

Dr. Chanca regarded the cacique sternly.

"You must not lie to us!"

"I do not lie," Guacanagarí said. "Caonabo attacked us and burned the fort and our other village. Ask my people if a big stone did not hit me in the leg."

"You can walk well enough to visit the Admiral on his ship," Dr. Chanca said.

"I invite him to come and visit me," Guacanagarí said with as much dignity as he could muster.

Behind me, the soldiers muttered angrily among themselves.

"The old fraud! Let me but get my sword out, and you'll see how fast he can run."

"I bet he burned the fort himself."

"Why don't we kill them all?"

Don Melchior quelled them with a glance. "Why should the Admiral come to you?" he asked.

Guacanagarí's eyes darted from side to side as he thought quickly. "Because I have gifts for him," he said, "that are so great and heavy I cannot bear them all."

"Leave a couple of armed guards behind to escort him to the flagship," Dr. Chanca advised. "They will make sure he gets there."

"We must return to the fleet ourselves," Don Melchior pointed out. "Better to report first to the Admiral and see if he prefers to receive the rascal or pay a state visit and scare the clout off him. Has he seen horses before?"

"No, sir," I replied, for we had carried none on the first voyage.

"Good." Don Melchior's tight smile did not bode well for Guacanagarí. "I believe a troop of horse with mounted men in full armor will convince him that we are not to be trifled with."

Chapter 25

Once convinced that every man who had remained in Hispaniola was dead, the whole company was eager to quit the blackened ruins of La Navidad. Some wanted first to kill Guacanagarí, others to fire the village, reasoning that all the Taino must have participated in the slaughter. Others wanted only to bury what remained and be gone. The Admiral alone was persuaded, after much reflection and questioning of the cacique and his chief followers, that in spite of his attempt to gain our compassion by pretending to be wounded, Guacanagarí had spoken the truth about the attack on the fort. The Admiral's opinion, of course, prevailed.

I did not believe that Guacanagarí's story of an attack explained the bound bodies on the riverbank. In the heat of battle, would warriors have paused so far from the fort to capture and bind prisoners, and having done so, then leave them to rot? But I shared these thoughts only with Rachel.

The Admiral and the cacique visited each other with great ceremony. Guacanagarí was duly terrified by the horses. There were no large animals on Hispaniola, and not only the great teeth and stamping hooves but also the horses' obedience to the heavily armed men upon their backs made a great impression. In any case, now that the lascivious and violent garrison of the fort was gone, Guacanagarí had no reason to rebel against us. He entered eagerly into discussions of where Cibao might lie and where we might hope to find the most salubrious location for a new settlement. His followers plied us with fruit, woven cotton cloth, and gold, both nuggets and thinly beaten sheets worked into ornaments.

Because the whole fleet lay at anchor and no danger threatened, we sailors had a great deal more liberty than had been granted until now. On the day before the Christians' Sabbath, while the company attended the funeral mass for the dead, Rachel and I were able to steal away. Our pretext was to search for a spring to add to our supply of fresh water. Our true intention was to celebrate our Shabbat. We didn't think Adonai would mind hearing the *b'rucha* over the candles on Saturday morning instead of Friday night.

Rachel had smuggled two wax candle stubs out of the Admiral's cabin. I had brought my tinderbox as well as my *tallit* and *t'fillin*. We walked for two hours before we decided that we had gone far enough that none of the crew, even those who might have set out to hunt birds and such small animals as the hutia for the table, would come upon us by chance. It felt exhilarating to let our voices ring out in the *Sh'ma*. "*Sh'ma Yisrael, Adonai eloheinu, Adonai echad.*"

"Such freedom!" Rachel echoed my thought. "Better than freedom—this feels like homecoming."

"I'm glad you came with me, Rachel," I said. "I mean to the Indies, not only today. Together, we are at home wherever we may be. After all, we are not the first Jews to be wanderers."

"No, indeed," she said. "Moses and those who fled with him from Egypt wandered for forty years in a wilderness more barren and less beautiful than this."

"And then," I said, "the Temple in Jerusalem was destroyed and our people dispersed."

"And now we are dispersed again from Spain," she said.

"Don't worry, little sister. We shall find a new home in Italy when we return. With the great purses of gold we bring them, Papa and Mama will be able to build a house even finer than our old home in Seville."

I hugged her, and she nestled into my arms. "That feels good," she said. "It is *tiring* being a boy."

"Once the site for our new settlement is chosen and construction begun, we will be able to live ashore, and you will not be so closely observed at every moment."

"Do you think so? It would be heaven indeed to share a tent with you, or perhaps a Taino hut." Her face fell. "But perhaps the Admiral will choose not to leave his cabin. It is very comfortable, you know." She added, "Especially for him, since he doesn't sleep on the floor."

"We will ask him to find someone else to serve him," I said.

"He has grown so accustomed to me," Rachel said, "that I believe he forgets half the time that I am not a boy."

"Then I shall remind him," I said. "You have served him well, and it is time someone else picked up the burden. I will recommend the best of the gromets to take your place."

We fell silent. In a nearby thicket, a bird was singing its heart out, liquid trills pouring from its throat. I laid my cheek against Rachel's curly hair and closed my eyes. The warmth of the sun caressed me.

"Diego! Wake up!"

My head jerked up. My eyes flew open. "I wasn't sleeping."

"Yes, you were," Rachel said. "Your mouth hung open, and you were snoring. Now, listen. Shh. Don't make a sound. Listen, and tell me what you hear."

At first I heard nothing but the wind soughing in the trees. Then the faintest sound of what might have been cheers and whistles came to me, not from the direction of the shore from which we had come, but further inland.

"That is odd indeed," I said. "It sounds like the crowd at a bull-fight in Seville. What could it possibly be?"

"Not my imagination, since you can hear it too," she said. "Let's go and see."

"Is that wise?" I asked. "We are only two and not well armed." For I had only my knife and the tinderbox.

"You worry too much, Diego," Rachel said. "It is such a happy sound, I cannot believe it is dangerous."

"It could be the Canibale having a feast," I said. "That would be a happy occasion for them, but not for us."

"You don't believe that," Rachel said, "and neither do I. After all, they say with as little reason that Jews kill Christian babies."

She started walking briskly in the direction of the mysterious sounds. Unwinding my *t'fillin* and carefully rolling up my *tallit*, I followed her.

We made our way through the forest, pushing hanging vines out of the way and ducking the occasional green fruit that the black-faced monkeys swinging overhead threw at us as they scolded and chittered. The noise grew progressively louder, still sounding cheerful and not unlike a bullfight.

Breaking through a glowing green veil of vines, we emerged into the dazzling brightness of an open space that I can only call a plaza. The central court was a great rectangle of packed earth sur-rounded by stones of varying sizes. At least two dozen Taino ran this way and that upon it in patterns that at first appeared random to me. As I watched, I realized that they contested possession of a large sphere of some marvelous substance, for when it struck the ground, it didn't roll, but instead sprang upward. The crowd of Taino spectators, both men and women, as well as many children, watched with keen interest, cheering, catcalling, or groaning as the ball passed from one man to another, now in a kind of dance, now almost too fast to follow.

"It is a game!" Rachel exclaimed in delight. "Look, those with the red face paint are trying to keep the others from hitting the great stone on that side of the court, and the others in the white are defending the stone opposite it. Are they not skillful?"

They were indeed, for they were bouncing the remarkable ball not only off the earth and the surrounding stones, but also their shoulders, knees, hips, and even foreheads with astonishing grace.

"They don't use their hands at all," Rachel observed. "It must be forbidden."

"Your eye is quicker than mine," I said, "but you are right."

At that moment, a young man in white face paint leaped high in the air, butting the ball with his head as it came flying at him. As he fell, half laughing, half exclaiming with pain as his buttocks hit the earth, the ball smashed into the opposing goal stone with a mighty thwack. All raised a cheer, and the game came to an end. The white-marked players had evidently won, for they embraced each other and raised the laughing hero to their shoulders, while the red-marked players shook their heads and shouted insults at their competitors. Some of the spectators appeared to have wagered on the outcome, for tokens ranging from fish-head spears to gold nose rings changed hands. All seemed good humored, which impressed me mightily.

Children leaped to smooth the scuffed earth of the court and what I took to be Taino priests performed a ritual with chanting and gestures. Next came a feast. This took place beyond the court, close to the shade of the green forest surrounded by its ring of mountains. Those who had been tending the cooking fires came forward with spits of roasted meat, pots of stew, and all manner of roasted roots, grains, and fruits. Both players and spectators fell on the food and soon became engrossed in eating, though they continued to jest and jeer about the game.

Rachel and I had crept forward without realizing we did so. The young man who had won the game looked up and saw us.

"Diego!" he exclaimed. Pushing those crowded around him aside with hip and thigh as he had the bouncing ball, he came toward us with outstretched hands. "I am glad to see you."

I was dumbfounded. "Hutia?" For it was indeed he. "My friend," I said in Taino, "I am happy to see you again. You have changed greatly."

He had been a well-grown and comely youth when we had worked together on the building of La Navidad. Now he was becoming a man, not bearded, as in that respect the Taino differed from the Europeans, but confident in his bearing and corded with muscles under the skin still gleaming with sweat from the game.

"So have you," he replied, "for you now speak our language fluently. Is this your wife?" He grinned down at Rachel, who was staring, fascinated.

"No!" she said.

I realized that Hutia had never seen a European woman, for none had accompanied us on the first voyage. For all he knew, an open shirt, breeches, and leather boots were our women's customary garb.

"Am I to guess?" he asked. "Your playmate? Perhaps your mother?"

"I'm Rachel," she said, not at all disconcerted at his teasing. "I am Diego's sister."

"I am glad to know you, Rachel," he said, with a courtly bow that he had learned from me the year before. "You too speak Taino. How can it be?"

"I learned it from your father," Rachel said.

"My father! I was so surprised to see you that I forgot to ask. I know he is not on the ships, for I have watched all that has happened since your winged boats arrived, and I did not see him. Did he remain in Spain?"

I was amazed to learn he had been watching us. But I could not question him on this subject, for the moment I had dreaded had arrived. Rachel bravely took the burden from me.

"He is dead, Hutia." She touched his arm lightly, and her eyes filled with tears. "I am sorry. He was a brave and gentle man."

"What happened? Did they kill him?" He drew in a sharp breath as he awaited our reply.

"No, indeed!" Rachel cried.

"He became ill," I said, "and we could not heal him."

"*Anki*, the evil one, told me he would be a slave," he said, "not free to come and go."

I wanted to deny it, but I could not. "He was treated well," I said. "I cared for him myself when he became ill. He was my friend. But he missed his family and longed for home."

His shoulders slumped. "The *anki* but taunted me, then."

"He was a cruel man," I said.

"Your father wished greatly to return home," Rachel said. "He was on the Admiral's ship with us and died within sight of land."

"I have long believed him dead," he said. A single tear ran down his cheek. "I am glad he has returned to Quisqueya. Atabey cradles him, and I can meet his spirit by the guayaba tree."

In the silence, I could hear birds chittering and small animals scuffling through the underbrush at the edge of the forest.

"But come," Hutia said, his expression lightening. "You must meet my friends and feast with us."

Rachel immediately started toward the Taino, now lying relaxed and replete in small groups in the grass around the court. I held Hutia back, my hand on his arm, when he turned to follow.

"I have much to tell you," I said, "including your father's last words for you, and I have many questions for you as well."

"Yes, indeed," Hutia agreed, "we must find a time to speak alone, and soon. But for now, let us be merry and rejoice that we have met again."

"Hutia," Rachel called over her shoulder, "what is the name of the marvelous game we saw you play?"

"It is called *batey*," he called back, lengthening his strides to catch up with her. "It is more than a game. It is an important part of our harvest, the solstice, even marriages. But today we played it for sport."

"And the ball, what is it called?"

"That is *batu*. It is made of the sap from one of our trees."

"May I hold it? I want to see if I can make it bounce."

"Of course you can. Are you not married at all?"

"Certainly not!"

"Why not? Is it that you don't bleed yet?"

"Not yet," she said. "Do Taino girls marry as soon as that happens?"

I sighed. Could she not have said simply that our women did not speak of such things? I quickened my pace. Rachel and Hutia had already reached the nearest group of Taino, and they were welcoming her with cries of delight.

Chapter 26

Rachel would have been happy to spend the night in a *bohio*, the large round Taino huts that sheltered several families. By the end of the day, she had discarded much of her clothing and had the Taino girls screaming with laughter as she attempted to paint her face, fix gold rings in her ears without actually allowing them to bore holes in her earlobes, and bounce the *batu* off her knee in such a way that it would not hit her in the face.

But if we didn't return, we would be looked for. The whole company was jumpy since discovering that Indians could kill Europeans if given sufficient surprise and motivation. Fernando would realize that I was missing, and the Admiral would certainly notice Rachel's absence.

Hutia and two of his friends escorted us as twilight faded to dark to where we could not miss the shattered bulk of La Navidad and the campfires around it. They even showed us a spring that lay closer to the shore than those the Spaniards had found so far, where we filled our water skins and washed away some of the sweat and grime of the day.

While Rachel chattered with the Taino youths, who clearly found her as fascinating as did the young women of the tribe, Hutia and I had time to talk. The bond between us held in spite of my absence and the increased tension and distrust between the Spanish and the Taino. I found I was able to bare my heart to him, including my fears for Rachel and my concern about the behavior of my fellows.

"The Admiral is a good man," I said, "but he doesn't treat your people as he ought. He did so at first, but now he is becoming consumed with the quest for gold and his desire to bring something of value back to the King and Queen of Spain."

"My father and his companions," Hutia said drily, "and the many gifts we gave him, including the gold you so value, did not win him sufficient merit in their eyes? These caciques of yours are hard to please."

"I am ashamed to say that you are right," I said. "But they are not my caciques." And I explained to him, as I had to his father, about the Jews.

"It is strange that they so lack respect for all gods except their Jesus," Hutia said. "They have not yet found the village where we play *batey*, but I was there when one of your *bohiques*, your priests, visited a *yucayeque* not far from where your winged boats sleep on the water. Or should I say," he corrected himself, "the Christians' priests."

"Which priest?" I asked. "I hope it was not a tall, dark, proud one." Fray Buil was a chronically angry man, more interested in discovering gold than in saving souls. I knew he would not have made a good impression upon the Taino.

"No, it was a little meek one, like a hutia but not so swift, who looked as if he would not be much good at *batey*."

"That is Fray Pane," I said. "He is a good man, but you are right that he is timid and resembles a small animal. In Spain, we would say a mouse or a rabbit. What did he want?"

"He wished to make us Christians," Hutia said. "We explained
to him that we have a religion of our own and have no desire to
change it for his. We serve Yucahu and Atabey, for they made
everything, and they are all around us." His sweeping hand encom-
passed the earth and sky. "He listened carefully and made many
scratchings with a quill on folded leaves, so perhaps he understood
and will not ask us again."

Later, I asked Fray Pane about this visit and asked to see his
journal. Sure enough, he had written much about the Taino gods
and religious observances.

"I believe they will come to trust me," he said happily, "as I
show interest in their superstitious tales and fancies. Eventually I
will win them over to Christ, since they have no religion of their
own. And when we return to Spain, I will have my collection published. There is a fellow in Germany who has found a way to make
many copies at once with letters made of wood or lead. I believe he
is dead now, but others have taken up his work. I will become the
author of the first book of folktales from the Indies."

"Hutia," I said now, as we drew near to where the Taino would
leave us, "may I ask a question that you might not care to answer?"

He did not pretend to misunderstand me. "You wish to know
who killed those at the fort."

"I will tell no one," I said, "for I left it in your hands whether
or not to reveal to your people that Cabrera raped and murdered
your sister."

"I did not," he said. "I didn't have to, for every one of the strangers behaved almost as badly. Many of the women the Spaniards
took had babies at home. Some escaped. But if they were caught
trying, the Spaniards beat them so badly that they could not run.
Their weapons were far superior to ours, so we could do nothing
until Caonabo attacked Guacanagarí's village. Then we saw our
opportunity and took it."

"Did your people take the women back when the Spaniards were all dead?"

Hutia looked at me as if he didn't understand the question. "Of course. They are our wives, our sisters."

"In Spain, a woman who has been raped is considered ruined. No man will have her as a wife, and she is shamed forever. What about the babies the Spaniards got on them? There must have been some, for it is a full eleven months since we left La Navidad." I added, "More than two hands of moons," to make my meaning clear.

"We don't play against babies," Hutia said.

I learned later that the Taino used the word "play" for fighting as well as for sitting in judgment. Disputes between caciques and their tribes were often resolved on the *batey* court. There were raids, like that of Caonabo's folk on Guacanagarí's, but they had no word for war.

Before the fleet could depart on its continued explorations, we had to wait for a favorable wind. This took several days, in which I met with Hutia daily. Rachel could not shirk her duties for the Admiral, but she managed to pay two more visits to the inland village. She even got a chance to play *batey*, when the women and girls formed sides. Not being hampered by clothing, they were as agile as the men, if not quite as strong. They looked like goddesses to me as they spun and twisted in the air, the *batu* shooting off a rounded hip or checked by a golden knee. The men commented freely on the women's game, but their remarks were confined to the players' *batey* skills. I reflected that even the Taino's rudeness was unimaginably polite and respectful compared to what Spaniards would say in a comparable situation, were it possible for such to arise.

When I told Hutia why our ships sat idle with sails drooping, he said, "Your priests must pray for wind."

"They have," I said, "but so far without result."

"Perhaps the breath of their God does not reach so far." He grinned broadly. "You must pray to Juracan, who is so powerful that when he wishes, he can send *bohios* and even trees flying through the air."

That did not seem likely to me, but Hutia said, "If you remain in our land until his angry season, you will see."

Although Rachel and I would be glad never to see La Navidad again, we were unhappy at the thought of leaving our new Taino friends.

Hutia reassured me. "Your Admiral seeks a place to build his village along the shore, does he not?"

"I would suppose so," I said, "for he doesn't wish us to be cut off from our ships."

"From the *yucayeque*, it is not much farther to one point along the shore than to another. I will find you."

When God's breath, as Hutia put it, finally blew upon us, it did so from the east. This was unfortunate, as the Admiral wished to sail in that direction, rather than continue westward, which he believed would take us farther from the region where we might find gold. So we had to beat against the wind in order to keep our sails filled. In twenty-five days, we made only thirty leagues, little progress despite great effort.

By then, the whole company was in great misery. Many were ill, and the cattle, which had not been let out to graze at La Navidad, were starting to die. The Admiral, pressed by all to go no further, chose a site with no harbor of its own and no water nearer than a river a mile away. These deficiencies he considered less important than the assurance of the local Taino that abundant gold could be found nearby, to which they would be glad to guide us.

When I disembarked, I found Hutia waiting for me. So many Indians flocked to the ships that no one took note of his comings and goings, which was as he wished it.

"You got here faster than we did!" I exclaimed.

"I walked," he said.

Indeed, the Taino were well suited to their environment. They moved easily through the varied terrain of the island and thrived on the fish, yuca, and sweet potato that wreaked havoc on the bellies of so many of our men, as did the local river water. The Spaniards were exhausted by the rigors of our difficult passage eastward. In addition, we had been plagued by a period of rain, which further weakened our men, although it had no effect on the Taino.

The Admiral waited only three days after we came ashore to send a company with Taino guides inland to seek gold. A soldier, Alonso de Hojeda, was given the command of this force. The rest of us who remained able-bodied were sent ashore to begin construction of the new settlement, which the Admiral named Isabela, for the Queen. Rachel soon joined us, happy to fetch and carry along with the gromets who were too small for heavier work. Hutia often chose to work beside me. No one thought to make any kind of roster or tally of the Indians. Indeed, many of the Spaniards could not tell them apart. Since it never occurred to them to offer the Taino payment for their labor, there was little reason to keep track of them, save to make sure enough hands and backs were available when wanted. I had only to act as if Hutia was under my orders, and he was able to come and go as he pleased.

"Why do you work for us at all?" I asked him one day as we rested on our hoes, for the company was set to planting as well as building.

"You cannot come to me," he said, grinning, "so I come to you." Growing serious, he added, "We are brothers, as my father told you." For I had repeated to him Cristobal's dying words. "Beyond that, my people help yours for *matu'm*, not for reward."

I had not heard the word before and asked him to explain it. It meant generosity, a virtue that the Taino valued highly. For the first time, I understood why the Taino had greeted us with gifts and served us willingly from the moment we had arrived on their shores in 1492.

"The Christians could benefit greatly from such a virtue," I said.

While we dug the foundations of permanent buildings for the new colony, we were allowed to erect temporary huts or shelters, so we could live ashore. Fernando shared mine, and the Admiral allowed Rachel to join us, discharging her from all duties to his person with praise and thanks for her service on the voyage. He did this loudly on the deck of *Mariagalante* in front of many, putting "the lad" under my supervision. While our hut was under construction, he paid an equally public visit of inspection in the course of his rounds to oversee the general building. His nod of approval gave us tacit permission to keep our shelter small so that we need have no other companions.

Rachel and I discussed the possibility that we might have to reveal her sex to Fernando. Not only might we have need of an ally, but Rachel was getting older, and we were lucky that it had not already become apparent she was a woman. The most obvious sign was a gentle swelling of her chest. She took to binding it with a cloth under her shirt, which she took care never to remove in company. As well, she told me that her courses had begun, as we had both known that they must. It seemed this monthly burden required additional cloths and running water. Luckily, Hutia was able to show us a spring hidden in the forest, far closer than the river where many went for water. Since Rachel no longer had access to the Admiral's chamber pot, we dug a trench behind the hut, which backed up to an impenetrable thicket at the edge of the settlement. This gave Rachel privacy to attend to her needs. I assured her of Fernando's loyalty and discretion. Our friendship dated from the voyage on the *Santa Maria*, when he had hidden my *tallit* and *t'fillin* from Cabrera so that I would not be exposed as a Jew. I suggested we tell him as soon as Rachel took up residence with us so that she might relax her guard in his presence. Rachel begged me to wait until some situation arose that made it necessary for him to know.

"He is a pleasant young man," she said, "but he is not like us, Diego. Have you noticed that when Hutia is with us, he never speaks to him directly?"

"He doesn't have our gift for languages," I said. "After all this time, he knows only a few words of Taino, which he pronounces badly."

"Hutia's Castilian is excellent," Rachel said indignantly, for she had made it her mission to teach him. "He understands everything that is said, even when it is not addressed to him. And his vocabulary increases every day."

"Fernando tended Cristobal when he was ill."

"Because it was his duty," Rachel said. "If we told him we loved Cristobal, he would be bewildered. Don't make excuses for him, Diego."

I had been about to mention that Fernando came from Granada, which had been governed by the Moors until early in 1492, and therefore might be expected to have a more liberal attitude. But I held my peace. She would likely say that he might just as well perceive the Moors as enemies, who had fought against the King and Queen's Christian armies in the streets of his native city.

"Very well," I said. "I am only saying that you must not fear to trust him."

"I will take your word for it," she said, "but let us not put it to the test until we must."

This occurred sooner than she had hoped. Fernando returned to the hut before me one night to find Rachel unwinding the bandage from around her breast and singing, which she no longer did in company since the gromets' voices had started changing. She had no lantern, undressing in the dark for greater privacy, but he carried one with him. I was not there, for we had taken our evening meal with the company around the campfires, and I had lingered. I didn't want a reputation for associating only with a Taino and a young boy, for that might draw precisely the attention that none of us wished for. I came in to find them confronting each other, Rachel clutching a hastily gathered up cloak against her chest and Fernando red-faced and stammering.

Fernando jumped when I clapped a hand upon his shoulder. It would be better to assume his allegiance than to beseech it.

"I see you have found us out," I said in a comradely tone. "If my sister has not yet told you, Admiral Columbus is a party to our little deception. He agreed I had good reason not to leave her behind when we quitted Spain. She had no other guardian, and as you can see, she is little more than a child."

Fernando's embarrassment suggested that he saw no such thing. But Rachel, quick to take my lead, managed to throw her shirt over her head and thrust her arms into the sleeves without dropping the cloak until it was possible to do so modestly. She thrust her hair, which had grown long enough to braid again, into a cap.

"This will make no difference," she said, making her voice gruff so that he might still perceive her as the lad Rafael whom he knew and liked, "if you will continue to stand our friend."

Fernando was recovering from being so greatly startled. The color in his flushed cheeks started to subside, and the hand that had flown to the hilt of his dagger fell to his side.

"What must I do?" he asked me rather than Rachel.

I grinned, keeping all hint of entreaty out of my eyes. "Continue to order young Rafael about," I said, "and cuff his ear if he fails to hop to it quickly."

Though I owed Fernando my life, never had the words "Jew" or "Inquisition" passed between us. Nor did they now. He stood in thought for some time while Rachel and I watched him, scarcely breathing.

"Very well," he said at last. "I came back to our hut seeking a gourd of spirits made of yuca. The Indian I had it from swore that if I drained it without stopping, it would make me forget my name as well as all that I had done for the past two hours. I will take it back to the fire, where I plan to get drunk. This means I will fall silent. Next, my head will start to whirl. Then I will vomit upon the ground, fall into a stupor, and lie where I drop till morning."

When he had gone, Rachel pulled off her cap and shook out her hair with a sigh of relief.

"How can we be sure he will fall silent, once he is drunk?" she asked.

"That is his nature," I said. "I have seen him under the influence of strong drink before."

"And in the morning?" she asked. "Will he not curse the world and all in it? A man with a splitting head doesn't feel kindly toward anyone."

"You have been too long among men," I said. "You should not know such things."

"Perhaps I should try it myself," she said, "and see whether it has the same effect on women."

Just in time, I perceived that she was teasing me. "Brush your hair and go to sleep," I said. "It might be well for us to be the ones to rouse him in the morning. We can carry him back here, so he will speak to no one until he has his wits about him. He will be glad of dark and privacy too."

"Do you suppose he will be grateful?" Rachel asked, head tilted to one side as she combed tangles out of her hair.

"No man is grateful the morning after," I said, having made the experiment for myself and concluded that the elation of spirits was not worth the ensuing sickness. "Or if he is, he will not admit it."

But in the morning, we did not need to rouse Fernando. We arrived at the biggest fire, now reduced to smoldering embers, to

find everyone onshore assembled and shouting except for several
of the cavaliers, who were mounted and galloping toward the ships.

There was such confusion that at first we could not tell what
had occurred.

"What is it? Are we attacked? What has happened?"

"Gold! Gold! Hojeda is back, and they have found gold!"

Chapter 27

Isabela, January 20–March 16, 1494

"Cibao is real! It's not just a legend!" I swung Rachel into the air and whirled her around.

"Did you not believe it before? Diego, put me down!"

All around us, men were laughing and crying, hugging their fellows or pounding them on the back. Some capered in a clumsy dance, chanting, "Gold! Gold! Gold!"

"Diego, have you heard? We will all be rich!" Fernando rushed up to us, no sign of the night's excesses in his beaming face. "Gold! Gold! Gold!" He too seized Rachel and swung her around.

"Have they found a mine, then?" I asked. "Have they all returned?"

"Have you seen the gold?" Rachel asked. "Can we see it?"

Fernando laughed. "Not a mine, not yet, but it is surely there, for they found rivers of gold, mountain streams carrying a bounty of nuggets down the mountainside. Captain Hojeda turned back because he came to a river in flood that the men could not cross. But he left a small group under Captain Gorbalan seeking a way to go farther. I have not seen any of the gold yet, for the men who brought it are besieged, and Captain Hojeda has taken the greatest part of it to Admiral Columbus."

"It seems to me," Rachel said with mock solemnity, "that the Admiral must have great need of his page's services and those of a scribe or two even more, for this news changes everything. Diego, will you accompany me?"

I did not resist. There would be no digging, building, or planting done today. Already the captains were declaring a general holiday. Gourds of *chicha*, the local brew, were being handed around. We found the Admiral in the large hut that had been built as his residence ashore, surrounded by his chief advisers, including his brother, Don Diego, Dr. Chanca, Captain Torres, several of the other ship's captains, and Fray Buil, as well as Captain Hojeda. The twinkle in his eye suggested that he guessed our arrival had more to do with burning curiosity than with devotion to our duty. But he shared the general benevolence to such an extent that he beckoned us forward so we could see the three great nuggets that lay on the table.

"Excellency, the savages who gave me these," Hojeda said, "assured us that we would find abundant gold higher up the mountain."

"Thanks be to Christ Our Savior and the Blessed Virgin," the Admiral said. "Fray Buil, will you lead us in a prayer of thanksgiving?"

Having invited ourselves to this celebration, Rachel and I could do nothing but kneel with the rest and join in the prayers. None sang more fervently than the Admiral. He fairly glowed with the joy of this discovery, which vindicated all his claims about the worth of his mission to Spain and to the Church. Perhaps, like me, he had secretly doubted that Cibao was more than a chimera. Not having brought back the expected riches on our return last year, he must have feared failure and disgrace. Now success was assured, not only for the expedition but for the establishment of a

Spanish colony on Hispaniola, which the Sovereigns had promised the Admiral would govern.

The gentlemen continued to confer as Rachel busied herself preparing paper and ink and I took out my knife and started sharpening the finest quills. We needed no orders to know that as soon as he dismissed his advisers, the Admiral's next task would be to compose a letter to the King and Queen.

"What will you do next, brother?" Don Diego asked.

"Let us await Gorbalan's return. The proof of Cibao is already conclusive." The Admiral nodded to Captain Hojeda, who bowed in return. "But the more information we have, the better. I would like to send gold as well as news to Their Majesties."

"Excellency." Dr. Chanca stepped forward. "Many of the men are sick. Flux and fevers have left them too weak to march, much less mine or farm or labor at building a city. Might we not send those who are ill back to Spain along with the report? Their condition and testimony will be eloquent when we ask for what we need most: foodstuffs and supplies. The men cannot remain well on the fish, maize, and roots that the Indians eat."

"I don't understand it," the Admiral said. "On our first voyage, hardly a man took cold. Now we have hundreds sickening and some dying. If the native food is indeed the source of all this illness, we must beg the Queen to send us what they crave: wheat flour and salt pork, along with olive oil, nuts, honey, and rice."

"The yam and yuca or cassava that grow here are nutritious enough," Dr. Chanca said. "But the men are ill at ease eating only foods they are not accustomed to. This causes their humors to become unbalanced. They complain that they are tired of fish."

"I am tired of fish myself," the Admiral said. "But I don't believe that the fish are to blame for my taking to my bed."

"You were struck down by exhaustion due to overwork," Don Diego said. "You are not yet fully recovered. You must take better care of yourself if you wish to be strong enough to lead an expedition to the mountains and perhaps build a second city near the gold fields."

"Yes, yes, of course I will go myself to see this wonder," the Admiral said. "How can I rest when there is so much to do? I am both Admiral and Governor General, so I must be conversant with every detail."

"You must delegate, brother," Don Diego said, a criticism that none of the rest would have dared level at the Admiral, though there was much truth in it.

"Very well, brother," the Admiral said. "While I lead a greater expedition to Cibao, you shall remain as governor of Isabela in my absence."

"I don't seek advancement," Don Diego protested.

This was true. All knew that the Admiral's brother was a devout and unambitious soul, who did not even want the bishopric the Admiral begged on his behalf. This very fact might make him a wise choice for leadership of the colony, for he would be unlikely to abuse his power, as some of the others surely would.

Later, Rachel and I talked over what we had heard.

"If he sends part of the fleet back to Spain, you should go with it, Rachel," I said. "You cannot pass for a boy indefinitely. How old are you now?"

"I will turn fourteen in June."

"You are fast becoming a woman. We have seen how easily Fernando unmasked you. You cannot hide away in our hut forever. You must work while the Admiral is gone. The ship's boys are already developing manly muscles, and their beards are starting to grow."

Rachel sniffed. "And do they not put on airs about the scraggly patches on their cheeks, like fields in a drought or perhaps the fuzz on a peach."

"You have turned boy enough that you make everything into a contest," I said. "But in this, you will never compete with them, and the more time passes, the more noticeable it will become. You can neither march with the soldiers nor linger in close quarters on the ship, even if the Admiral would give you leave to do so."

"Don't send me away! I will not feel safe, so far from you. Besides, what would I return to? They will land, most likely, in Cadiz. How, then, will I make my way to Italy? Doña Marina has surely long since returned to Barcelona. I will have no friends, no means, and no way to explain myself."

"Then what shall we do with you?" I expected no answer, for I could not argue with her reasoning.

"Send me to the Taino," Rachel said. "I will learn more of their ways, and Hutia will make sure I come to no harm."

I could not think of as many objections as I would have liked to. "You already know more than enough of their ways," I said. "If I leave you there for any length of time, you will end in going about naked. And you will never learn to be a lady."

"That cause was lost," Rachel said, "the moment I left the convent in Barcelona. So it is really all the King and Queen's fault. If they had not expelled the Jews from Spain and unleashed the Inquisition on those who remained, I might have become the kind of lady you imagine." She wrinkled up her nose and grinned. "But probably not."

Captain Gorbalan returned the following day with even better news. He had crossed the broad river with the help of the Taino, who not only offered him a canoa big enough for all his men, but swam across the swift current, pushing it before them. He had met yet more Taino who assured him that the higher one climbed, the more gold could be found. He had even watched a Taino goldsmith at work.

When we told Hutia of our good fortune, he shook his head. "There is not as much gold in those mountains as you believe."

"But the rivers are full of it," Rachel said.

"That is because it has been washing downstream for more suns than anyone can count, since the time of my ancestors. We take out very little, just enough to adorn ourselves and honor the gods."

I believed Hutia spoke the truth. I did not like to think of how the Spaniards would react when they learned the gold supply was not limitless. Instead, I hoped that Hutia's estimate of the quantities involved was mistaken. The Taino were no mathematicians, as far as I knew.

"Diego says I may not march with the soldiers to dig the gold," Rachel said. "May I come and stay with you and your family while he is gone? And learn to play *batey*?"

"Of course you may stay, little sister," Hutia said. "But you already play *batey*."

"I mean well enough to *win*," Rachel said with such determination that Hutia and I both burst out laughing.

"Shall I find her a husband, brother Diego?"

"No!" I must have sounded appalled, for this time both Hutia and Rachel laughed.

At the beginning of February, the Admiral sent a dozen of our ships back to Spain. Along with letters for the Sovereigns and sufficient gold to impress them, the fleet carried the men too sick to remain, three score colorful but noisy parrots, and two dozen unhappy Indians. If the Admiral needed to salve his conscience about enslaving them and sending them so far from home, probably to die as the previous captives had, he did so by insisting they were cannibals. But Hutia told us they were men of the islands like any others, only that they had resisted us instead of making us welcome, so the Admiral reckoned them fierce and warlike. Thus we might subdue them rather than befriend them.

The expedition to Cibao became the focus of all our efforts from the moment the ships sailed. I was ordered to make ready to march, along with Fernando and every other man not too ill to travel and labor, except for the soldiers needed to defend Isabela and sailors to guard the five remaining ships. The Admiral wanted no repetition of the slaughter at La Navidad.

So we struck inland, climbing to a pass that led over the range of rugged peaks and down into a fertile valley that rivaled in beauty even the Andalusian spring. We looked down upon trees heavy with rose-colored blossoms and a rich black land in which every kind of vegetation grew to an astonishing size, from low shrubs with enormous leaves to towering hardwood trees. Marching among the farmers who had come as settlers, I heard them exclaim over the richness of the soil.

"We can grow sugar cane here and make our own molasses," one said.

"And wheat for bread," said another, "or even that infernal biscuit the sailors eat."

They all laughed heartily at this.

"In this soil," said a third, "every seed and slip we brought with us will flourish."

On the near rim of the valley, the Taino greeted us with their usual generosity, though only I realized that this virtue was an important part of their religion. The others believed that the Taino, as heathen savages, were an inferior breed who would naturally yield the most precious thing they possessed to their superiors, that is, the Christians. They deemed the Taino's failure to prize gold an indication of a lower intelligence. They made no apology for helping themselves to the Taino's gold. Thus the Taino would pick up a shirt or knife or wineskin that caught their eye, thinking the exchange of possessions must be customary among us. But when they did so, we were quick to punish them.

This reputation must have preceded us to the far side of the valley, for we found the Taino had barred their doors against us and fled when we approached. In fact, the sticks or canes that crossed the open doorways of their huts were less a barrier than a signal any Taino would have known to respect. My heart was troubled at this sign, another among many, of the fragility of the Taino's defenses against us should we choose to overpower them completely.

Marching farther into the mountains beyond the valley, we found a grassy tableland on a river bend. We stopped there to water both horses and men. As we bent to drink, first one man, then another exclaimed as we spied grains of gold gleaming in the sandy river bottom, clearly visible through the water. With a shout, one of the troopers held up a nugget as big as his thumb. "Look at this! I didn't believe it, but it must be true, for here is the proof."

Admiral Columbus, who had remained mounted while one of the boys refilled his water skin, held out his hand. "We are but servants of the Crown, gentlemen, and to the Crown belongs all treasure that we find." As the reluctant trooper laid the nugget in the Admiral's palm, Columbus added, "Any man found keeping gold in secret for himself will be punished by whipping, and if the offense be repeated or the stolen amount substantial, by having his ears and nose slit."

None dared grumble at this pronouncement. The Admiral set the interpreter Diego Columbus, who for all his faults I could not suspect of harboring a lust for gold, to collect the grains the men had gathered in their hats or kerchiefs, as well as a few small nuggets less than the size of a currant or seed. When the leather pouch was full, he hung it at his own saddlebow.

The Admiral looked about him with a nod of satisfaction. "Gentlemen, here we will build a fort. And for the Doubting Thomases among you, whose doubts have been confounded on this spot, I name it Santo Tomas."

Chapter 28

When the Admiral returned to Isabela, leaving a Catalan soldier named Margarit as commander, I remained to work at the building of Santo Tomas. I would have worried about Rachel, had not Hutia come to assure me that she was well and happy among the Taino. He had no difficulty finding me. Our presence must have appeared to the Taino as a black and stinking scar on the landscape, for wherever we went, they quickly appeared—or ran away, as happened more frequently as they got to know us.

Hutia told me that Rachel kept all the women laughing as she insisted on learning to do everything they did, from making yuca bread to bouncing the *batu* off her forehead. I was afraid that the Admiral would insist that I accompany him back to the coast. Sooner or later, he was sure to ask about Rachel. I could not tell him she was living with the Taino. But he did not seek me out. He had other preoccupations than two young marranos whose father he had once known. As the lust for gold consumed him, he seemed to become a different man from the kind patron and protector I had known.

Since our number was small, discipline was relaxed at Santo Tomas. Hutia introduced me as his friend and brother at the Taino village of Ponton, near the river its residents had helped us cross. I spent my leisure hours there, playing *batey* and eating much better than my comrades who remained close to the half built fort.

As can happen with sport, I quickly formed a bond with the young men on my side. I became especially fond of two of them. One was a handsome young man they called Iguana for the ugliest creature in the islands, a lizard that must surely be closely related to the dragon. The other was a happy-go-lucky fellow with a prominent nose whom they called Aguta. The *aguta* was a furry animal with a long snout and venomous fangs, and Aguta's teeth were very white. Neither minded jokes about his name, which made all of them shout with laughter. The fellowship of sport must be universal, for these Indians constantly shouted insults at each other as the bouncing ball flew from one to the next around the *batey* court.

In short, I was happy. Constant sunshine and soft breezes made it hard to dwell on anger, fear, or sadness. Everywhere I looked, I saw the bright colors and flashing movement of abundant birds and butterflies. Flowers heavy with scent, lush vines and grasses, and towering trees that provided shade as we cut down the smaller ones to build a palisade made this place a true paradise. It rained every afternoon, but the water was warm and didn't fall for long. The brief downpour left every leaf sparkling like a jewel and the air suffused with rainbows.

This idyll soon came to an end. As I learned later, the Admiral and his company had had a terrible time making their way back to Isabela. The weather had been miserable once they crossed the mountains, and delays due to the flooded streams had caused their stores of wine and biscuit to give out. At Isabela, they found food enough, for the crops we had planted were growing well. But illness was still rife, and many of the men had died. Grumbling had increased, and Don Diego, whom the Admiral had left in

charge, had not the force of character to quell what might become
a mutiny. Some of the most discontented were the best armed, for
the caballeros would do no work that they could not do on horse-
back. This naturally caused great resentment in the rest.

The Admiral, ever decisive, sent several hundred men under
Captain Hojeda to join us at Santo Tomas, thus ridding Isabela
of the loudest grumblers and giving them occupation and proximity to the source of gold. He hoped this tactic would stop them
from demanding to go home to Spain. What happened before they
reached the new fort was entirely Hojeda's fault. I saw it all, for I
happened to be in Ponton. I had stripped to a clout and painted my
face like a Taino to play *batey*. My skin, never fair, had grown as
brown as an Indian's from running about half naked. The Spanish
soldiers who marched into the village did not recognize me.

Hojeda knew that the Taino didn't regard property as we did.
On his first visit to Ponton, scouting for the gold of Cibao, he had
received many gifts from the people there but reprimanded them
for trying to take the Spaniards' possessions in return. The Taino
truly did not understand the Europeans' lack of *matu'm*, nor did
they have a word for theft. So the tragedy that unfolded that day
could not have been prevented.

When Hojeda and his men arrived in Ponton, the cacique of
the village came out to greet him. As always, the Taino bore gifts of
gold and food. But Hojeda didn't even look at these offerings. What
caught his eye and aroused his ire was the fact that the cacique was
garbed in Spanish clothing. This had been a gift from villagers who
had taken a fancy to these garments when they had helped the
Admiral's men cross the river on their way back to Isabela. Out
of *matu'm*, they had not kept these treasures for themselves, but
bestowed them on their chief.

At first, Hojeda dissembled, smiling as he asked the cacique
who had given him these splendid garments. The Taino were
deceived, and to my dismay, my friends Aguta and Iguana stepped

forward. Perhaps they thought they were to be commended in some way. Nor did the chief see any secret to be guarded in this act of generosity. Hojeda became enraged. Roaring about ingratitude and thievery, he ordered soldiers to seize and shackle not only my friends but the cacique himself. He demanded to know the principal offender in stealing the garments. Now realizing that the Spanish captain meant them harm, Aguta stepped forward to spare Iguana, who was the younger of the two. Hojeda then ordered the soldiers to cut off Aguta's ears.

As the rest of the villagers and I looked on in horror, the sentence was carried out on the spot. Aguta wept with the pain but stood as straight as he could out of pride. Nor did he scream, for his mother and sisters were among those who witnessed this cruelty, and it was evident that he did not want to make their distress even greater than it was. When it was done, Hojeda told a well-armed guard to escort the prisoners back to Isabela to submit to the Admiral's justice, while he and the rest continued on to Santo Tomas.

I could do nothing, dressed as I was. As soon as the Spaniards had quitted the square, I was besieged by the cacique's family and advisers as well as Aguta's and Iguana's families, all begging me to do something. I assured them I would do whatever I could and shook off their clutching hands so I could hurry into my European clothes. I could help them better by reaching Isabela quickly than by staying to comfort them. I hoped I could persuade the Admiral not to punish these poor souls further for what they could not even now understand we considered a crime.

The prisoners' guard had horses and mules, and I had only my two feet. But strengthened as they were by the months of working, marching, and playing *batey*, they carried me to Isabela in time to learn that the Admiral had condemned all three of the Taino to be beheaded. Sick with horror, I swallowed my feelings, squared my shoulders, and went immediately to see the Admiral.

I found him in his hut, quill in hand. He greeted me as if nothing out of the ordinary had happened. "Ah, Diego, my boy," he said, raising the quill from the paper. "I am reduced to being my own scribe. I have sorely missed your services and those of, er, Rafael."

"I have been at Santo Tomas, Excellency," I said, "and young Rafael is safe with me. Do you wish his return, sir?"

I felt obliged to ask this, though I hardly knew whether I would prefer to see Rachel under his direct protection or in the Taino village. In neither place would I have wished her to behold such a piteous spectacle as I had at Ponton. Even the more remote villages might not be safe if this incident were repeated, or worse, became policy. I dreaded to hear what Hutia thought of the business.

The Admiral tapped his quill against the writing desk. "Better not, perhaps," he said finally. "Matters are volatile here in Isabela. And I must shortly sail on with as many as can be spared. Many islands must remain to be discovered, and we have yet to reach the mainland. Why, there might even be greater deposits of gold there than those we have already found. I must press on, and it would be inadvisable for your, er, Rafael to be close quartered on shipboard. He must soon reach an age when young men have their growth spurt, you know."

"Indeed, Excellency," I said, "I am aware of that and deeply grateful for your concern."

In truth, I was both dismayed to hear he was departing and relieved that we were not to sail with him for the dangers of unknown shores. The dangers at hand were bad enough.

"How can I help you today, my dear lad?" He gazed at me with benevolence as I stood before him. With one hand, he caressed a gold nugget no doubt given him by the Taino. "You look in the very bloom of health, the airs of Santo Tomas must agree with you. We are in bad case here in Isabela, I must tell you, for many continue to fall ill and die, and the hotheads never tire of complaining.

But I have put a spike in their treasonous plans, as I must if I am to leave them at my back."

I took a deep breath. His benevolent mood might change in an instant when he heard my petition. But I must speak up. "Excellency," I said, keeping my voice firm when it wanted to quake, "I beg of you to allow me to speak my mind and not become angry at me. There is a matter of great concern to me, and I believe it affects our whole expedition as well."

"What is that, my boy?" His expression was one of mild surprise and bafflement. "Don't fear to speak. I know you have my interests and those of our great work at heart, and you have shown yourself loyal and diligent."

"I thank you greatly, Excellency." I bowed low, feeling even more intimidated. As I straightened, I spoke quickly, before I could change my mind. "It is the matter of the unfortunate Taino who have been condemned for appropriating a few garments."

"You have a kind heart, Diego," the Admiral said, "and I don't fault you for wishing to spare them. But the Indians must learn we will not tolerate theft. We must make an example of these wretches so that others will not repeat the offense, once they know how it will be punished."

"I don't believe their execution will have that effect, Excellency," I said. "Sir, they don't understand our notion of property. They cannot comprehend that we—" I bit back my true sentiment: that we are not as generous as the Taino. Instead, I said, "that we set such great store by our personal possessions, as they hold all in common. Please, Excellency, I beg of you, don't let them die. The Taino—" Again, I had to watch my words. I would not betray the Taino by revealing how easily they communicated with their fellows throughout the island.

"I believe that the Taino who know of this will conclude that we are cruel and arbitrary. They will not understand the justice of it, no matter how many times it is explained to them. Rather, they will conclude that we plan to kill them all. If they believe they have nothing to lose, they will likely turn hostile. So far, they have been our friends. But should they suddenly become our enemies, we are not in fit condition to make a quick end to any conflict that ensues."

The Admiral frowned at this. At no time did he consider any of the Indians, even the supposedly man-eating Canibale, a match for Europeans. And in the end, he was right.

"You have said yourself, Excellency," I said, "that our men are sickly. Our forces are divided between Isabela and Santo Tomas, and you wish to continue the discoveries, which means those who remain will lose the support of most of the ships."

"There is something in what you say," the Admiral admitted, tossing the gold nugget and catching it again as he mused on my words.

"Please don't execute these men, Excellency. They have been sufficiently frightened. And by taking one of their chiefs so easily, you have demonstrated our superior might. Release them instead, and you will have the gratitude and loyalty of all the Taino."

I was not proud of myself, appealing to the Admiral's self-regard. A year ago, I would never have dreamed of such a sly measure working. I would have trusted his compassion and integrity to keep him from making such a grievous mistake. But the Columbus I had known was no more.

"Oh, very well," he said at last, "but only because you have pleaded their case so eloquently. We could send them back to Spain as slaves. But no, I believe you are right. The Indians will be more impressed by a grand gesture. You may run and tell the guard—no, I will go myself." He slipped the gold nugget into his pocket and took up his hat and sword. "I shall announce that in my magnanimity, and in light of the service that some Taino have done on our behalf in the past, I commute their beheading. They will be released."

Chapter 29

The Taino could not forgive the Spaniards for Hojeda's act. Wherever we went, they no longer greeted our men with smiles and gifts. They were more likely to flee when they heard the tramp of marching feet, the whinny of horses, and the clang of metal weapons. The Spaniards, in turn, perceived the Taino's new unwillingness to provide them with gold and information as sullenness or insolence. This opinion reconciled any who might have been inclined toward compassion to the view that the Indians were fit for nothing but slavery.

Nor were they held back by any reluctance to harm fellow Christians, for Fray Pane had still not succeeded in baptizing a single one. He continued to collect their "charming folktales" among Guacanagarí's villagers, for that cacique continued to cooperate with us. In other words, the Taino still attempted to explain their religion, and Fray Pane persisted in believing they had none.

Perhaps, in time, the Admiral might have seen that a punitive policy yielded more problems than rewards. But he did not stay to witness the full consequence of the disastrous misunderstanding in Ponton. Two weeks after the incident, he assumed command of the *Niña* and two other caravels and sailed away. Having taken the measure of Hispaniola, he burned to discover islands that might yield more abundant gold and inhabitants more willing to embrace Christianity. Most of all, he longed to find the mainland, for he was still certain that the lands of the Great Khan lay somewhere beyond the horizon.

Once he was gone, Rachel and I had more liberty than we had yet enjoyed. We showed ourselves in both Isabela and Santo Tomas often enough that Don Diego thought that we were still engaged in the building in Santo Tomas, and Captain Hojeda, who had taken over command of the new fort, believed that we stayed in Isabela. If he assumed that we served Don Diego as scribes and interpreters, we did not undeceive him. In fact, it didn't occur to Don Diego that he might enlist our aid in these tasks. A man with a great desire to please his great brother and no talent for governing, he was clearly overwhelmed by the chaos for which he had assumed authority. We pitied him and stayed out of his way.

We did not return to Ponton. It lay directly on the path between Isabela and Santo Tomas. This made it vulnerable to repeated forays by troops in search of food, gold, and forcible pleasure. Indeed, every village within range of the soldiers and caballeros became a village under siege. The simple, joyous existence that was natural to the Taino was snuffed out, and a bewildered, helpless fear took its place. They had no experience and no defenses.

With Hojeda in charge at Santo Tomas, the Catalan soldier Margarit had orders to scout for food and discover more of the terrain as well as products that might prove serviceable or fit for trade. Before leaving, the Admiral had charged him to treat the Indians well, for he still believed that in time they might be turned into Christians. Instead, Margarit's musketeers, crossbowmen, and well-mounted gentlemen became marauders, sowing terror among the Taino.

As Hojeda had proved when he seized the cacique of Ponton, rank was no protection. Nor, for the women, was youth or marital status or even age, for rape was part of the day's business for Margarit's men. The Taino men and boys were terrorized, even tortured, as the invaders demanded gold. The Taino kept little of it in their villages and had never made any attempt to mine it. But when they said so, Margarit's bullies accused them of lying and took satisfaction in causing them pain.

I could not stop it. In the Admiral's absence, I feared that if I called attention to myself, Rachel would be exposed. We could not risk the unknown consequences, for these reckless men's license knew no bounds. A Jewess who had immodestly passed as a boy might appear to them as legitimate prey, like the Taino girls and wives. Even if Rachel were not involved, any protest I made would be greeted with blank incomprehension or laughter.

So we fled. It was as if we came to dwell on a different island, no longer Hispaniola, but Quisqueya, which was the name the Taino called their home. Hutia became our constant companion and guide as we slipped further and further into his people's ways. He had a great web of kin throughout the region. As we retreated deeper into the mountains, toward the caves where the Taino believed their first ancestors had been born, we were made welcome everywhere. I hunted with the men and learned to spear fish in the streams. Rachel spun thread of a kind of cotton from a local tree and wove it into cloth. She pounded yuca with the women, an activity accompanied by much gossip and laughter, and baked it into the round, flat bread that was a staple of Taino fare.

We both became skilled at *batey*. In such perilous times, one might think that sport would be abandoned. But *batey* was a religious observance, the game a ceremony like the Christian Mass or carrying the Torah. In troubled times, spiritual practice is a necessity. My father had told me so, and the Taino understood this as well.

Once we were beyond the daily threat of depredations by Margarit's band, it became hard to remember that we were in danger. I didn't worry about our being missed. The expedition was now so scattered that no one, certainly not the harried Don Diego, kept track of any individual. Fernando might wonder what had become of us. But he knew of our friendship with Hutia as well as Rachel's reason to remain inconspicuous. He would say nothing.

I tried to keep track of the days, but in that land of endless summer, it was hard to do so. By my reckoning, it was in late June, not long past midsummer and the year's longest day, when we came to rest at a *yucayeque* so peaceful and unspoiled that we believed we had found sanctuary. It was built like any other Taino village: a ring of circular huts set around a *batey* court, with a *caney*, a larger rectangular hut, for the cacique. All the buildings were spacious, as several families lived in each of them.

We were welcomed in the home of one of the *nitaino*, a sort of nobleman, who commanded great respect. His name was Tiboni, which meant "great high waterfall." He immediately demonstrated his *matu'm* by presenting us with our own *hamaca*, the surprisingly comfortable hanging net beds, and urging us to make his *bohio* our home for as long as it pleased us. His extended family, all living under the same roof of woven straw and palm leaves, was so large I could not keep track of all of them. Rachel immediately learned all their names, down to the smallest baby. To see her settle happily into Taino family life loosened a knot in my belly that had been clenched so long I had forgotten I could feel otherwise.

"Diego, guess what I have made for dinner!" she exclaimed one afternoon, bounding up to me as I returned to the *bohio*. Hutia had been showing me how the Taino cultivated their crops, planting in rows on great mounds called *conuco*. "Tanama only helped me a little bit."

"I cannot guess." I smiled at her and then at Tanama, a young woman of no more than seventeen whose beauty and serenity had caught my eye from the first time I saw her, on our arrival in the village.

"You had better tell him," Tanama told Rachel.

"If Rachel wants to surprise me," I said, "I have the patience to wait until it is time to eat to find out what the fare is."

"I believe you," Tanama said, "but Rachel will burst long before then. She, not I, should be named for the *tanama*. She has the patience of a butterfly."

"I do not!" Rachel said, indignant but laughing too.

"Less, then?" Tanama laughed back at her.

"I would like to know, Rachel," Hutia said.

"Hutia stew!" Rachel burst out.

"No!" Hutia cried. He clutched at his breast and staggered. "You have killed and skinned me, and I did not notice. I have been simmering in a pot these last hours."

"With nuts and wild honey," Rachel said.

"Then it must have been his ghost walking the fields with me just now," I said.

"Everybody knows that spirits fly only at night," Tanama said. "Perhaps it is not Hutia in the pot, but an *arijua*, a foreigner."

We had all been enjoying the lighthearted foolery, but at mention of the strangers, a shadow seemed to pass over all of us. Hutia shook it off first.

"Come," he said, putting his arm around Rachel. "Let me taste this stew of yours and see if it is as sweet as I am."

I stared after them as they strolled off toward the cooking fires, a new and unwelcome thought in my mind.

"She is a young woman," Tanama said. "He is a young man. What is there to be surprised about?"

I turned to look at her, as surprised by her perceptiveness as by my realization that Rachel and Hutia were drawn to each other.

"Rachel is but a child," I said. "She and Hutia have been as sister and brother."

"Yesterday, perhaps," Tanama said, "but not today. I have not myself seen the *arijua*, except for you and Rachel, but to me you don't seem very different from us." She smiled. "Except for your hair."

She reached up to touch my tight curls, fingering a lock of her glossy, straight black hair with her other hand. I felt a shiver go through me.

"We are not the same as the other *arijua*," I said. How could I explain to her the difference between Jews and Christians?

"I already know that," Tanama said. "For you are kind and *matu'n*, and from all I have heard, the strangers are neither."

"In a way," I said, "we worship the same God. But we do not agree about His nature."

"You don't know Yucahu and Atabey?" Tanama raised her brows in surprise. "But Yucahu is in the cassava and Atabey in the earth. If you eat, you must know them."

"We come from far away," I said, "as the others do."

"In the winged canoa," she said, "across the great water. So I have heard. I have never seen the great water."

Now it was my turn to be astonished. "You have never seen the sea? But it is only a few days' walk from this village."

"Why would I leave my home? Everything I need is here, and so is everyone I love."

Words came to me unbidden: Could you love someone whose home is far away? I didn't allow them to pass my lips.

"Hutia and Rachel," I said at random. "It is not to be thought of. She is much too young."

At the same time, Tanama said, "They say the great water tastes of salt, like tears."

We both started to speak again, then fell silent at the same time. Tanama's eyes met mine. Then I was drowning in those great dark pools, forgetting what it was like to breathe. Her skin was smooth and golden as honey, her lips like the blossoms of a flowering tree. The top of her head was level with my chin.

Tanama drew a deep, shuddering breath, as if she too had momentarily lost the skill of it. "Rachel has begun bleeding," she said. "I was no older when I took a husband."

"You are married?" It was hard to speak calmly.

"My husband is dead," she said.

"Oh."

"I am as free as the butterfly I am named for," she said, regarding me steadily, "but less careless of where I alight."

I could not look away. The shape of her mouth and the curve of her breast were the very definition of sweetness. She wore nothing but a clout and a few ornaments of gold and bone, as did all the Taino women. I thought I had gotten used to it. I now learned that I had not.

"My touch would be gentle," she said. "I would cause no pain or harm."

Your presence could never cause me pain, I thought. Your absence might be another matter.

"Let us go and eat some of this hutia stew," I said, "or Rachel will think we scorn her cooking."

We did not touch as we walked side by side to where the others had already begun their meal. But I felt the warmth of her like fire upon my skin down the whole length of my arm.

Chapter 30

"Why is Tiboni named for a waterfall?" I asked Tanama one day. We were making poisoned arrowheads. She pressed the grated yuca to extract its venom, laying aside the pulp to be used in making bread. I dipped sharpened fish bones, bound to wooden arrows fletched with bright red feathers, in the venomous juice. Mundane our task might be, but I could smell a thousand perfumes in the air, hear every rustle in the forest, and feel the breeze like fingers on my skin. I felt it whenever Tanama was near me.

"You have not seen our waterfall?"

"No," I said. "Is it nearby?"

"Neither too far nor too close," she said, "and known only to the people of the *yucayeque*. To get there, you must cross the first river and follow the second downstream until you come to a cliff top and hear a great rushing sound, like Juracan roaring but more steadily."

"And Tiboni?"

She laughed. "His mother swore that he was conceived there. It is a popular place for lovers."

"Can we go there?" I spoke without thought. Once the words were out, I had no intention of taking them back.

"I have not been there since my husband died," she said.

"How did he die?"

"Juracan sent a great wind," she said. "He was hit by a falling tree."

"I am sorry," I said. "Did you love him very much?"

"We had known each other our whole lives."

She said no more. But that night, as I lay in my *hamaca*, I dreamed that Juracan's breath, as the Taino called a storm, blew so that trees crashed all around me, lightning flashed, and thunder rumbled. I woke to find Tanama blowing gently on my face. When I opened my eyes, she smiled and put a finger on my lips to keep me silent. All around us, Tiboni's kin lay snoring. I raised myself on one elbow, setting the *hamaca* rocking. Tanama slipped her warm hand in mine.

"Come," she whispered.

We stepped out of the *bohio* into a world bathed in moonlight. All color had been leached from trees and flowering vines. The homely shapes of the huts and all the tools and vessels the Taino used in daily life had taken on a ghostly radiance. A full moon rode high in the sky, lighting the *batey* court so brilliantly that we could have played a game then and there.

The light was less when we entered the forest, but Tanama drew me onward, sure-footed in the darkness. Like her, I wore only a clout, and the air was warm and caressing. The eyes of small animals gleamed at me from high in the trees. I could not tell how long this dreamlike journey lasted before we came to a river that flowed like silver in the light of the moon. An intoxicating smell of earth and damp and the sweet perfume of flowers rose to my nostrils as we stood on the bank.

"Now we swim." Tanama tossed her hair, a shimmer of silvery black in the unearthly light, and flashed me a gleaming smile. Then she plunged into the current and started across, head bobbing.

She had not asked me if I knew how to swim. Luckily, I did, though many sailors did not. As a boy in Seville, I had spent many hot summer afternoons splashing in the Guadalquivir. I lowered myself cautiously into the water. It was cool but not unpleasing. I began to swim, parting the silken water with steady strokes.

On the other side, she shook the water off with a sinuous motion of her body and took my hand again. "It is not far to the second river," she said.

"You look like a mermaid," I said, for her wet hair fell streaming around her breast and her body seemed the color of a dusky pearl.

We no longer whispered but still spoke softly, not to shatter the magic of the night.

"What is a mermaid?" she asked.

"It is a woman with the tail of a fish," I said.

She chuckled, the dancing of moonlight on water made into sound. "That does not sound very nice."

"Mermaids are very beautiful," I said. "They live far out in the sea, and the sailors say that no man can resist them."

"If they are made like a fish and not like a woman, the man who catches one must be very disappointed." She chuckled again. "Come."

When we reached the second river, we turned downstream and walked along the bank. The silvery flow drew us on. The earth was soft and still warm from the day. When we crushed grasses underfoot, a faint scent arose from them like a memory of sunlight. It did not seem long before we heard a rushing, then a roaring. The water flowed ever more swiftly until we came to the falls. The river seemed to come to a halt in midair. Tanama beckoned me onward, indicating branches, vines, and jutting rocks that I might use to steady myself, until we could peer over the edge. The water fell to a pool far below, sending a white spray foaming upward, as if Ha'shem were pouring milk from a pitcher.

"Can we get down there?" I asked.

"Yes," she said. "There is a path, but it is hidden. You must follow me."

Cautiously, we picked our way downward over jagged rocks and through tangled foliage. The river roared louder as we came closer to where it met the pool. Tanama said something that I could not hear. I shook my head and pointed to my ear. Leaning close, she put her lips to my ear. "There is a cave behind the falls. Be careful. The rocks are slippery."

The rocky ledge had indeed been worn smooth by the ceaseless tumbling of the falls. I slipped several times on the wet path. She tried to take my hand, but I didn't let her. If I fell, I didn't want to take her with me. Sheer rock rose above us to the cliff top on our left. On our right, moonlight shone through the falling water, turning it to a curtain of silver. I kept my left hand on the rock face for balance, so I felt it curve inward. I had been watching my feet as well. When I looked up, I saw Tanama standing under a crystalline overhang. At her back, the dark mouth of the cave yawned.

"Come," she said once more, her voice audible now but echoing a little.

The roar of the falls subsided as we walked deeper into the cave. Spears of crystal rock thrust upward and hung down from the low ceiling like giant fangs. The cave was dry, but I shivered, and Tanama put her arm around my waist, pressing herself close to my wet, naked body. When we reached a point where the cave mouth behind us was no more than a dim circle of moonlit darkness, Tanama came to a halt. She pressed her palm against my chest. "Wait." She knelt.

I heard the striking of flint against stone. A spark flared, then a flickering light as Tanama lit a torch of rushes held upright in a crevice in the rocks. She knelt on what seemed to be a heap of dried rushes and wildflowers strewn on the floor of the cave. She beckoned, and I knelt facing her. The torchlight turned her skin to flame. Her smiling eyes, her lips, her whole body reached out to me with an urgent, loving hunger. She took my trembling hand and laid it against her breast.

Papa was right. There is much pleasure when it is done correctly.

After this, we went often to the cave. Once the full moon passed, the night was too black to risk the climb by night. But we had the days. The Taino made little distinction between work and play, nor, indeed, worship, and none remarked on it when we left some task to finish later and disappeared toward the river. My joy and reverence for Tanama's body resembled worship. I was glad that Adonai did not frown upon pleasure and call it sin, as the Christians did. I loved her with all my heart and all my senses. And I believed that she loved me, though I did not press her to tell me so. She called me her beloved, and that was enough.

"What is it, *nanichi*?" she asked one day as we lay sunning ourselves on a flat rock in the pool below the falls, drowsy with the act of love. "Why do you look troubled? This moment is perfect."

"I am thinking that this perfect moment must end."

"You must not," she said, rolling closer so that she could draw her lips across my forehead, kissing away the thoughts that wrinkled my brow. "It makes no sense, for we have only this moment. So it is always. Do your people believe that tomorrow has a soul, that the future can fly like a bat in the guayaba trees? We are not so foolish."

"The Taino have a gift for happiness that we lack," I said, kissing her. "I cannot help thinking about the future. Rachel and I must go back."

"But not today."

"No. But I cannot be easy, not knowing what is happening at Isabela. I don't even know if the Admiral has returned." I could not bring myself to speak of my fear that Margarit and his rapacious band might be roving deeper into the mountains. They might fall on this peaceful village without warning unless I found a way to protect it.

Tanama kissed me. "Why can you not stay with us forever? Are you not happy?"

I kissed her back, holding her to me so fiercely that she had to push me away, laughing, to draw breath.

"I have never been happier," I declared. "I wish with all my heart that I could stay. But it will not do. Rachel, especially, must go back. Our parents must grieve for us, thinking us dead."

"Why can she not marry Hutia? She is already one of us. We have all seen the way they look at each other."

"It will not do," I repeated. I had been trying not to see the way Rachel and Hutia looked at each other. Tanama but confirmed what I feared. Rachel was only fourteen. I could not let her bear Hutia's children and perhaps one day be slaughtered by Spanish soldiers. Even now she demanded to go bare breasted, a fashion I had forbidden her to adopt.

"You think that we are doomed."

A shadow seemed to fall upon the sunny day.

"I have not said it."

"You don't have to speak for me to know your mind, especially when your thoughts concern the Taino."

"Hutia will return soon." When he offered to travel to the coast and bring us whatever news he could, I had accepted eagerly. I realized now that I had been as eager to separate him from Rachel for a while as I was to hear of the progress of the colony. "I must know more before any decisions are made."

"Then think no more of it until then," Tanama said. She slipped into the water and laughed up at me, droplets sparkling like diamonds in her hair.

"You look more like a mermaid than ever," I said.

She was right. Our happiness was a gift from Ha'shem. I must not throw it away by letting a future I could neither predict nor control intrude on it. I pushed myself off the rock and landed with a splash beside her, treading water to remain afloat as I took her in my arms. Her legs curled around mine.

"I believe I know how your fish-tailed mermaids make love," she said. "Would you like me to teach you?"

Chapter 31

Quisqueya, October 3–6, 1494

Hutia returned three days later. "I have much to tell you," he said.

We sat on a log outside Tiboni's *bohio*, Hutia sitting much closer to Rachel than he was to me. Their clasped hands were tucked into the narrow space between his thigh and hers. I pretended not to notice. Hutia's news was more important, for the moment, than what I could see only as a calamity I must somehow prevent.

"Has the Admiral returned?" I asked.

"His ships appeared off Isabela three days ago," Hutia said. "I did not wait to see what happened when he came ashore. I thought you would wish to know as soon as possible."

"We must go back," I said.

Rachel opened her mouth, no doubt to protest, but Hutia squeezed her hand, and she didn't speak.

"There is more," Hutia said. "Three ships arrived three moons ago. They bore food, for none of the settlers trouble themselves to cultivate the land, and they will not even let the Taino who serve them build *conuco*, which allow our crops to grow without much labor. They also carried the Admiral's brother, along with many more of the *arijua*." He held up a hand, forestalling my question. "Not he who is already here, trying to govern in his absence, though none obey his will. Another brother, Don Bartholomew."

"I have not met him," I said, "but he is said to be more forceful than Don Diego. Has he restored order?"

"Perhaps now that the Admiral himself has returned, the two together may be able to do so. But until now, Don Diego has been at a loss, for the evil Margarit has continued to do whatever he pleases. But a hand of suns before I reached the settlement, he and the angry *bohique* stole the three flying ships Don Bartholomew brought with him and returned to Spain." *Bohique* was their word for priest.

"Mutiny!" I exclaimed. "This is worse than I expected. I am surprised that Fray Buil made common cause with Margarit."

"They are both Catalans," Rachel said. "From a region in the northeast of Spain," she explained to Hutia, "where they have their own language and customs."

"So they are brothers." Hutia nodded. "I understand."

"At least," I said, "this must mean that Margarit no longer ravages the Taino *yucayeques*."

"I wish that were so," Hutia said, "but the men who followed him have not all returned to Spain. They do not wish to leave without as much gold as they can."

"How fares Santo Tomas?" Rachel asked. "Have they found the mine at Cibao?"

"No, for there is none," Hutia said. "We have tried to tell them that the gold they are fast stealing from our rivers is all we have. But they will not listen. They are fools, but dangerous fools, as they think torture will make us speak a different truth."

"Did you talk with our friend Fernando?" I asked.

"Yes, though he seemed ill at ease to be seen speaking with me. None but the little *bohique*, he who questions us about Atabey and does not believe our answers, talk of making us into Christians and therefore treating us decently."

"Fray Pane," Rachel supplied.

"They now say that because they have but a small store of gold for your caciques," Hutia said, "they will send all of us to them as slaves."

"No!" The horrified exclamation came from both of us at once.

"Surely the Admiral will not allow it," Rachel said.

"Your friend Fernando said that all speak as if the Admiral had already planned it when he sailed away five moons ago."

"Surely they will never come so far into the mountains," Rachel said. "Can we not stay here? If they come close, we can help the villagers to hide."

Hutia and I both shook our heads. Rachel's fervent belief that this could end happily for any of the Taino showed how young she still was.

"They range farther every day," Hutia said. "I will speak to the cacique and the *nitaino* as soon as I may. This village will not remain safe for long. I hope to persuade them to abandon it and hide more deeply in the mountains, perhaps near the sacred caves."

"You would not wish to be safe while others are suffering, Rachel," I said. "The thought is not worthy of you."

Rachel looked at me with tears in her eyes. "You are right, Diego." Her voice fell to a whisper. "But what if we go back and find that we can do nothing to stop them?"

"We must at least try," I said.

So the decision was taken. But we lingered, making no preparations for departure. I was reluctant to leave Tanama, and Rachel loved every soul in the village. Indeed, all returned her affection. Hutia lent a willing ear to all my plans and worries, but I knew that he too wished us to remain among the Taino.

"The most difficult task," I told him, "will be turning Rachel back into a boy. She has grown as a woman does. When she stands among the gromets, it will be apparent that she is different."

We crouched on the bank of a stream near the village, spearing the fish that darted through the shallows. Hutia laid down his spear before he spoke.

"The boys from the ships are scattered," Hutia said. "Some went with your Admiral, some with the evil captain of soldiers. Others have sickened and died. But you cannot turn Rachel back into a boy, no matter how you change her appearance." He picked up a handful of pebbles and sifted them through his fingers. "The tree cannot become a seed again."

"All the more reason to get her home." I cast my fishbone spear at a wily fellow bigger than the rest and missed. My aim was getting better, but I still hit my target only one time out of three.

"She is happy here," Hutia said.

"Nonetheless," I said, "it is my responsibility to restore her to her intended life."

"A life in which she cannot run or play *batey* or go where she chooses." Hutia pitched a pebble at the trunk of a nearby tree with such force that it broke the bark.

I opened my mouth to say, A life in which she can count on being warm and fed and clothed. But the Taino lived in a land that was always warm and offered food in abundance. As for clothing, they saw no need for it.

"It is her life," I said. "She belongs with her people. Our family longs to see her."

"She must go where Adonai can hear her voice," Hutia said. "But Rachel says Adonai is everywhere."

"I fear there may soon be no more happiness among the Taino," I said. "Truly, Hutia, I wish it were not so."

"I fear you are right," he said. "And I do not blame you."

He picked up his spear, and for the next few minutes, we devoted our attention to fishing.

"If only women had been included among the settlers," I said, my mind turning back to the difficulties of rejoining the colony without calling attention to ourselves. "Then she could be herself."

"If they had," Hutia began, "would the soldiers—"

He froze, head up, eyes narrowed, nose twitching as he scented the air. In a moment, I too could discern what had caught his attention: the crashing of booted feet through the brush, a horse neighing, and the clang of steel. A deep voice shouted, another answered. I heard laughter.

"Soldiers!" Hutia said almost soundlessly. "They come to attack the *yucayeque*."

"It doesn't sound as if they know that it is there," I said. "But they will find it. We must warn them!"

"You go!" Hutia said. "You must get Rachel—and your European garments. They must not find you dressed like the Taino. And tell Tiboni—he will know what to do."

"Do you not come with me?"

"I will follow the soldiers," Hutia said. "I will try to distract them before they reach the village. Go!"

He slipped away, moving silently through the trees toward the source of the sound. I ran as fast as I could toward the village.

Chapter 32

Quisqueya, October 6, 1494

Hutia sought stillness in his mind even as he ran as fast as he could without making any sound that could not have been caused by a creature of the forest. Not that the *arijua* were listening. They blundered through the forest like some blind, deaf, sharp-toothed caiman, oblivious to its surroundings but nonetheless lethal to any man or animal unlucky enough to stumble upon it. He must not panic! He must not fail! He must lure the *arijua* away from the *yucayeque* or at least slow them down in their monstrous march until Diego warned the villagers and got Rachel away.

For a moment he wondered if allowing the soldiers to see him, even to kill him, would provide a better distraction. He did not want to die, but if it saved his friends, he would not mind allowing his spirit to fly to Coaybay and feast on the guayaba. No, his death would serve no purpose. Nor could he allow himself to be taken captive. These strangers from across the sea used people up and tossed them away like empty husks. They had taken his father's life, not even by honest cruelty but heedlessly, by neglect. They would not take his. The Christians, as Diego called them, made much of their belief that men had souls. But how twisted was their understanding to think that only a Christian had a soul. Like the Taino, they were only men. And what were men but animal flesh animated for a little while by spirit?

Hutia shook his head to rid it of these buzzing thoughts. When men thought, they lost their animal instincts. He needed every advantage he could summon against the Christians' sharp, unbreakable weapons and their terrible horses. He had not admitted to Diego how much those great beasts' massive heads, rolling eyes, and stamping hooves frightened him.

The soldiers were still on the other side of the river. Because of the horses, which could run so fast they almost flew and made good time even in the forest, Hutia had to make haste to keep up with them as he ran alongside the river, taking care to stay in the shelter of the forest. He leaped over a log, his bare toes not even skimming its mossy surface, and ducked under a low frond of palmetto. Where the underbrush grew thick, he slithered through it. Where it was impassable, he sought a way around it, sometimes finding a thick, well-anchored vine on which he could swing himself over the obstacle.

From the shouts of the soldiers and the clatter they made, he could hear that they were approaching the river. It would delay them for a short while, since the *arijua* made heavy weather of crossing rivers. They would hardly have made it past the beach, no less into the mountains, without Taino help. But the horses could swim. And once across the river, their column would point like a spear straight at the *yucayeque*.

Hutia took a deep breath and slid rather than dove into the river, drawing in a deep breath and slipping underwater without the slightest splash. A few quick strokes took him to the other side without needing to take another breath. Now he must slacken his pace and fall far enough behind them to circle around and make them think there was something of interest on their other side, away from the village.

The strangers would destroy Quisqueya. He had known the first time he set eyes on them that they were cruel as well as dangerous. Even the image of their God was a man in torment. They must have thought the Taino as cruel as themselves, to believe such an image would persuade the Taino to abandon Yucahu and Atabey in favor of their Jesus. Then the man called Cabrera had murdered Hutia's little sister. Every time Hutia saw a golden flower, *anacaona*, he grieved anew. He would have killed Cabrera on the beach as soon as Diego had told him the truth, if Hutia's father had not been already on the ship. Hutia had settled that score later, when Caonabo's raid had given the Taino the opportunity they needed to punish the greedy interlopers and bring the women home.

Diego had tried to tell him that Cabrera was a man of pure evil, different from the rest. But Hutia had seen no kindness in them, except for Diego, who in any case was not of their tribe. And Rachel, of course. Whatever happened now, he knew that he would lose Rachel. It was a minor cruelty compared to all his people had already suffered and would suffer in the time to come, but it broke his heart.

The noise of the cavalcade sounded on his other side. Now they marched between him and the river, as he had wanted. He bent and picked up a rounded stone. It sat warm and comfortable in his hand, a friend, a weapon, a small piece of Quisqueya. He stood for a moment, steadying his breath and making sure his muscles were relaxed, his body in balance. Then he raised his arm and hurled the stone with all his strength ahead of the soldiers.

As he had hoped, they halted.

"What was that?"

Hutia held his cupped hands to his lips and produced a cascade of twittering, as if a hunter had disturbed a flock of birds.

"If it is a savage, there may be a village nearby."

"Let it be one ripe for plucking."

"With plenty of them naked girls."

"No, it was probably an animal, a big ugly lizard or one of those long-snouted things with the poison teeth. Not worth shooting for the pot, either one of them."

Hutia threw several more stones. He dared not imitate the animals or birds again, or the soldiers would ride straight to where he stood, rather than where the stones had landed, as he hoped.

Some of the soldiers wanted to seek out the source of the sounds. Others argued against investigating. If they came his way, they must not find him. He climbed a tree, shinnying up it with fingers and toes finding purchase in its rough bark. They would not look up. Meanwhile, Hutia had bought the village a little time.

"We will continue," a decisive voice said finally. "We are not far from the river we glimpsed earlier. Let us cross it. The savages must have water. We have seen that many of their villages lie beside a river. Come!"

As he watched from his perch, the soldiers reached the river-bank and began milling about, making ready to cross. He could do no more here. He must return to Isabela. When Rachel and Diego got there, they would need his help. If only they were not mistaken for Taino and cut down on the spot! No! He would not think it. They must live, and so must he. He dropped lightly to the ground. Turning his back on the soldiers, the river, and the *yucayeque*, he started making his way toward the sea.

Chapter 33

Quisqueya, October 6, 1494

I burst out of the trees, heart pounding, each breath like a knife in my chest. The scene before me was one of cheerful industry and play. For a final moment, the doomed village remained ignorant and at peace. Frantic, I looked around for Rachel. I heard a peal of laughter that could only be hers coming from the cluster of cooking fires where the women spent much of the day. I found her pounding yuca.

"Danger!" I cried. "Rachel, come!" I seized her hand.

The circle of women stirred but continued working, not comprehending that the emergency involved them. I realized that I had spoken in Castilian.

"Soldiers come!" I said in Taino. "You must hide! Quickly! Somebody tell Tiboni and the cacique. And get the children!"

Now they began to move, more slowly than I wished them to, putting down their tools and beginning to collect the babies and small children who played in the dirt nearby. Someone ran toward the cacique's *caney*, another toward the *batey* court, where shouts and laughter indicated that older children played. I didn't wait to hurry them along but pulled Rachel after me toward Tiboni's *bohio* where our possessions lay. Most had been untouched for months, although I always carried my tinderbox and my dagger of Toledo steel.

"We must dress in our Spanish clothes and hide," I panted. "They must not see us like this."

Rachel tugged at my hand, trying to draw me back toward the center of the village.

"We must fight! We cannot leave the others to face them alone!"

"We can do nothing! They have swords and horses. With luck, the villagers will be able to hide in the forest or get to the caves. I must keep you safe."

"I don't want to be safe if everyone I love is killed!" But she was running with me now.

We reached Tiboni's *bohio* and ducked inside. It was empty. I fumbled my way into my shirt and breeches, and Rachel did the same.

"Hutia!" she exclaimed. "Was he not with you? What has happened to him? If the soldiers have taken him, I *will* go back."

"*No*, Rachel! Hutia is fine. He is tracking them and will try to create a distraction to slow them down." I tossed her a sloshing water skin. "Here. We must have water if we are to reach Isabela."

"Then they will be hunting *him*!" Rachel wrung her hands. But in the next moment, she threw the last precious remnant of Espinosa soap into her tinderbox and stuck a fishbone-headed knife into the leather belt she had already wrapped around her waist.

"Boots!" I said, burrowing through the pile to find them and tossing the smaller pair to her. "We cannot cross the mountains barefoot."

"Will this do?"

I looked at her and saw a ragged European boy—with a face painted in white and ochre.

"Your face! And how is mine?" I snatched up a crumpled kerchief and poured water onto it from the water skin I had slung
across my shoulder.

"You are still smudged from yesterday's *batey*. Here, let me."
She took the damp rag from my hand and scrubbed at my face. "It
will have to do. Come." She pushed away my hand as I reached to
help her and dabbed at her own face as we ran.

"We cannot stay to look for Hutia!" I told her, guessing the
reason for her willingness to run toward the woods rather than the
center of the village. "He will find us at Isabela."

At that moment, from behind us came a burst of cries and
shouts, the clash of weapons, and then a series of women's screams.

Tanama! I had not thought of her in my anxiety to get Rachel
away.

"Stay here!" I told Rachel fiercely. "Climb a tree!" There were
vines and low-hanging branches everywhere, but I didn't wait to
see if she obeyed me. I was already running back toward the noise
of the fray, my dagger in my hand.

The unequal fight was already almost lost by the time I arrived.
The Spaniards' swords ran with blood. The horses' hooves were
caked with blood and dust. Taino men lay in a tangle of broken
limbs before the doors of the *bohios*, where they had evidently
tried to make a stand. Soldiers were herding the women and young
boys into the center of the *batey* court, beating at them with the
flat of their swords or snapping leather whips that left raw welts
on their flesh. Smaller children wandered about, screaming and
crying. The soldiers made no effort either to herd them with the
others or to step aside when they stood in the way of the horses'
hooves. From the numbers, I guessed that some of the Taino had
reached the shelter of the forest in time, but not many. I prayed
that Tanama was among them, for I could not see her anywhere.

Tiboni and several of the other *nitaino* had evidently tried to
protect the cacique, for they lay in a welter of blood in front of the

caney. The only man the soldiers had bothered to take prisoner was the cacique himself. They had loaded him down with chains, although it looked as if both his arms had been broken.

"Hey! Where did you spring from? Have you lost your horse?" A bearded face grinned down at me below a battered helmet.

It was a soldier I knew by sight, but not by name, though all of them knew me as the Admiral's sometime scribe and interpreter.

"I became separated from my company," I said, "except for the lad Rafael, the Admiral's page. Can you lend me a mule?"

"Help yourself." He lifted his chin toward the mêlée.

I could see that a mule or two wandered riderless. I grabbed at a dangling bridle. My chosen mule brayed once in protest but bowed its head and allowed me to lead it when I gathered up the reins and tugged sharply on them.

"Here," the soldier said. "You speak their jabber, don't you?" He nodded at the weeping huddle of captives. "Tell them to stop howling, for they are going to Spain, whether they like it or not. And tell those pretty girls that if they smile sweetly, they'll get some real men riding them. I wouldn't mind going for a gallop myself, but we'd better get this mess in order first."

"Don't call me by name," I told the women in Taino. "I will do what I can for you, but I fear it will not be much. And try to calm yourselves, as they will not hesitate to subdue anyone who causes trouble. If you are compliant, most of them will be less cruel."

I felt bitterly ashamed to give them such advice. But I could envision no happy outcome for them, unless Rachel and I could somehow free them on the march back to Isabela. But as the soldiers were even now attaching iron chains to their arms and necks and linking them together, I didn't see how that could be accomplished. At my words, they did their best to sob more quietly. The soldier grunted with satisfaction and turned away as I mounted my mule.

"Has anyone seen Tanama?" I asked the captives softly.

"She went to the stream for water," a young woman said, "before the *anki*, the evil ones, came. I did not see her return."

"I must march with them," I said. "I will make them give you water, and I will try to get them to loosen your chains."

I kicked my heels into the mule's sides, forcing it to a gallop back toward the nearest stream close to where I had left Rachel.

I found Rachel and Tanama both struggling with a single soldier. He had flung his sword aside, as well as his helmet, or else it had fallen off in the course of his exertions. He bestrode Tanama, forcing himself upon her as she screamed and fought. Rachel had leaped on him from behind and clung to his back like a monkey, beating at his head with a rock as he tried to shake her off without ceasing his assault on Tanama. I dismounted, for the mule, unlike the caballeros' horses, was not trained to battle. How could I join in the fight without hurting one of the women, pressed between them as he was? But I must! Tanama screamed again. I circled, seeking an opening, hardly aware that I was screaming too.

"Your knife!" I called out to Rachel in Taino. "Draw your knife. Push it straight in behind his ear, if you can."

I drew my own dagger, hoping for an opening. Rachel drew her knife from her belt with some difficulty, as the soldier, who was built like a bull, kept trying to buck her off. As I watched in horror, he reached behind him, pried her flailing fist open, and seized the fishbone knife as she loosed it. With a twist of his shoulders, he flung her off his back. He raised his arm high above his head and plunged the knife into Tanama's chest.

With a howl of grief and outrage, I threw myself upon him and buried my dagger in his back, just below his left shoulder blade. With a grunt, I drove it in up to the hilt. It must have found his heart instantly. The soldier flopped forward onto Tanama. I rose shakily to my feet so I could kick him off her. Trembling, Rachel came forward and added the force of her boots to mine. But by the time we rolled him onto the ground, Tanama was already dead.

Chapter 34

Quisqueya–Isabela, October 6–12, 1494

The nightmare journey over the mountains and down to the coast took six days. While we were on the march, I was in no danger of being betrayed by grief. Indeed, I felt numb. Rachel and I were both shocked by the suddenness of the tragedy and horrified by the villagers' fate. But we could not afford to allow the soldiers to see how we felt. The Taino understood this. Only in the darkest hours did I allow myself to think of Tanama. When the camp was quiet except for the cry of night birds, the scream of small hunted animals, and the occasional stamp of a horse's hoof, I grieved for her bright spirit, so heedlessly extinguished. My body ached with the memory of wanting her. I tried not to weep, because once I started, I could not stop. Sometimes I had to bite my arm to keep from sobbing aloud.

The Spaniards were in good humor at having taken many slaves. In the villages they had raided before reaching ours, they had tortured enough people to locate and seize every grain of gold in the vicinity. This success too raised their spirits. They joked and laughed incessantly, in marked contrast to the misery of the Taino, who stumbled along, scarcely able to move for the weight of their iron chains. Many had been wounded in the fight at the village, and their captors would not allow them time or freedom to seek healing herbs or make salves that might have alleviated their pain and weakness.

I feared that Rachel would be exposed if we came too sharply to the notice of the soldiers. But she insisted on bringing water to the captives, binding the worst wounds with such cloth as she could find, and going among the wretched Taino with words of compassion, if not comfort.

"I cannot believe the Admiral would allow this treatment," she said to me.

A second mule could not be spared, so she rode behind me. This gave us the opportunity to talk privately as the mule picked its way through streams and down precipitous slopes. As I held the reins, she often carried a baby in her arms. Some of the women had snatched up their infants as they were herded into the plaza. Even these rough men were loth to tear mother and child apart. Babies make inconvenient slaves, as they need constant tending. But none had the heart to abandon them in the forest, nor kill them outright, were it not in the heat of battle.

"Don't promise them," I warned her, "that the Admiral will relieve their misery. He didn't authorize the men to make such raids, but he may choose to believe that it is all in the name of Christianity, and that it is the Taino who have transgressed by withholding gold from the soldiers."

"I can't believe it," she said. "The Admiral is kind."

"The Admiral is devout," I said, "and ever conscious of his debt to Ferdinand and Isabella." I looked around to make sure no one had overheard me speak so disrespectfully of the Sovereigns. But truly, their policies had caused great misery to all but Christians. "He must justify the expense of his voyages in one way or another."

"Surely they have found the mine of Cibao by now," Rachel said. "Is that not enough?"

But they had not. We stopped briefly at Santo Tomas, which was now a serviceable fort from which parties of men went forth, not only to coerce gold from the Taino but to gather it from the rivers and streams whose bounty had made us so certain that the legend of Cibao was fact. The mine, however, remained elusive.

We arrived at Isabela dirty, weary, and discouraged to find many captives penned up there already. The men, following the Admiral's example, had taken to referring to them as Caribe, to create the illusion that they enslaved only the fierce enemies of the gentle Taino. But I doubted any of them was much troubled by conscience. The Admiral, as we soon found, saw no contradiction between his original intent and his current policy.

We were admitted to the Admiral's presence without difficulty, once he had explained us to his brother, Don Bartholomew, who had become his chief adviser. He did so without revealing that Papa, his companion in the fateful shipwreck in his youth, was Jewish. This in itself was a kindness for which I was grateful, although I wondered if the Admiral had perhaps managed to forget that inconvenient fact. But how could I fault him for lying to himself, when the account I gave him of our activities over the past six months was a farrago of lies?

We found the Admiral in bed. He had been stricken with gout on his summer voyage of exploration and frequently had to direct the running of the colony without leaving his quarters, though he did so with great energy in spite of his obvious pain. His face lit up when he saw us. He had no such mixed feelings about us as we harbored toward him, but saw us only as loyal and useful followers of whom he was particularly fond.

I would have liked to speak with the Admiral about Rachel's increasingly precarious situation. But I could not, as both Don Bartholomew and Don Diego were present. To me, Rachel appeared unmistakably a young woman. But I could discern no puzzled frowns or sly looks when the Columbus brothers gazed on her. The Admiral invited us to sit by his bedside on wooden stools while we recounted our supposed adventures in detail. I was running out of invention when there came shouts of great excitement from the direction of the shore.

The Admiral raised himself, wincing with pain. Don Diego hurried to support him. Don Bartholomew looked at us, clearly expecting the humblest of those present to find out what had happened and bring word back to the great ones.

The Admiral shook off Don Diego's arm. Wincing, he pulled himself up to a sitting position. "Barto, Diego, be so good as to go and see what has occurred. If it is a matter of any import, we must control it immediately. Not all the malcontents sailed home with Margarit."

"Of course, brother," Don Diego said, making immediately for the door.

Don Bartholomew looked surprised.

"I would talk with these lads further," the Admiral said. "Leave them with me."

"As your Excellency pleases," I murmured.

Rachel bowed. Like me, she realized that we needed Don Bartholomew's good will, and a show of humility would go some way toward attaining it.

Don Bartholomew shrugged and turned to go.

"So, young Rafael," the Admiral said blandly. "You have grown in these last months, but I see that you have not yet started your beard. Ah, well, you are yet young."

"Yes, Excellency." Rachel made a hasty bow to him and another to the Admiral's brothers as they hurried away.

When we were certain they were out of earshot, I went down on one knee. Rachel copied me.

"Excellency," Rachel said, "before we speak further, what can we do for your comfort?"

"Ah, I have missed my page." The Admiral's features, steely with pain as well as the habit of command, softened into his most kindly smile. "Very well, assist me to lie down."

We both sprang to do so.

"Ah, that is better. And that pillow under my leg will ease it greatly. Now, what can we do for your protection? For I am mindful that you are not as young as I would have my brothers believe."

"Excellency, we must contrive something," I said, "but I am at a loss as to what that might be."

"Shall I send you home?" he asked. "Ships have now returned to Spain without my guidance, and more will go when I can send sufficient treasure to please Their Gracious Majesties. We must also beg for more provisions, though my brother's arrival with three laden caravels has relieved our immediate needs."

It would be some time till a caravel departed. Before that happened, Rachel's bosom might swell to unmistakable proportions, or some rough sailor or soldier might come upon her washing a bloody rag. Besides, to return to Spain would be to exchange one kind of danger for another.

"Excellency," I said, "I don't know what to do for the best."

The Admiral assured us that we could rely on his protection if we remained, but it seemed to me that if the matter were made public, it might be taken out of his hands. As we discussed the dilemma, the shouting, which had grown louder and more excited as we talked, became an uproar moving toward the Admiral's quarters.

Don Diego burst into the room. "Ships! Three caravels have arrived!"

The Admiral sat up abruptly, crying out with pain as the movement put pressure on his gouty leg. "Help me up, and hand me those sticks."

"Captain Torres leads them," Don Diego said. "He brings settlers—and among them are women!"

All of us made haste to help the Admiral to his feet and then, once we had him leaning on his sticks, to let him walk without our assistance as he commanded.

"It is our opportunity!" I whispered to Rachel.

Necessity made both of us think quickly. Rachel had left a few possessions, including the traveling dress she had worn in Spain, in the hut we had shared with Fernando. Praying that he and none other still occupied our haven, I sent her running to change her clothes. Her whole body concealed under a hooded cloak, she could make her way through the settlement and join the new arrivals without being noticed. Meanwhile, I followed the crowd streaming toward the shore.

When I arrived, several boatloads had already landed. The travelers, looking wan and exhausted after several weeks at sea, either clung together or looked around with apprehension rather than wonder. Many trees had been felled in the building of Isabela. The newcomers would not get the impression that they had arrived in paradise. But the beauties of the forest and the richness of the soil would no doubt put heart in them soon enough.

The resident men looked curiously at the twenty or thirty women who climbed the bank and made their way toward the center of the town. I heard a few ribald comments, but most regarded the newcomers with sympathy and awe. I had no doubt that Christian women would be treated very differently from the Indian women. What kind of woman, I wondered, would embark on such a precarious journey into the unknown? None of them looked like loose women or the kind who attach themselves to armies, yet none was dressed richly. Most wore drab gray or brown woolen cloaks and carried sacks that no doubt contained the sum of their worldly possessions. They had broad peasant faces. I had no doubt that the rough cloaks covered sturdy arms and backs used to labor. Many of the men carried tools for farming. A few of the women seemed to be the farmers' wives. Men of Isabela

greeted one or two others with great excitement. These must be wives or sisters who had crossed the Ocean Sea to join their menfolk in making a new life.

Several of the women had children, not babes in arms, which I thought wise, but boys and girls who clung to their mothers' cloaks or helped to carry their bundles. One woman in particular caught my eye. Two children walked by her side, one a boy of perhaps ten who bore a bundle that looked too heavy for him. When his mother reached out to assist him, he shook off her hand and held himself a little straighter as he marched along. The other was a girl of five or six, half hidden in her mother's skirts. In one arm she clutched a poppet made of rags. It had button eyes and hair of brown wool, and it wore a grimy, salt-stained blue garment that perhaps had once been a cotton kerchief.

This woman's face looked kind. I watched her approach. The newcomers must climb to reach the fort, and since all bore burdens, their passage was slow. The sun burned high in the sky. The procession halted raggedly as the voyagers paused to remove their heavy cloaks. The woman I observed stopped perhaps a hundred yards away. She removed her cloak and draped it over her arm. The boy tried to take it from her to add to his own burden, but she refused. She bent to tie a white kerchief around the little girl's head and unwind the shawl that the child had worn for warmth.

I felt Rachel nudge me. Glancing to the side, I saw that her hands were hidden beneath a bulging gray cloak.

"I brought all my things," she said.

"Was Fernando there?"

"No, but his Taino mistress was."

"What?" I kept my voice low with an effort. "I don't believe it. Fernando?"

"She assured me that it is true," Rachel said. "She is seventeen, and she says he treats her kindly."

"That doesn't surprise me," I said, though I was not quite sure if this news meant that Fernando had become a better ally to the Taino or a predator like the soldiers.

"What now?" she asked.

In a moment, I made my decision. "Do you see that woman, the one who has just kissed the little girl? When she passes us, fall into step with her. As you do so, slip off your cloak and lay it over your arm. You might offer to carry hers as well. She is heavily burdened already."

"I will do better." Rachel needed no explanation to comprehend and improve on my plan. "I will offer to carry the girl. See how her little feet are dragging with weariness and the poor poppet is trailing in the dust."

It was quickly done. In another minute or two, Rachel had the child, poppet and all, in her arms. She turned a sunny smile on the mother. "May I walk with you? I am Raquel. You must have crossed on one of the other ships. What a lovely little girl—what is your name, sweetheart? And a fine son too. You are fortunate. I traveled alone, for I have no family back in Spain, and I am determined to make a better life for myself here than I could have done if I had remained."

"So am I," the woman said, smiling back with great warmth. "We are happy to have your company. My name is Pilar. I am a widow, and these are my children, Ana—don't suck your thumb, Ana, and thank the pretty young lady for carrying you—and Benito. It was a long journey, was it not? Yet there is something in being out of sight of all land, surrounded by sea and sky, that lifts the heart, do you not think so?"

"I do indeed," Rachel said. "It seems that we are meant to be friends."

Chapter 35

Isabela, October 15, 1494–January 15, 1495

We spent a tedious winter enlarging the palisade around Isabela. We built new huts, storage rooms for roots and grains, and smoke-houses for fish and the scanty amount of meat we slaughtered. We also constructed an armory much like the *caney* in the *yucayeque* but reinforced with hardwood logs and bands of iron. The women, Rachel among them, planted, hoed, and weeded in hopes of grow-ing enough food to feed the whole colony and end our reliance on provisions sent from Spain. Most still refused to eat yuca or plant their beans and maize in *conuco*. But Rachel persuaded Pilar and one or two of the other women to do so, and their harvests yielded double the crops of the others.

Children worked alongside the women. Rachel not only made the work into a game for Benito, but also amused Ana, who was too little to work but could not be left behind. For this, Pilar thanked Rachel over and over, saying she didn't know what she would do without her. Most of the women married shortly after their arrival, putting themselves under the protection of some sturdy farmer, a sailor with a ready smile, or a soldier who had amassed a greater hoard of gold than the others. But Pilar, who had been happy with her dead husband, was neither ready to replace him nor eager to lose her independence. I think for a while she had hopes of me, though she was my elder by ten years. But I gave her no encouragement. I had no intention of remaining in the Indies. Besides, my memories of Tanama were still too fresh. Yet I was always welcome at her table and was happy to perform any tasks on her behalf or Rachel's that demanded a man's strength.

We told Pilar, the children, and any others who expressed curiosity that Rachel was my cousin. I had not known, we said, that she planned to settle in the Indies. Nor had she known that I had sailed with the Admiral, not only on this expedition but on the first voyage, which all the newcomers wanted to hear about.

"The day your ship arrived at Isabela," I told the wide-eyed children, "was two years to the day after we made our first landfall, after sailing many leagues with no notion of whether we would ever reach land."

The children regarded me with as much awe as they accorded the Admiral, on the rare occasions they saw him at a distance. Rachel and Pilar both assured me that they were unusually well behaved when I was present. I formed the habit of taking my evening meal with them. Afterward, we would sit by the fire, little Ana on my lap or Rachel's, until both children grew drowsy and I realized that I too must sleep, for I could always count on a long day's work the next day.

In theory, I still shared Fernando's hut. In truth, I gave him and his Taino companion as much privacy as I could. He seemed fond enough of the girl, though their conversation was limited, as Fernando had never managed to learn much Taino. Instead of giving her a Spanish name, he called her Yayama, his little pineapple, declaring that like that curious fruit, she was prickly on the outside but sweet and succulent within. I found occasion to ask her privately in Taino if she was happy with her situation. Later, I learned that Rachel had done the same. The girl swore to both of us that she was content, although like Cristobal, she would not tell us her original Taino name.

"My family is gone," she said. "That name is no longer mine. Only Atabey remembers it."

During these months, Hutia came and went between Isabela and the remote villages and caves to which the Taino who resisted subjugation had retreated. He avoided being penned up with the captives by telling any Spaniard who accosted him that he was my servant and interpreter. Though I saw little of the Admiral these days, I was still known to all as his favorite. Indeed, it was understood that I was especially precious to him since the young page, Rafael, had reportedly sickened and died while on an errand to Santo Tomas. We made sure that those at Santo Tomas heard that Rafael's demise had occurred at Isabela. Either way, none doubted this, as many had died. Fray Pane and his newly arrived fellow clerics performed many more funeral masses than weddings. At any rate, if Hutia's excellent command of Castilian did not give sufficient credibility to his story, the suspicious were welcome to apply to me for confirmation.

Somewhat to my surprise, Rachel seemed to be tolerating the tedium of a life that consisted only of work, interspersed with meals and sleep. It took me some time to realize that she had found a pastime of which she knew I could not approve. When I asked how she fared, she admitted that the unremitting round of work made her restless and cranky. She did not crave leisure, for Rachel had no use for idleness. But she longed for freedom.

"Let me but spend an afternoon in the forest talking with the parrots and weaving myself a garland of flowers, and I will take up my hoe more willingly," she said.

"You cannot wander through the forest alone," I said. "It is not safe."

"I can take care of myself!" Rachel said. "After our time with the Taino, I have as much woodcraft as you."

"My concern is not the dangers of the forest," I said, "but the men you might encounter there. And before you say it, I don't mean the Taino."

"Nonsense," Rachel said. "None would accost a Spanish lady. But if you wish, I shall take Benito with me. I am sure he has as much desire to run and shout as I do."

"Oh, so now you are a lady?" I had not outgrown my pleasure in teasing Rachel and seeing her grow red-faced and sputtering with indignation. "Doña Marina would be pleased to know that we have found a more effective method of training a wild girl to be a lady than convent schools and lessons in manners. Rather, the girl must cross the Ocean Sea and be set to work in the fields."

Rachel seized my ear and twisted it. I responded by tickling her as any brother would, and the conversation ended in laughter and good humor. But the next afternoon, I saw her set out, two water skins slung across her shoulders and Benito at her heels, a sack that probably held cassava bread on his back. I could not like it, and I was not certain which of them was supposed to protect the other if danger arose. But the forests of Hispaniola held no predators other than our compatriots, and Rachel had certainly proven herself competent in an astonishing number of situations that would never have arisen had she been an ordinary Spanish girl. So I objected no more to her expeditions after she and Benito returned from the first one tired, dirty, and happy.

One evening we sat at Pilar's fireside, replete with hutia stew and dumplings made of maize.

"Who would have guessed that an animal such as the hutia would make such a delicious stew," I said.

"I dreamed I had a pet hutia of my own," little Ana said from her seat on her mother's lap.

"Hush, you did not." Pilar dropped a quick kiss on the top of her head.

"I gathered the nuts we eat in the forest," Benito said, jealous of his sister's bid for attention. "And I can almost hit a hutia with a stone."

"Can you indeed?" I said. "Bringing down game for dinner takes much skill and practice. Is Rachel teaching you on your excursions to the forest?"

"No," Benito said, "Hutia is."

For a moment, I thought that he spoke nonsense, saying that the furry little animal supervised its own demise. A quick glance at Rachel undeceived me. She frowned fiercely at Benito, but he was throwing nutshells into the fire, aiming at a knot on the biggest log, and did not notice.

"So you met Hutia in the forest yesterday?" I spoke softly.

"Oh, we meet him every time," Benito said. "He gives me a lesson in hitting what I aim at. I usually hit something, but often it is a bush or rock I did not even see. Then Rachel tells me to gather as many stones that fit my hand as I can and practice until she comes for me. And I am not to move more than thirty paces from the big tree, so she can find me."

I could not find words. Rachel's cheeks were burning, as well they might. Pilar was humming, paying no attention to the conversation as she rocked Ana into sleep.

"Rachel!" I was so angry that her name issued from my tight throat as a croak. I took a deep breath, telling my shoulders to drop and my fists to unclench. "It is time for me to seek my bed. Walk with me."

She was not foolish enough to argue.

It was late, and few people were about, though from open doorways came flickering firelight and the occasional burst of singing and laughter among men whose evening recreation was to drink wine or *chicha* until they fell into a stupor. We walked silently, side by side, until we reached the shadow of a great tree fifty yards from my hut.

"What have you been up to?" I demanded. I kept my voice low, but I trembled with the effort.

"Hutia is my friend as well as yours!" Rachel burst out, as angry as I. "Why should I not meet him?"

"You have been deceitful and irresponsible." Remembering what made me feel the worst when Papa caught me in some transgression, I said, "I am disappointed in you."

"You are not Papa!" she shot back. "If you had asked me, I would have told you the truth."

"You left Benito alone in the forest. He is just a little boy!"

"I thought you meant him to protect me." Her tone shifted from withering sarcasm to sullenness. "We didn't go far. If he had cried out, we would have heard."

"That is the feeble defense of a child," I said. "I thought better of Hutia, however."

"Hutia has done nothing wrong!" she said. "What ugly thoughts do you harbor, brother?"

"I don't know what you have done," I said. "You had better tell me, for it seems I don't know as well as I thought what you are capable of."

"We have only kissed. But I wish to do more. And so I would, if Hutia didn't care more about your good opinion than he does my happiness."

My anger deserted me. "He does care about your happiness, child. And so do I."

"You do not! I love Hutia, and I am a woman! I am!"

"Don't be silly, little sister. Your happiness does not depend on your indulging in pleasures that belong to the marriage bed."

"You didn't marry Tanama!"

I felt as if she had struck me. She clapped a hand to her mouth and burst into tears.

"I am sorry, Diego! Truly, I didn't mean to say anything so hurtful. It is not only that I love Hutia. I see the misery of the Taino every day, and we can do nothing. Nothing! I cannot bear it! At least when Hutia kisses me, I forget about all the cruelty in the world for a little while."

I put my arms around her. She laid her tearstained cheek against my chest. I rocked her, crooning, "Hush, little one. I know. I know."

Presently, I said, "The Admiral plans to send ships back to Spain in a month or so, as soon as he deems the winter gales on the Ocean Sea will not prevent them from reaching a Spanish port safely. You should go with them."

"Without you?"

"I still have to make my way in the world," I reminded her. "I can send you back with enough gold for safe transport to Italy and an ample dowry."

"I don't want to leave Hutia!"

"If Hutia loves you," I said, "he will encourage you to go. There is no future for you here, Rachel. If you but think, you will see that for yourself."

"Then why can't Hutia come with us? On the ship, he must pretend to be our slave, but once we reach Italy, he can be free. Surely Papa must see he is as fine a man as any we have known."

"I too think Hutia is a fine man," I said. "But I know what Papa will say: he is not Jewish."

"He could convert," she said without much conviction. Unlike the Christians, we did not encourage conversion.

"You know what Papa says," I reminded her. "Who would have the fortitude or folly to wish to be one of us, if he were not born to it?"

"Maybe one whose people have suffered as much as ours," she said. "Maybe one who loves a Jewish girl enough to leave his homeland."

"As our people have done over and over," I said, "in order to survive, ever since the destruction of the Temple in Jerusalem. But I don't think Hutia will wish to leave this land. I will speak to him. In the meantime, you walk no more in the forest."

Chapter 36

Isabela, January 16–February 24, 1495

I did speak to Hutia, but only to tell him he must not dally with my sister.

"Jewish girls of Rachel's age don't perform the act of love," I said. "Nor do Jewish women outside of marriage. A single marriage between one man and one woman," I added, remembering that Taino customs were often otherwise.

Hutia did not pretend to misunderstand me. "I am not an animal!" he said. "I esteem Rachel greatly. I can control my desires."

"But she, perhaps, cannot," I said.

"I will be wise for both of us."

"I have told her she must not meet you alone at all," I said.

Hutia sighed. "I know she is not for me. But she is courageous and beautiful and quick-witted. How can I not love her?"

This left me somewhat at a loss, feeling as I suppose all brothers do when a man first courts their baby sister.

"Setting Rachel aside, you might consider returning to Europe with us." I had not meant to make this offer, but I could not help wishing Hutia well. "If things continue as they have lately, you might have as little future on Hispaniola as Rachel."

"Quisqueya," Hutia corrected. "I fear that you are right, but I cannot give up all hope yet. And even if we are doomed, I must stand with my people."

So the matter rested until, early in February, the Admiral announced that four caravels would return to Spain under the command of Captain Torres.

"I am sending Yayama away," Fernando said to me one afternoon as we labored at thatching the roof of yet another storeroom.

"You will return to Spain?"

"Yes. I have obligations in Granada, and I confess I don't think the colony will succeed. They are doing everything wrong!"

"On that point, we are in complete accord." I sat back on my heels and wiped sweat from my forehead with my forearm.

He, too, paused in his work.

"Have you heard the rumors about demanding tribute?" He threw back his head and raised his water skin, gulping as water poured in a steady stream into his mouth.

"It is more than a rumor," I said. "Every Indian man on Hispaniola will be required to give a certain quantity of gold several times a year, and wear a token that he has done so, or be killed or enslaved. I wish I could tell you that it was not the Admiral's idea."

"I hope Yayama will be safe," Fernando said. "She says that there are caves far back in the mountains that the soldiers have not yet found."

"I wish Hutia would go with her. I fear it is only a matter of time before we control the whole island, seizing or destroying everything that made it seem like paradise when we first came here."

"One cannot deny that Christians have a natural superiority," Fernando said, "and thus a right to dominion over lesser folk. But matters could have been settled with more discipline and less confusion."

I had nothing to say to that, and my silence reminded Fernando of the unspoken fact that I was not a Christian. His face reddened, and he turned back to his work without saying more.

"What obligations have you in Granada?" I asked presently, hoping to ease things between us, for in spite of his prejudices, he was a good friend.

"My father is a merchant," he said. "When the Moors governed the city, his prospects were limited, but now his business prospers. He wishes me to learn his trade so that in time I may take over the direction of all his enterprises." He reddened again as he added, "And I am betrothed."

Matters quickly became worse for the Taino. Fernando and I did not speak of Yayama again, and I had no chance to urge Hutia to seek greater safety in the mountains. The decision to send ships to Spain gave the Admiral an opportunity to report in full on matters in the Indies and beg the Sovereigns for further supplies in as great detail as possible. This made me valuable once more as a scribe, especially since, without discussing it, both the Admiral and I thought it unwise to press Rachel into service. Those who saw her at his desk might notice her remarkable resemblance to young Rafael.

Description of the islands and harbors he had found in his explorations flowed readily from his lips to my quill and paper. But when it came time to enumerate the proposed cargo of the ships that would sail back to Spain, the Admiral grew fretful.

"We sent Their Majesties thirty thousand ducats' worth of gold last year," he said, more to himself than to me. "Perhaps we can amass the same amount again, if we press the Indians hard. They deserve no better, for some of them have killed Christians. But it is not enough! Not enough! The trade goods I have already sent have found no favor, except for the cotton cloth, and that is paltry. A trading colony must have goods to trade. Very well, I will send them what can be found in abundance here—slaves."

"Excellency!" I had to speak, though I feared his anger. "Is that not unworthy recompense for the welcome the Taino have given us since we first set foot on their shores?"

"No, no, Diego." He looked at me in mild surprise. "We take no Taino, only Caribe, those fierce fellows who have the impudence to resist us."

This was a delusion, and I marveled that he seemed to believe it.

"And those who have killed our soldiers, of course," he went on, "like that rascal Guatiguana, must die."

This was a cacique who had defied and killed a group of soldiers who came to plunder his village. The Admiral's logic left me bewildered and appalled. The folk of the island must give gifts, but the Christians need not. The Christians might kill, but the Indians must not.

"Find my brother Bartholomew and ask him to attend me," the Admiral ordered. "We must organize the taking of the captives, so that we can choose the best specimens to send to Spain." He added kindly, "You have labored so long on my behalf that your fingers must be stiff with cramp." He himself had been ill throughout the winter, with extreme pain in his joints, especially when the weather was damp.

"Excellency." I bowed and went upon this errand without saying more. No matter how eloquently I pleaded on behalf of the Taino, it was clear he would not relent.

By the time the ships were ready to depart, Rachel had received three proposals of marriage from men of the colony. More would have offered, had she not made it generally known that the suitor of a girl not yet fifteen could expect only quick rejection, and if he protested, ridicule.

Hutia departed for the mountain caves, after a tearful scene with Rachel. I witnessed it because my fear for what might happen if I left them alone together exceeded the discomfort of being present while she pleaded with him to accompany us to Europe.

"So you go with her," Hutia said. "You have had enough of paradise."

"We have already destroyed paradise," I said. "Hutia, I bitterly regret it, and I can no longer stomach being part of that destruction. Spain can send unlimited ships with horses and armored men, until the last Taino in the deepest cave, whether hiding or resisting, is subdued."

"Hutia, please come with us!" Rachel said. "They will kill you or make you a slave. How can that be better than starting a new life in Italy with us—with me?"

"You would have me betray my people?"

"Is survival itself a betrayal?" Tears streamed down her face. "I don't think so."

"Rachel, I cannot." He looked at her with longing in his eyes. "Perhaps I am not meant to survive."

"No! Don't say that!" Rachel sobbed.

"Brother," Hutia said, "will you too try to persuade me?"

"My heart tells me to beg you to save yourself, but it is your decision. I would be glad if you chose to trust yourself to us, but I honor you for your loyalty to your people."

"Honor!" Rachel said on a flood of tears. "Oh, you stupid, stupid *men*! We could have been *happy!*"

She fled, sobbing, I hoped to Pilar's motherly arms to weep away some of her pain.

"I didn't tell Rachel the worst," Hutia said when she was gone. "Some of my people have so given in to despair that they have taken poison, the juice of the yuca."

"Promise me that you will not do that!" I said, horrified.

"I will not. But it is a mercy to those they would execute, like the cacique from the village where—your village."

I could not speak. I gave him the embrace of a brother.

Happiness was in short supply when we boarded our caravel, Captain Torres's flagship, on the morning of our departure. The returning Christian soldiers, gentlemen, and sailors looked cheerful enough as they patted the pouches of gold hidden on their persons, for all had ignored the prohibition against amassing personal wealth. Yet there hung about them a kind of puzzled disappointment, as if paradise had somehow failed their expectations.

The five hundred naked Taino being herded aboard and prodded into the dank and lightless holds could not have been more wretched. Those guarding them had indeed picked "the best specimens," strong young men and women who might survive the voyage and bring good prices in Seville. Taino slaves would be a novelty among Africans from the Guinea Coast, Guanche from the Canaries, and Moors taken in the recent war.

"It is unbearable! Unbearable!" Rachel said under her breath. "Look, they are allowing the Christians to have the pick of those who are left on the shore. Ugh! That vile Cuneo has two girls by the arm. They cannot be more than ten or eleven!"

"I believe he is to sail with us," I said.

"*Baruch atah Adonai Eloheinu*, please, please, not on our ship!"

"Rachel, that is blasphemy."

"I don't care! Anyhow, Adonai heard my prayer. See, Cuneo is boarding the second caravel."

She was right. He dragged the two weeping girls along. I pitied them.

The Admiral had recommended me to Captain Torres as a scribe and also as an interpreter, "if indeed," he had said, "there should be occasion to address the captives." So I did not need to leap into action as the sailors went about raising sail and weighing anchor to get us under way. My position would also enable me to make Rachel more comfortable than she might otherwise be, as no other women were returning to Spain. Captain Torres had promised to look after her as well, at least to the extent of not allowing any on board to offer her insult.

"Come, Rachel," I said. "Let us find shelter at the lee rail near the bow and turn our faces toward home."

"Not yet," Rachel said. She took my hand and drew me after her toward the stern, where the green bulk of Hispaniola slowly receded. "I must finish saying good-bye."

We both leaned on the rail. I took a deep breath of the clean salt air and silently said my own words of farewell, as well as prayers that Ha'shem would carry me safely to the new life that lay beyond what could only be a miserable voyage.

"Diego, look!" Rachel shrieked. "Someone is swimming after us! I believe it is Hutia! It is! It is!"

It had been long since any Taino swam out to a Spanish ship in expectation of a warm welcome. Hutia looked not joyful but determined. Spray flew with every stroke of his muscular brown arms. If the caravel had not still been coming about to catch the wind, he could not have reached the ship in time. I threw him a rope. Luckily, nobody was watching as he clambered aboard. He was not naked but wore a dripping tunic of Indian cotton. Rachel flew to him, laughing and crying as she flung her arms about his neck. "You came back to me! You came back!"

"In the end, I could not leave you. I could only trust my heart." Hutia turned to me, hope and doubt warring on his face. "Brother, you will never be rid of me now."

"I am glad of it," I said heartily.

"So am I!" Rachel clung fiercely to Hutia. "Thanks be to Ha'shem, so am I!"

"Let him go, Rachel," I warned. "We must establish Hutia as our slave if he is not to be taken captive."

We were challenged only once as we led Hutia to the corner of the deck where we planned to establish ourselves.

"I will give you a dry shirt and breeches," I was saying when a couple of soldiers accosted us.

"Here, what's this one doing up out of the hold?" One of them held out a burly arm to bar our way.

"He is my servant," Rachel said, looking down her nose at him like a court lady, though he towered over her.

"Is that so, missy?" The other, furred like a beast with coarse black hair, was disposed to be amused. "Who says so?"

"I do." I stepped forward, hand on the hilt of the sword I now wore along with my Toledo knife.

Rachel raised her chin. "Do you doubt my word?" Her hand went to her back, where I knew she had tucked into her skirts an envenomed fishbone dagger.

Hutia forbore to cower but stood straight and calm beside us.

The soldiers looked as if they wouldn't mind a fight. I thought the outcome of such a fight could only be a sorry one for us, even if we overcame them. So we stood at an impasse until Fernando swung down from the rigging to range himself beside us.

"Be on your way, fellows," he said. "This gentleman and lady have the captain's ear, and I would advise you not to test their influence."

One soldier gave a growl of disgust, the other a bark of laughter.

"To the devil with it, then. What's one cannibal more or less? Mind he don't eat you for dinner, missy!"

They swaggered away.

"All right?" Fernando said.

I nodded. Rachel gave him a misty-eyed smile.

"Then I'll be about my duties." He clapped me on the shoulder before swinging back into the rigging. The three of us were left alone, or as alone as we could be on the crowded deck.

"So I am now your slave?" Hutia said.

"No!" Rachel and I spoke at once.

"No matter," he said. "I can buy my freedom."

I had thought he wore a tunic only to distinguish himself from the captives. But now he reached inside it and brought out a sack of gold so weighty that I marveled that he had been able to swim with it.

"No!" I said. "It is blood treasure. I will not take it. I don't want it."

After turning the matter over in my mind many times, I had taken no gold for myself when we embarked. I had not asked Rachel what she carried in her baggage.

"It is my gift to Rachel," Hutia said. "Let it be her dowry, for I mean to marry Rachel. It is mine to give, for it belongs to my people. I value it as little as ever, but you have taught me that in Europe gold can buy us what we will need most: freedom and transport."

"Take it, Diego," Rachel said. "You can carry it more safely than Hutia can."

"Very well." I stowed the sack about my person. I would have to find a better hiding place for it. "You are right. Hutia must not risk being found with it."

"So we are to marry?" Rachel smiled at Hutia in a way that made me envy both of them.

"As soon as you are old enough," he said, "and I can be baptized Jewish."

"We don't baptize." I could not help laughing. "We are not eager for converts like the Christians. You must study and learn first."

"Then you must teach me," he said. "I will learn to perform the ceremonies of worship for Ha'shem and Adonai."

"Our God is One," Rachel corrected him. "He simply has many names."

Hutia shrugged. The distinction made as little sense to him as the Christians' Trinity did to us.

"Besides," Rachel said, "you already have a religion of your own. You must continue to pray to Yucahu and Atabey."

"I have said my farewells to Yucahu and Atabey," Hutia said. "I am going where they will no longer be able to hear my voice. So I must pray to your Adonai to take me under his protection."

"That must be our prayer too," I said. "This voyage cannot be a happy one. Many will die."

"But we will survive," Rachel said. "The Jews have always been survivors."

"Then I will be a Jew," Hutia said.

"We are called the Chosen People," I told him. "In times like these, one would think we are Chosen only for suffering."

"So are we Taino, it seems," Hutia said.

Later, while Rachel and Hutia discussed what tasks would best allow him to be seen doing her bidding at all times, I made my way back to the stern. Hispaniola had vanished behind us, but we still sailed through turquoise seas past islands rimmed with scalloped shores of sand and set with blue-green mountain peaks. As I watched them stream by, for a moment it seemed to me that I saw a host of naked golden people swimming toward me. As they approached, they laughed with delight at the prospect of new friends and such curious treasures as red caps, glass beads, and hawk's bells. For such gifts as these, or simply for *matu'm*, they willingly offered not only gold, but love.

Historical Timeline

October 19, 1469

Marriage of King Ferdinand of Aragon and Queen Isabella of Castile

February 6, 1481

Inquisition holds first auto da fé in Seville

January 2, 1492

Ferdinand and Isabella defeat the Moors at Granada, completing the Reconquista

August 3, 1492

Columbus's first voyage begins when the *Niña*, the *Pinta*, and the *Santa Maria* set sail from Palos; all Jews leave Spain on pain of death

October 12, 1492

Ships make landfall at San Salvador (called Guanahani by the Taino) and are greeted by the Taino

December 24, 1492

The *Santa Maria* is wrecked on shoals on the north coast of Hispaniola (called Quisqueya by the Taino)

January 4, 1493

The *Niña* and the *Pinta* leave Hispaniola; forty men remain behind at the new fort of La Navidad

February 16, 1493
Columbus reaches the Azores
March 4, 1493
Columbus arrives in Lisbon
March 15, 1493
Columbus makes harbor in Palos
April 2, 1493
Passover, total eclipse of the moon
April 7, 1493
Easter Sunday, Columbus, in Seville, receives letter officially appointing him Admiral of the Ocean Sea, Viceroy and Governor of the Indies
April 15–20, 1493
Columbus arrives in Barcelona and is received by King Ferdinand and Queen Isabella at Court
May 23, 1493
Don Juan de Fonseca, Archdeacon of Seville, is appointed with Columbus to make all preparations for the second voyage
September 25, 1493
Columbus and a fleet of seventeen ships sail from Cadiz
October 7–10, 1493
Fleet sails from the Canaries
November 3, 1493
Fleet makes landfall at Dominica (called Caire by the Taino)
November 4, 1493
Columbus lands on Guadalupe (now called Guadeloupe); a shore party gets lost for four days
November 14, 1493
Fleet lands on Santa Cruz (now called St. Croix); first battle with the Indians

November 27, 1493

Fleet anchors off Hispaniola (called Quisqueya by the Taino), near the site of La Navidad in what is now the Dominican Republic

November 28, 1493

A shore party finds La Navidad burned to the ground and learns that all the Spaniards who remained there are dead

January 2, 1494

The fleet anchors off Hispaniola at the site of what will be Isabela

January 6, 1494

Hojeda and Gorbalan are sent to find the gold mine of Cibao

January 20, 1494

Hojeda returns to Isabela and reports that he has found Cibao; in reality, there is alluvial gold but no mine

February 2, 1494

Twelve ships under de Torres are sent back to Spain

March 12, 1494

Columbus leads an expedition from Isabela inland over the mountains

March 16, 1494

Columbus orders the building of a fort at Santo Tomas

April 9–12, 1494

Hojeda mutilates a Taino for stealing clothes and takes a cacique captive

April 24, 1494

Columbus leaves Isabela with three ships for further exploration, leaving his brother Don Diego in charge

June 21, 1494

Columbus's brother Bartholomew arrives in Isabela with three ships

September 1494

Margarit and Fray Buil seize three caravels and sail for Spain

September 29, 1494
  Columbus returns to Isabela
February 24, 1495
  Four caravels, under the command of de Torres, leave for
Spain with a cargo of five hundred Taino slaves, of whom more
than two hundred die at sea

Afterword

Besides the characters known to history, I have used historical details as much as possible. For example, there really was a merchant noble family in Seville called Espinosa, although the characters of this name in the book are fictitious. The real-life Espinosas dealt in olive oil and wine; other families manufactured soap. There was indeed a "bakery inquisitor" who prepared supplies for the second voyage, though his name is unknown.

To the best of modern knowledge, Columbus was exactly where I have said he was on the dates given in the story. My fictional characters had more freedom to move around, within the framework of the historical timetable.

Some of the historical details are so amazing that it would be hard to make them up. The *Santa Maria* really was wrecked on Christmas Eve, 1492, in calm waters after a wild party with the Indians on board. There really was a full eclipse of the moon on April 2, 1493, the first day of Passover that year.

Almost all the incidents involving historical characters are true. Melchior Maldonado and Dr. Chanca really visited Guacanagari's village and took the cacique's bandages off to see if he was faking his injury. Fray Pane really published his "collection of folktales."

Hojeda really cut off a Taino's ears for stealing a few articles of clothing.

Michele de Cuneo really committed the rape described in this book. He wrote his own account of it when he returned to Europe, and historians quoted it as an amusing anecdote as recently as the mid-twentieth century.

The treatment of the Taino from 1493 on is fact, including the taking of fifteen hundred Taino in February 1495. Five hundred of them were loaded onto ships under conditions as wretched as those of any African slaver, destined for the slave markets of Spain; two hundred died before the voyage ended and were thrown into the sea. Some of the Taino drank cassava juice, which contains cyanide, to avoid being enslaved or killed. The modern view that the Taino disappeared primarily because of disease from germs imported from Europe is at best a comfortable exaggeration. By 1496, at least one-third of all the Taino had been killed.

There is no record of the Taino names of any of the Indians who were captured and taken to Spain. Only the names of some of the caciques have survived. My fictional Taino names are based on words from the Modern Taino Dictionary (Millville, NJ: The Taino Language Project, 2009, available at http://members. dandy.net/~orocobix/tedict.html), e.g., "gold flower" (ana caona), "butterfly" (tanama). The hutia is a rodent that still exists in the Dominican Republic and other Caribbean islands, though many of its species are extinct and others threatened.

No two parties agree on almost anything connected with Columbus's voyages, although contemporary accounts exist, including extracts from the journal Columbus kept on the first voyage. My main references were Samuel Eliot Morison's Pulitzer Prize–winning biography *Admiral of the Ocean Sea* (Boston: Little, Brown, 1942, 1970) and Kirkpatrick Sale's *Christopher Columbus and the Conquest of Paradise* (London: Tauris Parke, 1990, 2006), along with J. M. Cohen's translation of the primary sources (which

include parts of Columbus's own letters and logbook, the biography written by his son, and other contemporary accounts),
published as *Christopher Columbus: The Four Voyages* (London:
Penguin Books, 1969).

Morison and Sale disagree on almost everything, including
whether the Caribe were cannibals. Morison was a man of his time,
with an unselfconscious Eurocentric and patriarchal view of events
and motives. He was also an experienced sailor. In 1939 and 1940,
he followed the routes Columbus took on all four voyages in his
own sailboat, so he speaks with authority about where Columbus
went and the conditions on land and sea. Sale is a radical historian
who challenges the traditional view of the "Discovery" with his
more contemporary perspective, made vivid by his blunt use of
such words as "rape" and his charge that Columbus was responsible for "the death and enslavement of many Indians and the
destruction of their culture," i.e., genocide.

My online sources ranged from the helpful but not always
reliable Wikipedia to scholarly articles and book excerpts. I found
websites maintained by those who claim Taino ancestry and are
in the process of reconstructing the tribal language and culture. I
found one scholarly article that made a case for *taino* not being the
name of an ethnic group at all, but just a word, meaning "good,"
that Columbus and his companions heard the people they met use.
I discounted this. According to Phil Konstantin, author of *This Day
in North American Indian History* (Boston: Da Capo, 2002), "Many
tribal names mean 'People,' 'Us,' 'human beings,' or similar words."

Passages from Mary Elizabeth Perry's *Crime and Society in Early
Modern Seville* (Lebanon, NH: UPNE, 1980), which I found on the
website of the Library of Iberian Resources Online (LIBRO), were
particularly helpful in orienting me to late fifteenth-century Seville.
On the same site, Ruth Pike's *Aristocrats and Traders: Sevillian Society
in the Sixteenth Century* (Ithaca, NY: Cornell University Press, 1972)
provided information about the Moorish and African slaves and the

manner in which they were sold in Seville. For information about the Roma, I relied on Rom-identified online sources, learning, among other things, that few generalizations can be made about this widely traveled and much oppressed people who originated in the Punjab region of northern India.

My impression is that each authority, including Morison and Sale, decided what they would believe and what they would disregard. This is understandable, because even Columbus lied. On the first voyage, he kept two logs, one with what he believed were accurate figures of how far they had sailed each day, and the other with more optimistic figures, which he made up and shared with the crew to keep their spirits up. According to Morison, Columbus's estimates were so faulty that, in fact, the false figures were more accurate than those he believed to be the true ones. Following the historians' example, I have adhered to those aspects of history that suited my story and adopted a flexible attitude toward the rest. Novelists make things up—it's our job.

Note: The Prologue of *Voyage of Strangers* first appeared in *Ellery Queen's Mystery Magazine* (January 2011) as the short story "Navidad."

Acknowledgments

My thanks and gratitude to Janet Hutchings, who brought Diego to life by publishing my stories of the first voyage, "The Green Cross" and "Navidad," in *Ellery Queen's Mystery Magazine*; to my blog sisters Sharon Wildwind and Julia Buckley and historical novelists Kenneth Wishnia and Annette Meyers, the fine writers who critiqued the first draft; to D. P. Lyle, MD, who helped me make a fifteenth-century death from asthma credible; to mystery author Rabbi Ilene Schneider, my go-to person for questions about Judaism and Hebrew; and, as always, to my husband Brian, whose love of history inspires me, even though (or maybe because) he gets his information from history books rather than novels.

Discussion Questions

1. Because the point of view in *Voyage of Strangers* is Diego's, the story is told from an outsider's perspective. What makes a person or a group of people outsiders? Are there outsiders in our society today? In your community? What is your own experience, if any, of being an outsider?

2. It was long believed that the Taino became extinct a short time after the Spanish conquest. Yet today, people in the Dominican Republic and Haiti, Puerto Rico, Cuba, and throughout the United States identify themselves as Taino and are determined "to protect, defend, and preserve the Taino cultural heritage and spiritual tradition." (You can learn more at the website of the United Confederation of Taino People at http://uctp.org.) What do you think defines racial, ethnic, cultural, and religious identity? How important is genetic makeup? Cultural and religious practices? Language?

3. "History is written by the victors." This popular saying, often attributed to Winston Churchill, can be applied to the discovery of America, which is usually celebrated today as a joyous commemorative occasion with special reference to Italian Americans.

To what extent does it matter what people believe about events in the past? What are the possible consequences over time of only one version being remembered? How important is it for the losing side's story to be told?

4. People's beliefs are colored and their actions largely determined by their time and culture. For example, King Ferdinand and Queen Isabella believed that their Christian faith was an absolute good. Some Jewish scholars today believe that Columbus himself was a secret Jew and that his hidden agenda was to find a homeland for the Jews. How does cultural relativism affect our perception of right and wrong, good and evil? How do our beliefs affect what we perceive as facts?

5. One of the most interesting aspects of Taino culture was their use of *batey*, a ball game resembling soccer, to resolve disputes as well as for sport. What effect would it have on our society if we replaced war or even elections with athletic competitions?

About the Author

Elizabeth Zelvin is a New York City psychotherapist and author of a mystery series featuring recovering alcoholic Bruce Kohler. Liz is a three-time Agatha Award nominee and a Derringer Award nominee for Best Short Story. She is currently working on the sequel to *Voyage of Strangers*. Liz is also an award-winning poet with two books of poetry and a singer-songwriter whose album of original songs is titled *Outrageous Older Woman*. After many years in private practice and directing alcohol treatment programs, she now sees clients all over the world online. Her author website is at www.elizabethzelvin.com. Visit www.lizzelvin.com for Liz's music and www.LZcybershrink.com for online therapy. Liz is a veteran blogger, posting weekly for seven years on *Poe's Deadly Daughters* and recently blogging on *SleuthSayers*.

Books and Stories by
Elizabeth Zelvin

NOVELS
Voyage of Strangers
Death Will Get You Sober (A Bruce Kohler Mystery)
Death Will Help You Leave Him (A Bruce Kohler Mystery)
Death Will Extend Your Vacation (A Bruce Kohler Mystery)

E-NOVELLA
Death Will Save Your Life (A Bruce Kohler Mystery)

SHORT STORIES
"Navidad"
"The Green Cross"
Death Will Tank Your Fish & Other Stories
    "Death Will Tank Your Fish" (A Bruce Kohler Mystery)
    "The Silkie"
    "Dress to Die"
    "The Saxon Hoard"
    "Choices"

"Death Will Tie Your Kangaroo Down" (A Bruce Kohler Mystery)
"Death Will Trim Your Tree" (A Bruce Kohler Mystery)
"Death Will Clean Your Closet" (A Bruce Kohler Mystery)
"The Emperor's Hoard"
"Shifting Is for the Goyim" (An Emerald Love Mystery)
"Girl Feeding Birds"
"A Breach of Trust"
"Death Will Fire Your Therapist" (A Bruce Kohler Mystery)
"The Man in the Dick Tracy Hat" (forthcoming)
"A Shifting Plan" (forthcoming)

MUSIC (AS LIZ ZELVIN)
Outrageous Older Woman (CD or MP3)